Just Like the Bronte Sisters

Laurel Osterkamp

Copyright

J ust Like the Brontë Sisters

a novel

by

Laurel Osterkamp

PMI Books, Boulder, Colorado

This book is a work of fiction. Names, characters, places and incidents are products of the author's imagination or are used fictitiously. Any resemblance to actual events or locales or persons, living or dead, is entirely coincidental.

eISBN (Kindle): 978-1-933826-63-9

ISBN (paperback): 978-1-933826-88-2

Published by PMI Books

an imprint of Preventive Measures, Inc.

254 Spruce St.

Boulder, CO 80302

Chapter 1

Skylar

"Come on, Skylar! Keep up!"

I tucked my ski poles under my arms, bent my knees and drove my shoulders forward. That would increase my speed. That would show Jo Beth that I was worthy of being her ski-partner. She wouldn't always have to urge me on or insist I keep pace with her frenetic energy. But it wasn't so easy; Jo Beth continued to race down the mountain, and yelling over her shoulder to me clearly hadn't slowed her down. I exhaled and tried to relax, tried to just enjoy this amazing day, one that I'd looked forward to so much that I could barely sleep the night before. Two feet of powder had dumped down late yesterday evening, so last night Jo Beth and I had shared an unspoken agreement to hit the slopes as soon as the sun was up. With snow like this, if we weren't skiing we might as well be dead.

But relaxing was hard because all the signs for an avalanche were there: the wind whipped around at high speeds, the early March temperature was on the rise, and a mini-avalanche had occurred at this very spot less than a week ago. I'd learned all about avalanches at school and I knew that they didn't simply happen by surprise. The mountain will first send out a warning sign. Plus, if one little misstep releases a lethal torrent of icy wrath, usually there's someone to point a finger at. A human is to blame. But Jo Beth wouldn't understand. My sister never really thought things through. Her mind was always on a straight path that only went forward and not to the side.

"Jo Beth," I hollered. "I think I heard a cracking. We need to get out of here!"

She halted and let me catch up. "You're not afraid, are you?"

I let my skis glide to a stop so that we were standing parallel to each other. The off-slope mountain was deserted except for us as we'd strapped our skis to our back and hiked up to the highest peak, just so we could race down. "Sometimes it's good to be afraid."

Jo Beth laughed. "Fear is for the weak, Skylar. If you could ever get your head out of a Brontë novel, you'd realize that."

Leave it to Jo Beth to mock me for my literary devotion. My parents were impressed with my reading skills, that at such a young age I was already consumed by classic novels. But Jo Beth loved to tease me about it. Even when she called me an "old soul"—something that ought to have been a compliment—she said it in a taunting voice, like I'd just farted or something. Now Jo Beth resumed skiing and I followed, sure that every crack, pop, and whoosh I heard was the beginning of a snow slip that would swallow me whole.

Why had I even agreed to this? I imagined what an avalanche would feel like. Would it be a form of drowning, of getting overtaken by the wet and the cold, of literally surrendering to a force of nature? The blades of ice would pierce my skin, but that would probably hurt less than the strong arm of the snow's cold, arrogant power.

It would make me disappear.

"Ta da!" When we landed at the base of the mountain, Jo Beth's gleeful cry rang out like a broken bell. "Everything was fine! We had nothing to worry about."

I said nothing. I couldn't yet verbalize what I already knew, that just because something had worked out, that didn't mean there wasn't ever reason to worry. Even if everything else was fine, you could still cause an avalanche.

Chapter 2

Jo Beth

Jo Beth couldn't get the look on Skylar's face out of her head. She'd rolled her eyes, puckered her lips, and scrunched her nose, like it was painful not to speak, not to say what she really thought: that Jo Beth was irresponsible, that even though Skylar was the younger sister, she was wiser and way more responsible. Skylar seemed to think it had become her duty to scold Jo Beth. Still, Skylar had remained silent and that was a silver lining, because it meant Jo Beth could stay silent too. It's better not to yell if you can help it.

Jo Beth yelled a lot. Many people called her a "passionate person," which was just a nice way of saying she had a wicked temper. So what if she felt things deeply? Life was for the living, and Jo Beth prided herself on her passions, for things like adrenaline rushes, well-timed naps, and winning every single one of her ski meets. Skiing, preferably with Skylar, was her number one passion. But in the winter of her sophomore year, Jo Beth developed a brand-new passion. What made this passion special, made it different, was that it was for a guy.

Things had started innocently enough, through the time-tested bandwagon effect. The way all the ski team girls were going on about the new coach, you'd think he was God's gift, capable of anything, like he knew how to execute the perfect kiss without slobber but with tongue, or he might be able to halt global-warming during his downtime, in between workout sessions, while he drank his protein shake. They spoke his name breathlessly, but in all caps: DALLAS.

It was the other girls' fault that Jo Beth had formed an epic-sized crush on him. And it wasn't just that he was her ski coach at Black Diamond High, twenty-three years old to Jo Beth's fifteen, an age difference as forbidden and exciting as whipping down an icy, closed-off jump. He also had that Adonis thing going on, and if Jo Beth was the sort of girl who accepted her own, personal limitations, she'd have known that Dallas was way out of her league. Instead, Jo Beth felt the swell of her competitive spirit. Flirting with Dallas was just one more game that she could win.

One afternoon after practice, Jo Beth decided it was time to make her move. All the ski-gear lockers were housed in the same spot, and boys and girls alike were simultaneously removing boots, stepping over puddles, and peeling damp mittens off icy fingers. Dallas stood only a few feet from Jo Beth, so she caught his eye and spoke like they were the only two people in the room. "Hey Dallas," she said, trying to sound both playful and bored, "why were you named after a city in Texas?"

He shrugged and smiled. "It's where I was conceived."

Rather than responding, Jo Beth simply maintained eye contact and kept her lips slightly parted. She figured she was too old to show shock at the mere insinuation of parental sex.

Dallas kept talking, his tone mischievous. "My dad's a businessman and he was traveling for work. My mom was an event coordinator at this hotel where he stayed. They hooked up on the first night they met and she got pregnant, so, well, you can guess the rest."

Jo Beth took off her boots and shoved them into her assigned locker, gleeful at the other girls' jealous stares as she and Dallas chatted. "Yeah, I *can* guess, but I'm not sure I want to," she said, laughing.

"No kidding," he told her. "My dad is thirty years older than my mom and he's always telling me this stuff about their sex life..." Dallas shook his head and grimaced. "It's really twisted."

In that moment, Jo Beth decided that she and Dallas must have a special connection. Otherwise, why would he overshare like that? She became even more confident of their bond at the next practice. One minute he would divulge a new dark secret about his family life, the next he would place his hand on Jo Beth's hip. "Don't put so much weight there," he told her. They were hidden by the curve of a hill, their words muffled by the cover of snow. "That will slow you down." His hand lingered against her butt cheek for a second too long, pausing before the rest of the high school team caught up with them.

The weeks passed in a pleasant haze, and when Jo Beth wasn't with Dallas, she counted down the minutes until she'd see him again. He was just so supportive, telling Jo Beth that she was meant for the Olympics. He encouraged her to get a private coach, to start training so she could compete at a higher level than she'd ever dreamed. Having him in her life was a ray of hope and maybe, with his help, she would someday get out of Black Diamond. Maybe, after graduation, she wouldn't have to settle for a job at the ski school and haunt the town, trying to resurrect her glory days. Maybe she wouldn't eventually morph into another high school ski-team captain turned ski-bum, completely ordinary, a cliché of a cliché.

Jo Beth wasn't about to report the stolen kisses behind the activity bus, or the "special" practice sessions after regular practice got out, or the silent pact between her and Dallas that the more sexual favors she granted him, the more he'd choose her over juniors and seniors to compete in ski events. If people found out, she'd be the villain, a slut who'd betrayed everyone, including herself.

One night she went over to his house. He still lived with his parents in a large, rustic A-frame with humongous windows, which gave passersby a glimpse into the decadent interior that contrasted with its log cabin exterior. Jo Beth and Dallas sat in the huge hot tub, which was out on the deck, positioned perfectly for a postcard view of the Rockies. But they weren't looking at the scenery. Dallas sat pressed up next to her, sliding his hand underneath the strap of her bikini.

"I want you so bad," he whispered into her ear. His hand traveled down Jo Beth's torso, into her lap, between her thighs.

Her mind raced. If she let Dallas have his way, she would lose her virginity in that hot tub. She'd already given him hand jobs, and the hand jobs had graduated to blow jobs, and now there wasn't anywhere else to go. What should she do? According to all the love stories that her sister Skylar read, a woman's virtue was her most prized possession, and these books preached that you should wait until marriage before submitting to sex. But come on: that was fiction, written hundreds of years ago. It was bunk, if you asked Jo Beth. Yet, she had to admit there might be something to those stupid romantic principles. Sure, nowadays nobody expected you to marry the guy you lost your virginity to, but maybe you should love him? Maybe he should love you?

She pulled away.

"What's wrong?" he asked, with just a pinch of testiness.

"Am I your girlfriend?"

"Of course, you are, Jo." He didn't miss a beat, just wrapped a lock of her wet hair around his finger. "We can't tell anyone, though. The world is against us. I would lose my job, maybe even go to jail." He tilted his head and leaned in for a supple kiss on the lips. "But I can't help it. I love you."

Jo Beth scrutinized him. With his blond hair, golden skin, and broad shoulders, he could have anyone. Had he really chosen her? "You do? Are you sure?"

"One hundred percent." He kissed her again, this time thrusting his tongue into her mouth. His hand crept back up and now it was underneath her bikini top, cupping her breast. The heat, the steam, and the liquor they'd drunk all swirled together into a cyclone, sucking away her ability to think or process, and before she knew what was happening, Dallas had removed her top.

She didn't tell him no because her body was already saying yes. She was vague on how exactly it happened, what led up to that moment when she straddled him and he shoved himself inside her, but she remembered thinking that she'd regret it, that it was wrong. She was so young, so ill-prepared for the pain, so shocked by the look on his face as he grunted and pumped. She cast her gaze up to the sky, at the millions of stars above, and soon they started spinning in circles, like a kaleidoscope. *I'm a woman now* was her last thought before she passed out.

When she woke, she was lying in an unfamiliar bed.

"You really didn't think this one through," a male voice said. He sounded like an older version of Dallas.

"Sorry."

"I knew it was a mistake, letting you coach high school. God, at least you could have picked a senior this time. What is she, a freshman?"

"Sophomore."

"Jesus! What if she cries to her parents and they contact the school?" Jo Beth heard a whacking sound of palm against skin. "What if someone other than me had caught you? You have to think!"

She sat up. Dallas was in the room and that had to be his dad standing next to him. Jo Beth grabbed at the covers, frantic to cover herself, frantic to flee.

"You're awake," the dad said. He lifted a glass of water off the night stand. "Here, drink." He handed the glass to a terribly thirsty Jo Beth, who took only a modest sip. "I apologize to you on my son's behalf."

Dallas just stood there, his hands in his pockets, his head hung low. When he wouldn't meet her eyes, the truth hit Jo Beth like the sudden onset of stomach flu. Dallas didn't love her and she'd been a stupid, silly girl to believe, even for a moment, that he had. Meanwhile, why the hell wouldn't the father look away? He was thicker than Dallas, gray hairs mixed in with his blonde, and lines creased his golden-tan skin. Yet their resemblance was uncanny; they were the same factory model.

"I should probably go." She looked from side to side. "Where are my clothes?"

"Dallas will get them for you." His father flicked his head in the direction of the door, and Dallas took his exit.

Jo Beth cocooned herself in the sheet as the dad sat beside her on the bed. "Dallas has this unfortunate habit. He says that the apple doesn't fall far from the tree, that we both like younger women. But you are merely a child, and I'm always pulling strings, trying to clear him of statutory rape charges. Do you understand?"

She didn't understand. Her brain still felt fuzzy, but she nodded her head in agreement anyway.

"Dallas got into some trouble during college in Vermont." He waved his hand dismissively. "Similar stuff. You should be aware... whatever he told you, it's a lie."

The dad was sitting too close, staring at the sheets stretched over her naked chest. Dallas came back into the room, holding Jo Beth's clothes in a bundle. He tossed them onto the bed, like somehow *she'd* offended *him*.

"Get dressed," Dallas said in a cold voice. "I'll drive you home."

"No." The dad sounded like a villain in a teen-slasher film. "I'm driving her."

The ride back was eternal. The space between her legs burned, her mouth was so dry she couldn't swallow, and her head ached with unshed tears. And he kept talking and talking, his voice like dull teeth gnawing through her skull.

"Dallas's coaching job is the only thing that keeps him from becoming a ski bum." He stared straight ahead, clutching the steering wheel so tight that he looked like he could rip it off. "He needs a sense of purpose and a scandal won't do anyone any good. If you say something, nobody will believe you but they'll have to look into it. You won't prove anything, but reputations will be ruined. You understand how that would be bad for you? Bad for the ski team?"

Jo Beth just pressed her forehead against the cool glass of the car window and stared out.

"That house is mine," she rasped, and he pulled up to the curb. She reached for the door handle a split second before she heard the click of automatic locks. Jo Beth turned and for the first time, looked this man in the eyes.

"Let me out."

"In a moment." He paused, staring her down. "First I need to know that we agree."

"Agree about what?"

He spoke low, clipping his syllables with precision. "That you won't say anything about what happened between you and Dallas."

"Why would I agree to that?"

He smiled like a cobra. "Dallas says you have potential. That you should get a good coach, that you're destined for the Olympics." He gestured towards her parent's modest house. "I'm guessing you don't have the money or the connections to make that happen. But I do. Don't say anything about Dallas, and I will sponsor you. If you're as good as Dallas says you are, we'll both benefit."

Up until then she'd almost been a romantic, believing true love could exist, that there was a possibility of happily-ever-after. But at that moment her cynicism emerged like an iceberg cutting through a mountain, leaving a huge, pragmatic ravine in its wake. "Fine." She reached out and shook his hand, sealing her deal with the devil.

That night was the real beginning of Jo Beth Blue, ski star extraordinaire.

More importantly, she'd learned a valuable life lesson. Hooking up with guys was fine, but she had to be the one in control. And as it was her job to protect her younger sister, Jo Beth took on the job of educating Skylar. Jo Beth realized this would be a challenge, especially after she took Skylar to see a production of *Romeo and Juliet*. Skylar ate it up. Cried, even. Afterwards Jo Beth yelled at her.

"Juliet killed herself over a guy she'd known for less than a week! And she'd only met him a few hours before they got married! Who does that, besides some lame Disney princesses? No! You will NOT be one of those girls!"

Skylar sniffled in the seat next to her as they drove home from the performance. "What do you mean? One of what girls?"

"One who buys all the fairytale, true-love crap."

"But I love a good romance," Skylar said.

Jo Beth gripped the steering wheel and clipped her syllables, not unlike how Dallas's father had done.

"Forget romance. You have to be strong, Sky. Only the strong survive."

Chapter 3
Skylar

My parents taught strength to Jo Beth and me every day, whether they meant to or not. They had no choice, not while raising us on a limited budget and in such an entitled environment. And they were so young when they had Jo Beth, yet they did okay. I loved hearing the story of how our family came about. We'd all sit at the kitchen table eating a fresh batch of snickerdoodles and drinking milk. I'd say, "How did Jo Beth get her name?" And even though it was a story told many times before, Mom and Dad would tell it jointly, trading off at various points, almost like it was rehearsed.

Many years ago—while they were still in high school—my mom, Elizabeth Simpson, and my dad, Joseph Reese-Wakefield, started dating. As graduation approached, they both applied and were accepted to C.U., but Mom got pregnant. The timing was bad but they were in love, so Mom and Dad decided it was more important to start a family than to go to college. Mom became a baker and Dad a preschool teacher/artist. They believed in equal rights and freedom of choice and, I don't know, sticking it to their fathers, neither of whom supported their decision to marry. So, Joseph and Elizabeth combined their own first names to form their daughter's first name, and they chose their mutual favorite color as her last name. Thus, Jo Beth Blue was born.

But how did she become a ski star? Well, both Mom and Dad liked to ski, so we spent most of our free time hitting the slopes. Somehow, they managed to budget in a family lift season pass every year, and we frequented the second-hand sporting goods shops to update our gear. I suppose Jo Beth and I both inherited a bit of talent, a bit of athleticism, and a penchant for snow. But Jo Beth got something else, a quality I would never, ever possess. Nothing intimidated her.

You could never say the same about me. Standing up to people was never really my strong suit. In my defense, Black Diamond is a wealthy ski town, girls are mean, and my middle school clique had my back until they realized that I wasn't wearing the right clothes, that I raised my hand too often in class, that I said, "no thank you" when they passed me a joint at the last party they ever told me about. One Monday morning in math class I opened my Algebra textbook to find a note inside. This was after weeks of being shut out, of being ignored if I dared to speak at the lunch table. "Sky" was hand-written in large, loopy letters on a piece of lined paper folded in fourths. I unfolded it eagerly, hoping to find an invitation to a sleepover, or some inside joke, or maybe just an "I miss you" from my best friend, Eileen. The note was in her handwriting.

Everybody hates you. You should just kill yourself.

I spent the rest of the day with my lips clamped shut and my eyes cast down, so as not to cry. As soon as school was over I raced home to find Jo Beth, who usually stopped at our house for a snack before she met with her trainer. I rushed in through the backdoor and into the kitchen. Jo Beth was standing in front of an open refrigerator, but she shut it as soon as she saw my face.

"What's wrong, Sky?"

Wordlessly, I showed her the note. Then I burst into tears.

Jo Beth's eyes turned hard and her voice was like concrete. "Who did this?"

Through sniffs and hiccups, I answered. "Eileen. Ever since she became friends with Becca, she hates me because Becca hates me too."

Jo Beth crumpled the sheet of notebook paper, shoved it down the garbage disposal, and hit the switch so that the note became nothing more than a memory forever stamped across my brain. "Forget those bitches," Jo Beth said. "They're not good enough for you."

"But I want to be friends with them."

"No." Jo Beth put her bony fingers underneath my chin and tilted my head up, so our eyes met. "You don't need them, and you're coming with me."

We spent the afternoon taking our aggression out on the slopes. For me, that precious time with my sister was enough to make me forget those mean girls, but not for Jo Beth. On Wednesday night, before I went to bed, Jo Beth came into my room, her urgency more glaring than usual.

"Hey," she said, trying to sound casual. "Was it Eileen you had over when you used the Ouija Board and tried to summon her dead grandmother?"

"Yeah," I said. "Why?"

"And I dropped you off at her house that one time? It has that big tree that's right outside her bedroom?"

I paused before answering. It was exactly like Jo Beth to be plotting revenge. "Don't do anything, Jo. Whatever you're planning, don't do it."

"Okay." She got up and went towards my bedroom door.

"Really?" Before, she'd never been easy to convince.

"I'd never do anything to hurt you, Sky." She stopped with her hand on the doorknob, turned, and winked at me. "You're my favorite and I love you best of all."

"I love you, too."

She walked out of my room and soon I fell asleep, confident that the world was right. But the next morning I woke, went to take a shower, and found Jo Beth in our bathroom. She was wiping off grey makeup that had been smeared all over face, covering her freckles. Her brown hair had been sprayed silver and the remains of black lipstick clung to her plump lips.

"What's going on?" I asked. "Did you go to a costume party?"

"No. Don't worry about it. But do me a favor, okay? If Eileen is suddenly nice to you, ignore her."

"Huh?"

Jo Beth smiled. "Refuse to be her friend. Promise me, Sky."

I should have been in the shower by now, letting warm water wash over me as I tried to wake up. Yet I was instantly alert as dread washed over me instead. "Oh my God!" I yelled. "You said you wouldn't do anything!"

She stepped forward and placed her greasy, soapy palm over my mouth. "Shush! If Mom and Dad see me like this, they'll know I sneaked out."

I spoke through her hand that pressed against my lips. "WHAT DID YOU DO?!!"

"I fixed things for you, okay? Relax! Your life would be so much easier if you stopped worrying so much. TRUST ME."

I relented. After all, what choice did I have? Whatever Jo Beth had done it was too late to take back now. Speaking of late, Jo Beth took forever to shower, so when I finally made it through the doors of West Diamond Middle School, first hour had already begun. But nothing seemed any different. Same groups of people ignoring me, same burnt out teachers spurting out their lesson plans, same sun shining up over the mountains and through the large picture windows, making it all the more difficult to sit inside rather than enjoy the day.

Yet at lunch time I was startled when Eileen set her tray down across from mine. "I have to talk to you," she said, and I noticed she was pale underneath the cafeteria's fluorescent light. I also noticed her perfectly painted magenta fingernails; she must have learned all about hair and makeup from her new set of friends. Speaking of which, why wasn't Eileen sitting with that pack of Abercrombie-clad Emmas?

Jo Beth's words from that morning rang in my head: *Don't be friends with Eileen.* I made fists, hiding my own nails, which were ragged from being chewed. And I kept my voice stiff, like an un-promising handshake. "Yeah?"

"Do you want to come over today after school?"

I had to pause for a moment and reign myself in. "No."

Eileen's face fell. "Please, Skylar? I sort of need you to."

"Why?"

She ran her fork through her mashed potatoes, keeping her eyes on the goopy white tracks. "You wouldn't believe me if I told you. Let's just say I heard from my grandma last night."

"But your grandmother is dead."

Eileen looked up. She had dark circles underneath her bloodshot eyes and she spoke in a vicious whisper. "Yeah... but I was woken by this bright light shining through my curtains, and when I looked outside, there was this figure."

"Your grandmother?"

"No." She shrugged. "Maybe. It was dark and I couldn't see much, but it was the creepiest face I'd ever seen, all grey and dead looking, like she was floating in the air."

I breathed steadily, trying to calm my racing heart. "Like, where that tree is?"

"Maybe, but there was this deep, scary voice, and she told me..." Eileen shook her head. "Never mind. Nobody is going to believe me, and if I tell anyone, I'll go to hell."

Eileen has never been the brightest bulb. She'd believed Noah Simmons when he'd told her that the school cafeteria imprisoned child slaves to make the popcorn chicken tenders for our lunches, because only tiny fingers could bread pieces so small. So whatever prank Jo Beth had pulled, it was plausible that Eileen would buy it, hook, line, and sinker. I looked at her face, all pinched with fear. I imagined Jo Beth outside her window, scaring her, but I could muster no sympathy for Eileen, only admiration for my brave, hilarious sister.

"Excuse me, but I'd really rather eat alone." I picked up my tray and moved down three spaces. Eileen twisted her mouth like she was about to say something, but I turned away.

I ate lunch by myself, with nobody to talk to, and I pulled out a copy of *Jane Eyre* for company. Yet as I read, I could hear Jo Beth's voice as clearly as if she sat across from me. *I just want you to be in control, Skylar. Never give away your power.* I resolved that I wouldn't give my power away, unless, of course, it was to my sister. She was the best company I could keep, and if I couldn't be with her, I'd keep company with my favorite authors instead, like Mary Shelly, Jane Austen, or most especially, the Brontë sisters. I imagined Jo Beth and me to be like them, for when Charlotte, Emily, and Anne first wrote their respective novels (each under a different male pseudonym) the literary community was convinced it was all the work of a singular talent. The Brontë sisters were competitive for sure, but their isolation and dependence upon each other was what made them capable of inventing worlds full of gothic romance, hauntings, and devastating love. They were complete individuals, seemingly sharing the same soul.

Just like Jo Beth and me.

Chapter 4
Jo Beth

Jo Beth was fine on her own, but if someone caught her eye it went against her nature not to pursue him. She would never again make the same mistakes she had made with Dallas, but what could be the harm of getting to know Blake? He worked as a bartender at The Outpost, a busy hangout at the base of Black Diamond's most popular ski run. They met when she handed him her fake ID. He took one look and handed it back to her.

"Sorry, Amelia," he said, calling her by the name on the driver's license she'd given him. "You don't look a thing like your picture."

"I do when I'm naked," she replied.

He ran his fingers over his super-short hair, rubbing his buzz cut. "That doesn't make sense," he said carefully.

"We're at a bar, and we're talking about nudity. It's not supposed to make sense." Slowly, she licked her lips. "Now can I please have a beer?"

He filled a glass with whatever was on tap and she drank it down in a few gulps. He kept filling and refilling it, and she sat at the bar, downing whatever he gave her. When his shift ended Jo Beth could barely stand, so he led her to his car and drove her to his apartment.

"I'm not a virgin," she slurred as they walked in through his door. She plopped down on his couch and started to remove her boots. She was sober enough to realize that her pants would come off way easier if she took her boots off first.

He sat down next to her. "Of course, you're not. You're way too self-destructive to be a virgin."

Jo Beth laughed at Blake's earnestness, at the way he stared at her with those baby blue eyes. "What do you care? You're about to get laid." She tugged at his long-sleeved t-shirt but he swatted her hand away.

"Not tonight," he said. "I don't take advantage of minors."

"You won't be taking advantage of me. I'll be taking advantage of you."

Still, he got up, went to the kitchen, filled a glass with water, and placed it on the coffee table.

"Goodnight," he said.

She couldn't figure it out. Why get her drunk in the first place? Her head was way too heavy to put together his motives, so she let it fall to the worn couch pillow, where she slept for several hours before she awoke with a stabbing pain behind her eyebrows and a mouth full of cotton. Jo Beth guzzled the water he'd left, put on her boots, and left.

Outside was cold and dark, not yet dawn. But she made a decision on her trek home. This guy, this bartender whose name she couldn't remember, was for her. He was honorable and kind, and she liked his military-ish good looks.

The next night Jo Beth returned to the bar. "What time are you off?" she asked him.

"Forget it," Blake replied. Blake. *Of course.* How could she have forgotten his female-soap-opera-character name? "I'm working all night," he said, "but even if I wasn't, I wouldn't go out with you."

"You're wrong," she told him. "You're totally into me."

The bar was crowded and a loud, large man shoved into her before he ordered his drinks. Jo Beth stood back and let Blake do his job. But once a stool opened up she sat there, waiting for closing time. When Blake finally acknowledged her two hours later, he said, "Why are you still here?"

"Because we're going to start dating."

Blake squinted at her. "How old are you, really?"

"Seventeen. But I'm going places, so you need to catch me now, before I leave you in the dust."

There was a hint of smile across his stubbled cheeks. "Oh yeah? Where are you going? To juvie?"

"The Olympics."

Then his eyes widened in recognition. "You're Jo Beth Blue, aren't you?"

"You've heard of me?"

He nodded. "You're like this prodigy, a ski legend at seventeen. Of course, I've heard of you. The whole town is talking about how you're going to win the Gold before you're a legal adult."

"There are lots of things I'm going to do before I'm a legal adult."

He laughed and that was it. Blake was hers.

They did everything together for almost a year. Even Jo Beth's parents knew about Blake, because eventually it became too much of an effort for Jo Beth to hide their relationship. But shortly before Jo Beth went to audition for the Olympic team, he cut things off.

"You're going to be a star," Blake told her. "You don't need a dead weight like me."

She swallowed back tears. She wouldn't beg him to stay because sooner or later, she knew she'd leave him anyway.

"Okay," she replied.

"Okay? Just like that?" He looked like a little boy, disappointed that she wouldn't search for him in a game of hide-n-seek.

Jo Beth glanced at the clock even though she knew what time it was. "I have to go. I'm supposed to pick Skylar up from school." She grabbed her purse, which had been lying on the same couch that she'd passed out on the first night they met.

He blocked her path. "Jo Beth, don't leave angry."

Honestly, she wasn't angry until he said that, but suddenly she could picture herself seizing one of his dull kitchen knives, wrestling him to the ground, and slitting his throat. The blood wouldn't faze her and the remorse would be fleeting. "Blake, either I leave angry, or I leave with your blood on my hands."

He looked into her eyes. Blake must have been able to see that she meant it, because he stepped aside. She rushed down the stairs of his apartment building, out to the parking lot, and into her car. As she drove towards Skylar's school, her surroundings blurred. There was no contrast, no difference between light and dark, only fear of self. It was the first time she ever felt capable of murder. And somehow, she knew with a scary certainty that it wouldn't be the last time.

Turns out, it was over a year later when her bloodthirsty feelings re-emerged. She was competing in the Olympics and it began during her chance at Women's Downhill. Jo Beth dug her poles into the ground and pushed off. She was a lightning rod, breaking the laws of physics. A gold medal was within reach, but then the spectators started to clang those damn bells. The noise echoed and reverberated, over and over, until Jo Beth swore the ringing came from inside her ears.

How could something so stupid faze her? This was the most important race of her life. Why couldn't she just tune it out?

She tried to focus as she skied in between pole after pole, first red then blue and then red again, never missing one, never falling, not bending too deep and refusing to hold back. Onlookers and fans stood to the side, ringing those God-forsaken bells to cheer her on. But she wanted to rip those bells from their hands, to shove those bells down their throats. Because when she neared the finish, the ringing became so loud, so intense, that she faltered for half a second as she skied around that last red pole. That half second cost her. It was the difference between silver and gold.

"Wow! That was quite a run!" The sports announcer gushed to Jo Beth at the bottom of the slope and shoved the microphone into her face. "You're already a legend, and only nineteen years old! How do you feel?"

Jo Beth held up her skis, fulfilling her sponsorship contract by making sure the name *Rossignol* was captured by the camera. Then she oozed out her answer. "Incredible! I couldn't be happier."

Nobody guessed her dark thoughts. And later, when she stood on that podium and they placed the silver medal over her shoulders, she smiled like the best thing in the world had just happened. Her face didn't even twitch; she gave no clue that she wanted to blow up the whole auditorium and take out the smug skier from Denmark whose half-second advantage made her the best in the world, and made Jo Beth an afterthought.

That was the first time Jo Beth truly felt fear. It was deep, soaking into her muscles and bones. It was the type of fear she could only escape if she learned how to escape herself.

Chapter 5

Skylar

"You can't trust anyone, Skylar. But you especially can't trust men." Jo Beth sighed, dropped her *People* magazine onto the table, and walked toward the kitchen counter. "I know he killed her," she said, as she refilled her mug with fresh coffee. "Look at his eyes. They're soulless."

I put down *Jane Eyre* and reached for her magazine. The cover held a picture of a beautiful couple, him in a tuxedo, her in black dress with a white sweater. He stood over a head taller than her, but they both had dark hair and gleaming white smiles. They obviously belonged to each other. "But they seem so perfect," I said.

"Anyone can seem perfect. But nobody actually is." Jo Beth jabbed her finger at the magazine. "I can't believe you haven't heard about them. They've been all over the news. You really do keep your nose buried in a book, don't you?"

I shrugged and glanced at the cover of *Jane Eyre*, with the young heroine in a black cloak and a shadowed man on horseback. They were surrounded by clouds and a castle sat in the background. "I guess I prefer the fictional world to the real one," I told my sister.

"Hmpf," she grunted. "I saw the movie of *Jane Eyre*. That story is fucked up."

I couldn't argue her point because I'd already thought it myself. True, Jane seemed destined for dank environments, and yes, she fell in love with a gloomy, secretive guy. I mean, not only was he married, but (spoiler alert) Mr. Rochester kept his wife up in the attic. Meanwhile, Jane was an innocent virgin, proving that the bad-boy/good-girl dynamic is a time-honored literary device. I wasn't beyond appreciating the romance yet I could also recognize the theme: men can violate, but women can't let themselves be violated. Was this a universal truth, or merely fiction?

Jo Beth reverted to her magazine, determined to fill me in. "He's on trial right now. They say he killed his pregnant wife so he could run off with his girlfriend; he made it look like she was missing for months. And then, when they finally found the bodies..." She shuddered.

"What do you mean? There was more than one body?"

Jo Beth nodded slowly as she used both hands to grasp her coffee cup. "The baby had been cut out of her. They found it first, and then they found her...with her head cut off."

"That's terrible." I took a sip of my orange juice, trying to wash down my queasiness. We were just finishing breakfast and the sun shone through Jo Beth's windows, as if to convince us that the world was a friendly place. But my sister knew better.

"This sort of thing happens way more than you know. The guy seemed like an ideal husband, but he was a cold-blooded murderer." Jo Beth leaned forward, pressing her elbows against her oak table, her eyes boring into mine. "Let's promise each other that we won't fall for the charming guy, especially not for the charming, handsome guy. They're nothing but trouble."

"Okay," I rasped. The orange juice still burnt my throat.

"Promise me, Skylar. You have to promise."

I wasn't sure it was a pledge I could stick to, but I was incapable of saying no to my sister. "Okay, I promise I won't fall for the charming, handsome guy."

Jo Beth slapped the table in victory. "Good. I promise too." Obviously feeling successful, she relaxed her pose and leaned back. "What do you want to do today? Should we go skiing?"

"Of course!"

Jo Beth hopped up from her seat at the table. "Great. They sent me some new fleece mittens and you can have them, Sky. They'll look perfect with your jacket and they're super warm." Jo Beth moved in a flurry, like she always did when she was in a good mood. On sunny days like this one, the world was made just for her and simply being in her presence turned me into royalty.

It took us very little time to don our gear and make the short commute from Jo Beth's condo to the ski resort that was practically in her backyard. "My condo is so much cooler than Mom and Dad's house," said Jo Beth. We now sat on the ski lift, floating over mountain tops that I knew so well, were I to close my eyes I'd still be able to see their rocky ridges and scattered evergreens. "And if you move in with me, it's walking distance to the lift." Right after Jo Beth scored her first big sponsorship she had bought her luxurious, celebrity-appropriate condo. Now it seemed to be more than her new home; those walls had become an extension of Jo Beth's fabulousness.

"That is a bonus." I tried to sound noncommittal. I knew I was too young to move from home, too unsteady to walk away from Mom and Dad.

"And you'll have your own room. God, Skylar, you'll even have your own bathroom, with a Jacuzzi tub, no less." She swept her long ponytail off her shoulder. "How can you possibly turn that down?"

I busied myself shifting one ski pole so that my left hand was holding them both, and using my mittened right hand to scratch just below my nostril. The damp fleece only irritated my nose and I made a face.

"Don't avoid me, Skylar."

I realized that Jo Beth was glaring at me, her cheeks red from the wind, small drops of moisture clinging to her eyelashes.

"How am I avoiding you?" I rocked our chair by moving my weight back and forth. "It'd be sort of impossible right now, even if I wanted to."

"I know you better than you know yourself. You're hesitating, buying time, trying to find a nice way to say no." Jo Beth transferred her gaze to her skis, which she'd raised and held vertically by straightening her legs. Then she attempted to remove the little clumps of snow that clung to her skis by knocking them together.

"I just don't get why you'd want me around all the time." I playfully nudged her shoulder with my own. "You're so popular. You don't need your little sister around, invading your privacy."

"I'm not that popular."

"What are you talking about? Everyone I know wants to be around you."

Jo Beth smiled for half a second, before her chin trembled and she bit her bottom lip to make the trembling stop. "The only person who even knows me at all is you."

We had reached the "Prepare to de-board" sign. My poles were both already in my outside hand and Jo Beth transferred hers. We lifted our skis, stood at the right moment, and glided off the lift. I was glad for a second of respite. Maybe I could collect my thoughts and find a way to say no thank you, without hurting Jo Beth's feelings, of course.

Yet by the time I'd caught up to her, the old Jo Beth was back. She gave me a smile of such glowing confidence, I figured I'd merely imagined her vulnerability back on the lift.

"We're doing the mogul run, right?" I asked.

"Sure, if that's what you want." She pivoted and prepared to launch herself down the mountain. I knew then that the issue was closed, that she'd already extended herself way more than she liked. I could just let it go. I could tell myself that Jo Beth wasn't really lonely; she was just trying to be nice. But suddenly the choice between living with Jo Beth and living at home became so clear, that it was barely a choice at all.

"Jo Beth!" I was as surprised at my volume as she was. When she turned toward me expectantly, I wasn't even sure what I meant to say. "Umm..." I stammered. "I just don't want to hurt Mom and Dad's feelings. That's all."

Jo Beth gave me a simple nod. "Sure. I understand, Skylar. Don't worry about it."

"But..." I swallowed roughly, knowing that once I made this concession, there was no going back. "But I'd rather live with you."

Jo Beth's eyebrows arched in victory and the corners of her mouth inched into a modest smile. "No worries. I'll talk to them for you." She lowered her ski goggles, so now her face was behind a mask. "Let's go." An immense stretch of powder extended before us. "Race you to the bottom!" Jo Beth cried.

"You're on!" I took off, aware that my sister was giving me a head start. She had to; otherwise, there'd be no contest. As I kept my skis parallel, gliding swiftly over moguls and around steep turns, I knew that Jo Beth was gaining on me.

It didn't matter. If most of the time I felt like Jane Eyre, with "features so irregular and so marked...poor, obscure, plain, and little," now I felt like the moon to her sun, borrowing her light so I could illuminate on my own.

Chapter 6

Jo Beth

She needed to convince her parents that Skylar should move out of their childhood home, to live in Jo Beth's swanky ski condo, which was too big and too quiet for just one person. To divide and conquer, Jo Beth visited her mom at the bakery first, in the afternoon when business would be slow.

"How are you going to enforce any rules?" Her mom, Elizabeth, stood behind her bakery counter, nearly done with a day's work of frosting cupcakes and refilling patrons' coffee. She looked like she needed a coffee of her own. Jo Beth figured that her mother had started her workday at four a.m., just like always. Elizabeth yawned, but Jo Beth refused to acknowledge the subtle social cue that she should save this conversation for a time when her mother was less exhausted. Because it seemed her mother was always exhausted.

Jo Beth just plowed ahead. "Come on, Mom. If anything, Skylar's the one who will be enforcing rules toward me."

"You're not exactly making a case for yourself here."

Jo Beth walked around to behind the bakery counter and removed the nearly empty coffee pot from its hot plate. There was just enough coffee left to pour two cups: one for her mom and one for herself. "I'm just saying that Skylar's not a rebel. I doubt I'll have to do much to keep her in line."

"What about curfew?"

"Curfew?" Jo Beth laughed. "Skylar doesn't ever go out, Mom." She leaned against the wall, then thought better and fixed her posture. It was time to stand tall. "Actually, that's one of the reasons I think she should move in with me. Skylar is great in every way and you've done a superb job raising her…"

"*Thanks,*" Elizabeth said sardonically.

"…but she isn't very happy. Maybe I could teach her some social skills, teach her to fit in a little bit better, so she has more of a life outside of skiing and books."

Elizabeth took a sip of coffee and winced, as if the hot liquid had scalded her tongue. When she spoke, it was with a choked voice. "I don't know, Jo Beth. I mean, I don't think it's books that are a problem. I think it's you."

Had she just heard her mother right? Indignation bubbled inside Jo Beth, but she tried not to get steamed. With as much composure as possible, Jo Beth simply asked, "What do you mean?"

"Skylar relies on you for everything. If she moves in with you, nobody else will matter."

"I won't let that happen, Mom."

"How are you going to stop it?"

She thought for a second. "Okay, maybe Sky idolizes me a little too much. But if anything, living together will knock me off that pedestal. I swear, Mom, this will be a healthy thing."

Elizabeth put down her coffee cup and turned away, toward the sink, so Jo Beth couldn't see her face. Jo Beth spoke to her back. "Haven't you always said that your relationship with *your* parents was ruined after they tried to keep you away from Dad?"

"It's not the same thing."

"But it's close. If you want to her keep her long term, you have to let go of Skylar, at least for right now."

Elizabeth spun around suddenly, grabbing Jo Beth with both hands, capturing her in a fierce hug. "I can't lose either of you," she said.

For a moment, Jo Beth was paralyzed, shocked into silence by this sudden show of desperate affection. Then she let her arms slowly float up and around her mother, returning the hug with an embrace not quite as tight. "You're not going to, Mom."

But Jo Beth knew that was a lie.

Chapter 7

Skylar

Shortly after I moved in with Jo Beth, she and I began this constant informal game of truth or dare. The only twist was we didn't get to choose "truth" or "dare" —we randomly assigned them to each other whenever inspiration struck. Jo Beth always won. But then one overcast February afternoon during my junior year of high school, we strapped our skis to our back and hiked up Tenderhook Ridge to ski off-slope. We were alone and a storm was approaching.

"Hey!" I cried. "Dare! You're going to jump over that ravine." I pointed up slope to a mess of craggy rocks and protruding branches.

"No thanks, Sky. I don't have a death wish."

"You're not accepting the dare? You forfeit? I actually win a round?"

She laughed but looked down, adjusting her ski goggles. "You can't just change the rules in the middle of the game."

"How am I changing the rules?"

There was a sudden gust of wind and a spray of snow slapped us both across the face. I flinched, but not Jo Beth. "We said that dares need to be doable." She pointed up the ravine. "That's not doable, that's suicide."

For some reason I felt especially stubborn, but I wasn't sure why. Maybe the moon was full, maybe my lunch wasn't sitting well, or maybe I was tired of always giving in. "Fine, I'll do it instead." I used my pole to snap off the locks of my skis, hoisted them up over my shoulder, and began the climb.

"Come on, Skylar," Jo Beth yelled. "Give it up."

I looked back at her, at the silver-medal Olympic skier in her sleek black Bogner parka, which the manufacturers had sent for free. Strands of her long, light brown hair were wind-blown and stuck to her face, and her freckles blended in with her cheeks, which had grown rosy from the cold. Many people forgot that Jo Beth was not beautiful, I suppose because her magnetism propelled her into rock star territory. Meanwhile, I was the younger, un-extraordinary version of my sister and I worried that was all I'd ever achieve. I turned back around, determined to reach a good distance above the area I had challenged Jo Beth to jump. Down below, she shifted her weight and checked her watch as if she were standing at the bus stop.

"You're insane!"

I could barely make out her words, even though the wind carried them to my ears rather than swallowing them whole.

"Mom and Dad better not blame me for your death."

She was just trying to scare me. I knew I wasn't about to die. Only one part of the landscape was very sharp; however, the scattered patches of crusty snow did add to its treachery. But I figured I could zigzag around the blotches of dirt and branches, which would give me enough velocity to hit the decline and fly over the bed of rocks, landing safely onto a plateau of snow at the bottom.

I closed my eyes, said a silent prayer, and took off.

It was like the out-of-body experiences I'd only ever read about. I could literally see myself skiing over this impossible slope, yet I was also the puppet master, controlling my movements from up above. My blood pounded in my ears and I discovered a powerful rhythm as I deftly maneuvered myself through the narrow, snowy path, avoiding the pitfalls, gaining speed, and flying over the rocky ravine that my sister had labeled a death wish. When I landed I returned to myself, laughing and whooping with victory. "Yes!" Then, in a sing-song voice I chanted, "I can do something you can't do!"

Jo Beth's mouth turned down and her chest caved, just slightly, before she jutted out her chin. Anyone else would have missed the moment, but to me, Jo Beth broadcast her annoyance as clearly as if she'd yelled it.

"Fine," she muttered, and made a big show of snapping off her skis and trudging up the mountain, to the exact spot where I had taken off moments ago.

The wind had picked up and snow was simultaneously blowing and falling. By the time Jo Beth reached her destination, the visibility was so bad I could barely make out her turquoise snowflake hat. Razor-edged foreboding jabbed my stomach. Why hadn't it occurred to me how much Jo Beth had on the line? She'd secured her spot on the ski team for the upcoming Olympics and was supposed to leave next week.

"Don't do it, Jo Beth," I yelled. "You won't be able to see like I could."

Either she couldn't hear me or she pretended not to. Jo Beth crouched down into her aerodynamic position and then she became a streak of black and turquoise. She went fast but I felt I was watching her in slow motion, sure of the impending catastrophe yet powerless to stop it. When the tip of her ski hit a patch of dirt she fell forward, her limbs twisting and flailing like they were reaching for something solid, not just grasping at air. She landed face down in a patch of rocks, with her left leg jutting at an unnatural angle.

It took us forever to get to bottom of the mountain. I had to support Jo Beth's weight as we traipsed gingerly down, abandoning our skis in the hope that they'd still be there when I managed to return. The storm had reduced things to near-white-out conditions. My face, fingers and toes were numb with cold and my limbs ached with fatigue. But my discomfort was nothing compared to Jo Beth's pain. By the time we'd made it home it was early evening, and much later still when we returned from Urgent Care. Jo Beth hoisted herself out of the car, hopping on one foot over patches of ice to retrieve her crutches from the back seat.

"Let me help you," I said.

"You've helped enough already, Sky."

And that was the last thing she said to me for two days. Jo Beth had torn a ligament in her knee and her face was bruised and scratched. She would be unable to do her photo-shoot for Rossignol, but more importantly, there was no way she'd win or even compete for the Olympic gold now. And she blamed me for everything.

"Hey," I said on the second morning of her stony silence. I'd brought up her breakfast of protein shake and pomegranate, which I'd made for her. "Should we drive into Denver today? Maybe there's a movie worth seeing. I could check the listings." No response; nothing even registered on her face. "Look, Jo Beth, I'm sorry. Really. Please talk to me."

I stood there, knowing I should get ready for school, knowing it was good that she hadn't responded, knowing that an unexcused absence could keep me from getting into my dream school, Cornell.

"Come on. Look at me, please. I really am sorry."

That word, *sorry*, always passed too easily from my lips, like a nagging, non-productive cough. Conversely, Jo Beth didn't know how to say 'sorry' at all, but up until then she would at least accept my apologies with grace. Her eyes would turn from steely gray to silver, sparkling as the light bounced off them, her smile warming her face. Not this time. I'd lost her unconditional support and approval, and the ground beneath me felt uneven as I searched, desperately, for a way to get it back. I shouldn't have bothered. Jo Beth had to be the one to determine the timing of things, and she decided to beckon me later that evening.

"Skylar," she belted, and I instantly abandoned my trek to the kitchen. I found her in bed, her knee elevated on a stack of pillows. But when I saw what she held, I tasted something sour. Jo Beth was reading my poetry journal.

I'd started keeping it after reading *The Bell Jar*. It was an outlet for all my rite-of-passage teenage cynicisms: a place to record my philosophical low points as I wrestled with adolescent angst. Even I knew that my writing was ridiculous, self-indulgent ramblings, but isn't that the point of poetry journals? Nobody but me was ever supposed to read it.

"How did you get that?" I stuttered.

Jo Beth shrugged. "I'm not an invalid and I have crutches. You were out all day, I was bored, so I snooped in your closet." She said this without apology, daring me to make a stink.

"Oh. That's okay. I mean, it's private, but I'm not mad. Can I have it back now?" I reached out, but she slid the journal underneath the pillows that propped up her injured knee. I didn't dare upset it.

"Calm down, Sky. You have nothing to worry about. You're really pretty good at poetry." She smirked and there was a trace of laughter in her voice, just like there was a trace of arsenic in the poppy seed bagel

I'd eaten for breakfast that morning. "But they're all written for Neal Morgan. What's that about?"

My cheeks burned. I'd told no one about my crush on Neal. He was a year older than me, a senior with a girlfriend, and completely out of my league.

"They're just stupid poems. Forget them, okay?"

It was like she hadn't heard me. She pulled my journal back out, leafed through it, cleared her throat, and began her recitation in a pretentious British accent.

"For Neal. #23.

In the twilight song of wraithlike aching,

Owls hoot their isolation while the beautiful find peace.

Meanwhile fog descends, shrouding me in a brooding mist, a lurking trepidation.

Your inky black hair beckons me. Your sturdy shoulders long to sag into my willing arms.

Our crimson lips will meet, parting faintly but with strength

To the taste of life.

Now on a night of pooled vivacity

I hunger for you."

She laughed and raised an eyebrow. "Not bad, but maybe stop reading so much Brontë. And your thesaurus is going to break down from overuse."

I forced a laugh. "Yeah. I'm sure you're right."

Jo Beth closed my journal and opened her mouth as if to continue. She noticed my non-existent poker face, which surely betrayed my distress, and something must have clicked inside her locomotive of a brain because her lips relaxed into a gentle smile. "Don't start crying. I thought you'd think it was funny."

"Well, I don't." I reached out my hand. "Can I have my journal back?"

"I'm not done reading it."

"Come on, Jo Beth."

Jo Beth examined her fingernails. The manicure she'd had last week was beginning to chip and she picked at the pale pink polish on her left thumb. "You should tell him how you feel. I don't think Neal has any idea that you're so into him. It took me by surprise and I know you like I know the back of my hand."

"And you know the back of your hand so well?"

She stretched out her fingers and gazed. "Maybe not as well as I thought."

"Jo Beth, I'm serious. Give me back my journal. Now."

I'd never used such a firm tone with her, but she just grinned like I'd made a joke she'd heard a million times before.

"Sit down." Jo Beth patted the side of the bed. "Sit down and talk to me. How long have you been pining for Neal? Tell me why you're so into him."

She was wide-eyed and guileless. Maybe she really cared. Maybe she actually wanted to know about my stupid, hopeless crush. And after days of the silent treatment, of blaming myself for her having to drop out of the Olympics, her interest in me felt like putting frozen toes in hot water: painful at first, but ultimately soothing. So, I sat and we talked.

I told her that Neal and I had been lab partners and we'd shared some inside jokes, that he'd noticed when I'd gotten my hair cut, and how he'd confided in me about a fight he was having with his girlfriend. Jo Beth was an intent, non-judgmental listener, and at the end of the night, when she asked to hold on to my poetry journal, I said okay. My sister wanted access to my innermost thoughts and I was happy to give her the key.

I fell asleep next to her in her bed. In the morning, after my shower, I went to my room to get dressed and found my poetry journal on top of my computer. *Oh good,* I thought. *She returned it without my asking.* I was running late so I hurried to school without checking my phone. But it didn't take me long to figure things out. The snickers and the pointing were my first clue. I stood at my locker, trying to convince myself I was paranoid, that the laughter and whispers were at someone else's expense. Then Neal approached. His face was grey and he clenched his jaw.

Like someone had died. Like he wanted to kill me.

"What were you thinking?" His voice seemed purposefully loud, inviting the whole school to overhear.

Instantly I realized I was cornered. My heart flung itself against my ribcage, desperate for escape. "I don't know what you mean…"

"There is NOTHING between us, okay? Stay away from me, freak!"

He stormed off to people's applause and high fives. I slammed my locker door shut, made a beeline for the bathroom, locked myself in a stall, and whipped out my phone. One look at Facebook confirmed my worst fears.

Jo Beth had posted three of my most passionate poems about Neal on his wall, using my account.

Two girls entered the bathroom, laughing. "I can't believe it," one said.

"I know, right?" said the other. "It's so ridiculous."

I flushed the toilet and exited the stall in a rush, before they could name me as the subject of their conversation. They did not give me a second glance as I washed my hands and left the bathroom, but I was sure they were laughing at me.

EVERYONE was laughing at me.

I made it through the day by keeping my head down and saying nothing. The moment the afternoon bell rang I raced home, a million thoughts racing through my head. But they were all variations on the same theme: what I was going to say to Jo Beth. I found her on the living room couch watching TV. I stormed past her and the Pottery Barn apothecary table where she rested her feet. Then I flicked off the huge flat-screen television mounted to the brick wall.

"Excuse you," she said. "I was watching that."

I spun around so I was both facing her and standing over her. "Do you hate me or something? Why would you hurt me like that?"

Jo Beth twisted her mouth into a neutral position before answering. She blinked a couple of times, but otherwise, her face stayed passive. "You're talking about the poems?"

"Of course I'm talking about the poems! The whole school saw them. Neal yelled at me and called me a freak! It was like..." my voice cracked. "It was the most humiliating thing that has ever happened to me and it happened because of you. Why did you do it?"

She sat up straight, flinging her shoulders back, but avoiding my eyes. "It was a truth. I called truth."

"Truth only works if I'm the one saying it. You can't say it for me."

She shrugged. "Well, this time I did. I changed the rules, just like you did last week."

"That's completely different."

Jo Beth raised her voice. "I thought he should know how you felt about him. If you don't let him know, then you're giving him all the power."

"You're lying!" I shouted. I took a step forward, menacingly close to where she sat. "You blame me for the accident. You're pissed that I got down that slope and you didn't. You're worried that I might be as good a skier as you, so you wanted to hurt me. That makes you vindictive, petty, and the most unlikable person in the world!"

It wasn't that I was yelling at her for the first time ever; no, I mentioned the possibility that my skiing skills might compare to hers. Such an unforgivable statement was like puking up hot coal. My throat burned, but my stomach felt a hell of a lot better. Jo Beth didn't lash out like I thought she would. Instead she retreated into herself, becoming smaller as her body sagged into the couch. Her voice was quiet, almost inaudible. "You'll never be as good as me, Sky. You're not strong enough for my kind of success." She kept her eyes down, using her right index finger to trace a polka dot on her flannel pajama pants. "If that makes me the most unlikable person ever, I don't care." She forced a tiny laugh. "I mean, I'm not more unlikable than Hitler, or Stalin."

"They're both dead."

"Are you saying I'm the most unlikable person alive?"

"I'm saying that right now, I wish you were dead too."

Jo Beth's mouth dropped open and she met my eyes. Her own eyes widened as she waited for me to take it back, to apologize. I ought to have. Because it was my own death I'd been wishing for all day, not hers. Yet for once I could not utter the word *sorry*.

"You'll regret this," she said softly.

I already did.

Chapter 8

Jo Beth

That moment when she'd flown over the rocky ravine had lasted forever and took no time at all. Jo Beth knew she'd fall yet was utterly clueless, also thinking she'd be suspended in the air indefinitely. But what goes up must come down, and Jo Beth was due for a crash landing.

Skylar had wanted it to happen. Here she was supposed to be Jo Beth's biggest fan, the one who would always cheer for her, but nobody is completely on your side. Sure, Skylar had felt bad when they'd trudged down that mountain and she'd shouldered Jo Beth's weight. But Skylar's help had done nothing to prevent Jo Beth's limbs from growing cold and stiff, which only exacerbated the pain in her knee. And yet, the worst agony took place inside Jo Beth's head, where she couldn't stop making lists of all the things that monumentally sucked. She'd have to drop out of the Olympics. She'd have to back out of her sponsorship contract with Rossignol. She'd have to find a new identity as she endured the buzz of the skiing community, all those jealous bitches who'd declared she was sure to win gold this year but then behind her back had whispered that she'd never seal the deal.

Turns out they were right.

"Oh, Jo Beth!" Chelsea, one of her Olympic teammates, called as soon as she heard the news. "I am so, so sorry. God, life is so unfair sometimes. I wish you a really quick recovery."

Like hell she did. At that moment, Chelsea was probably popping a bottle of champagne, sure that her chances of winning gold had just increased 100 percent. God, false sympathy was way worse than aggression. At least aggression was honest. The only people who *honestly* felt bad for Jo Beth were her parents and Skylar. Yet that also made her fume.

"What can I do?" Skylar kept asking.

"Leave me alone," Jo Beth replied, if she replied at all.

The full fury of Jo Beth's storm raged when Skylar thought she could cheer her up. "You'll be back," Skylar chirped. "In another four years, you'll be so strong and fast. You'll win gold for sure."

As she spoke, Skylar set Jo Beth's dinner tray in front of her, a bowl of tomato soup. Jo Beth wanted to throw it in Skylar's face and watch it drip like blood. She'd be strong again? Jo Beth was strong *now*, and if Skylar didn't see that, then the stars were seriously misaligned. It was up to Jo Beth to restore the balance. The universe needed fixing and the dynamic between her and her sister was the only place to start. Later Jo Beth could see that she'd acted rashly, that perhaps she could have been a little less cruel.

But she regretted nothing. Strong people don't have regrets.

Chapter 9
Skylar

Mostly Jo Beth slept, but when she was awake, her face was lifeless and her hair was droopy and greasy. She stopped showering and for weeks she languished, waiting for her knee to heal while she barely talked to me. It was like she was living her own version of *Becoming Ophelia* or *Prozac Nation*. All day she'd loudly sing along to the Ramones and take selfies, photos where she pouted for the camera and then posted them to Facebook, with captions like "so sad, can't talk about it..."

I found a lot of excuses to stay with Mom and Dad, until one evening I came home to Jo Beth's condo and found it empty, her clothing and prized possessions all packed up, except for her silver medal, which still sat in its display case.

She'd left a note on the refrigerator:

Sky,

I've decided to backpack through South America. I'll contact you when I can, but they don't have a lot of cell phone towers there and I hear the internet connection sucks. Feel free to stay in my condo as much as you want; in fact, it's better if the place looks lived in. And don't worry. I still love you.

Jo Beth

The moment I read the note I turned around and drove straight back to my parent's house. "Mom!" I yelled as soon I walked through their front door. I assumed, and rightly so, that Dad would be in his garage-turned art studio. But instantly I found Mom in the living room.

"Mom! Jo Beth is gone."

Mom sat in her favorite chair, an old fleece blanket with its permanent chocolate ice cream stains draped over her lap. She was reading the latest most popular novel. This was predictable behavior for her, since Mom spent most of her expendable income on books from the best-seller shelf at Barnes & Noble. I plopped down on the couch adjacent to Mom's chair and handed her the note. She took it without speaking and read it calmly, as if it was another page from the book she'd been reading.

"South America, huh?" She handed the note back to me. "Interesting choice. I would have picked Europe. It's much easier to get around and way more people speak English. She'll be so isolated in South America."

"That's precisely why she chose it. So we can't get a hold of her." Fat tears began their slow escape from my eyes. "It's all my fault. She left because of me."

Mom leaned forward and patted my knee. "I'm sure that's not true, Honey. Jo Beth has been unhappy lately, and not just because of what happened with the Olympics and the fight you two had." Mom took a deep breath, rolling back her shoulders as she inhaled. "She needed a change of scenery. Her celebrity has faded a little and I could tell she was getting stir-crazy." Mom's eyes shifted, straying off towards the distance. "Jo Beth can be like me in that way."

"What do you mean, stir-crazy?"

Mom bit her bottom lip for a moment, choosing carefully what she was about to say. "Just that her ups and downs are rather extreme, and lately she's mostly been down."

Perhaps I'd noticed this tendency in Jo Beth, but I was only sixteen, and I'd never really thought about it too hard. I certainly didn't know what Mom was talking about when it came to herself. She was the steadiest person I knew.

"What do we do now?" I asked.

"There's nothing *to* do," Mom replied. "If Jo Beth wants to explore the world, we can't stop her."

"But aren't you worried? What if she's the victim of a drug lord, or she gets Yellow Fever, or she falls into the Amazon?"

"Bad things can happen anywhere, Sky."

"Yes, but she's in way more danger there than she is here." Absently, I tugged at a snarl in my long brown hair. "And if Jo Beth did get into trouble here, we'd be aware and we could do something. But if she's in Argentina, or Brazil, or Portugal, we wouldn't even know and we certainly couldn't help."

"Portugal is in Europe."

"Mom! Take this seriously."

Mom pushed up her wire-rimmed reading glasses so they sat right below her forehead, and brushed a lock of her auburn hair (courtesy of Revlon, shade 5R) behind her ear. She gave me a thin-lipped smile and the seconds dragged out as I waited for her magic words, the ones that would make everything all right.

"Darling, you can move back in with Dad and me. In fact, I insist. You're way too young to be living in an empty condo all by yourself."

I didn't say anything; I just let the truth settle over me like a dense fog. Jo Beth was gone, and not even Mom could bring her back.

Junior year ended, summer passed, and then I was a senior, which meant a light at the end of the tunnel. I wanted to be somewhere different, somewhere with ivy-covered towers and stone pathways along a wide river, where I'd find people to pontificate with about the complexities of the Brontës' work versus Jane Austen. And maybe, if I wore a wool pea coat and leather boots instead of a parka and Sorels, I'd finally feel comfortable in my own skin. Consequently, I stayed focused, studied hard, finished my college essays, and kept my fingers crossed about getting into Cornell.

I spent my days with my chin down, eyes focused on my text books, working hard, and keeping up my GPA. My only social life came from ski club, because I'd occasionally attend a party after we won a meet. I'd never had a boyfriend, unless you counted guys like Nick from The Great Gatsby or Darcy from *Pride and Prejudice*. But I fancied myself a true literary heroine, and inside my mind I took risks, unafraid of where my imagination led me, ready to jump over the pitfalls of uniqueness on my way to maturity.

After the school day let out, if I didn't have ski practice I would walk to my mother's bakery and usually I'd help her by washing dishes or kneading bread. One afternoon the smell of pumpkin bars hung in the air for blocks before I reached the bakery's door, and I could almost taste the buttery, spicy, goodness that would become my after-school snack. Yet when I walked into the bakery, it wasn't my mother I found behind the counter, but a boy I sort of recognized as having graduated last spring.

"Um, hi," I said. "Do you work here now?"

When he smiled, his baby-face grew slightly leaner. "You're Skylar. I remember you from art class." He reached a hand over the counter to shake. "I'm Gavin. Your mom just hired me."

As we shook hands I gave him the once over. His medium brown hair was short in the back but flopped onto his forehead; his large, crooked nose gave his face character; and his plump lips looked soft. For a brief, unintentional moment, I imagined those lips on mine, but I shook that idea off quickly.

"Hello again," I said, pulling my hand away. "I didn't know my mom was hiring."

His grin expanded, making the right side of his mouth rise up half an inch higher than the left. "She wasn't, but I came in with a plate of these—" he pointed to the pumpkin bars,"—and I convinced her to take me on."

"Oh."

"Here, try one." He nudged the platter toward me and I took a bar.

"Oh my GOD!" I said, after my first bite. My taste buds were exploding. "How did you learn to make these?"

"I'm guess I'm pretty much self-taught," Gavin answered. "Trial and error, you know? And I read a lot."

"Yeah, me too." I wiped my mouth with the back of my hand, hoping I wasn't smearing cream cheese frosting across my chin. "I mean, I don't read books about baking, but I read a lot of books on my own, trying to learn about literature, and writing, and well, you know..."

I let my voice trail off, aware that I sounded pretty inarticulate, especially for a self-professed English scholar. Yet Gavin looked at me like I'd just uttered the wisdom of the ages.

He raised his eyebrows. "You're a writer, right?"

Oh, God. Did he remember the Facebook incident with Neal?

"I always saw you writing in your notebook," he continued. "Usually at lunch and you'd have such a serious look on your face that I assumed you were writing something really deep."

I laughed, embarrassed. "Not really. I never had anyone to sit with, so I tried to look busy, because that's less pathetic than looking needy."

"Yeah." He blinked at me and I marveled at how comfortable I felt. Admitting this truth to him was like a long exhale after holding my breath.

"High school cafeterias are the worst," he said. "I wish I'd known, though, that you were maybe up for some company. I'd have introduced myself a long time ago."

My smile started in my stomach, right at the spot where that pumpkin bar had landed. Now I'd be looking forward to my afternoon bakery visits for the entire day.

Chapter 10
Jo Beth

Jo Beth clung to a secret: She was glad for her knee injury, glad to be off the hook for the next Olympics. It wasn't just the fear of failure that drove her. Skiing itself had become way too scary.

It had started with winning the silver. She couldn't get over it. One pause, one hesitant turn, one bump to the right instead of straight ahead, and now she couldn't let go of the what-ifs and they led her down a dark path. *What if I'd planted my poles slightly forward on takeoff? What if I'd put more weight on my left thigh? What if I lost my balance, tumbled down, hit my head at an angle, broke my neck, and died?* The infinite number of possibilities played in a constant loop inside her mind and it dawned on her just how many ways there were to die while skiing. Why had she never seen it before? This was an unwanted paradigm shift, like waking up inside a horror movie without a credit roll. The only way to make it stop was to stop skiing altogether, but that was impossible. The world expected her to ski, so of course she did, but she'd come to hate every moment of it.

Except, that is, when she skied with Skylar. Somehow with her skiing was safe. But then Skylar won her stupid dare and Jo Beth crashed on that rocky slope, and skiing became a favorite jacket that no longer fit. Jo Beth tore more than just a ligament that day. Something else irredeemably ripped inside her, and both Skylar and the mountain had won. That meant Jo Beth lost, and if there was one thing Jo Beth was bad at, it was losing.

That's why she had to leave.

She never apologized for any of her behavior and her guilt was its own form of quicksand. When Jo Beth finally came home for Christmas she avoided Skylar, not wanting to be alone with her because she had no idea what she'd say to her sister. So, Jo Beth made plans with friends for Christmas Eve and on Christmas Day she feigned a hangover, not making it over to her Mom and Dad's until nearly dinnertime.

The instant she walked through the door, Skylar caught her in a hug. "I missed you so much!" she laughed and cried, squeezing her tight.

Jo Beth hugged her back and for a moment the constant, high pitched panic that had burdened her for the past few months diminished into a softer tone. Jo Beth pulled away and took Skylar in.

"You look exactly the same," Jo Beth said, which was a lie. Skylar had a new, pixyish cut that accentuated her hair's brown waves, and there were even more freckles splattered across her cheeks, which made her hazel eyes pop. To anyone else, Skylar would be a combination of girl-next-door and uniquely pretty, but to Jo Beth, she was heart-meltingly beautiful. She'd thought so the first time she ever saw her baby face, and she thought so now.

"And you look skinny." said Skylar. "Did you forget to eat in Chile?"

Jo Beth shrugged. "I just did a lot of walking and I got busy."

Actually, she'd been on a torrent. Every morning she woke with a list of things to do, places to visit, people to meet. With every goal attained there were five more added to her list and it was never-ending. There was barely time for rest and little time for food. Then she met Magda and life was even more of a loud rush, which was all the better to drown out the high-pitched panic.

Mom spoke up. "Well, let's feed you now. Dinner is ready."

"Wait," said Skylar. "We have to introduce Jo Beth to Gavin."

A medium-tallish guy with floppy brown bangs stepped forward, his hand extended. "Hello," he said. "I've heard a lot about you."

"Gavin has been working at the bakery so much that he's practically become a family member," said Mom.

"I'd give anything for that to be true," replied Gavin, his eyes planted on Skylar, who was oblivious to his gaze.

For the moment, Jo Beth could feel that she had Skylar's undivided attention, and in a good way. It meant Skylar didn't hold a grudge. Maybe the skiing accident, their argument, and Jo Beth's abandonment of her sister were all water under the bridge. But was it really possible for them to just move on, to not talk about it, to just sort of pretend that none of it had ever happened? Maybe their strong sisterly bond could endure such a strain, but there was always the possibility that stress fractures would surface later. And Jo Beth knew from experience that once something was cracked it was as good as broken.

Chapter 11
Skylar

My sister and I had been separated from each other for far too long. Our first moment alone together came on Christmas Day, after presents had been opened, the turkey eaten, and the dishes washed and put away. We sat outside on the patio, for it was warm that year, although cold enough that we needed blankets wrapped tightly around our shoulders. We were each protected in our own cocoon, sitting on the rickety wooden chairs as the tea lights Mom had strung through the trellis cast a faint glow over Jo Beth's face.

"So, where are you going to college?" Jo Beth asked. She'd spent all of dinner regaling us with stories of her travels: the villages she'd visited, the mountains she'd climbed, and the people she'd met. But once we were outside she immediately switched her focus to me.

"I've applied to Brown, Penn, and, of course, Cornell." I shrugged. "We'll see. I probably don't have enough extracurriculars. The only thing I've ever really done is ski team." I was trying to sound nonchalant, as if taking such a tone would make me feel less freaked.

"You should apply to Vista College. As, like, a back-up."

"They've already recruited me." Vista College is located at the base of the widest mountain in Colorado and has a very successful

Nordic team in the USCSA. If I went there, my commute would be non-existent and I could ski all I want. Plus, they were offering me a scholarship. "But I want to get out of Colorado, to the East Coast. I need somewhere with a strong English Lit program. Vista College is for people who want to study sports therapy."

Jo Beth nodded. To her credit, she didn't try to convince me that I was crazy pursuing a major with no future, while giving up on what could be a decent skiing career.

"What about Gavin? Won't you miss him?"

I looked down at my blanket-covered lap, so I didn't have to meet her eyes. "We're just friends."

"That's not what Gavin thinks. He stared at you all through dinner."

"No, he didn't." Actually, I'd barely noticed Gavin throughout dinner and I hadn't thought Jo Beth had either. It wasn't until dessert time, when Gavin's pecan pie was presented, that Jo Beth even spoke to him. "Does this have pistachios?" she'd asked.

"What?" Gavin's cheeks turned a baby-blanket pink. "No. Of course not. Just pecans."

Jo Beth pressed further. "What about coconut milk?"

"No. Only condensed milk," he replied.

She nodded, satisfied, and took a piece of pie.

"Jo Beth's allergic to pistachios and coconut milk," I'd whispered to Gavin.

Now Jo Beth giggled and it dawned on me how much I had missed that sound. "He did stare at you and you should cut him a break. Say you'll be his girlfriend, Sky."

I rolled my eyes heavenward toward the mass of stars twinkling brightly in the crisp, mountain night. "I don't want to be anyone's girlfriend," I replied. "And you're the one who convinced me not to trust men."

"But Gavin is innocuous and he's not bad looking. You could do a lot worse."

I didn't think too hard about why Jo Beth suddenly encouraged me to have a boyfriend, instead I thought of the Dorothy Parker anthology I'd been reading. Dorothy would have told me not to trust Gavin; she'd have said not to trust anyone who swore his love because vows of passion are inevitably lies. Not that Gavin had ever made a move, but I could sense that he was gearing up for one. Through the sliding glass door I could see him standing at our kitchen counter, bent over what I assumed was his recipe notebook. Earlier he and Mom had been discussing a new apple sage torte and I assumed he was now jotting down ideas. He carried that recipe notebook with him everywhere, as if a sudden baking emergency might happen and he needed to be prepared.

"You should go inside," Jo Beth continued. "Talk to him. Make him happy."

"I'd rather talk to you. You're not here for very long and we need to catch up."

Jo Beth rubbed her forehead with the palm of her hand, closing her eyes while doing so. "Sky, to be honest, I have a killer headache and I could use some alone time. But I'll still be here tomorrow and we can spend the day together. I promise."

Her voice sounded pained, so I pushed away the stab of hurt caused by her dismissal. "Are you okay? Can I get you anything?"

She opened her eyes slightly and squinted at me. "I'll be fine. I'm just going to sit here for a few minutes and then I'm going to bed."

"Okay."

Jo Beth leaned back in her chair and reclosed her eyes, and I knew that was my cue to leave. I got up, slid the door open, and walked back into the bright warmth of my parent's house. The smell of turkey and bread pudding still clung to the air. When Gavin heard me come in he looked up. Our eyes met and he smiled.

"Back so soon?" he asked. "I figured you and your sister would be talking for hours."

"She's not feeling well." I sat on a stool by the kitchen counter and gazed down at Gavin's notebook. "What are you writing? A recipe for that apple torte?"

He nodded and reached back to scratch the base of his neck. "I was thinking the sauce could be a caramel reduction and we could toast cheese and sprinkle that on top."

"Sounds delicious, but how can you even think about food right now? Aren't you stuffed from dinner?"

Gavin flicked his floppy brown bangs out of his blue eyes. "When I think about food it's not usually about eating. It's just, I don't know, about aesthetics. Does that sound stupid?"

"No. It sounds generous."

He laughed. Gavin's laugh always seemed to come from the pit of his stomach. It was one of the things I liked best about him. "How is it generous?"

"Because you're thinking about food for other people and not for yourself." I let my right index finger stray across the counter, so it brushed the taut skin over one of Gavin's knuckles. His hand was warm, like a conduit, and it made heat travel through my body. It was the first time I'd voluntarily touched him and I guess that was all the encouragement he needed. Gavin put down his pencil, closed his notebook, walked around to my side of the counter, took my hand, and gently tugged. I slid off the stool and put my feet against the floor.

He looked at me with such intensity that I stopped breathing for a second. "I'm going to kiss you now, okay?" he asked in a raspy voice.

"Kiss me or don't kiss me, but don't ask my permission."

I was expecting a gentle, tentative, messy sort of kiss, with too much saliva or an overly aggressive tongue. I'd never actually been kissed before, but I'd heard girls on the ski team talk, so I had some idea of how bad kissing could be. But Gavin used a confident strength to pull me toward him, and when we embraced, suddenly he was Heathcliff and I was Cathy. We were standing on the moors, hearts beating wildly in our chests.

Before I knew it, the kiss was over, and I was left with a tingly dizziness. "Your parents are watching TV in the basement," he said calmly, like nothing momentous had just occurred. "They said to join them if we want to."

"Do we want to?"

He shook his head no and then silently led me to the guest bedroom. My parents had issued a standing invitation for Gavin to use it any time, but I doubted that this was what they had in mind. Yet I followed willingly and let him close the door and take me in his arms. Then we were kissing again and it occurred to me that being so close felt like the red velvet cake he made last week: delicious, but after one or two bites, I'd had my fill.

When he started to walk me towards the bed I pulled away. "If my Dad catches us, you'll lose your guest room privileges."

His chest heaved up and down. "Why can't we just tell them about us?"

One kiss and we were an *us*? "I think that's a bad idea."

His smile disagreed with me. "Maybe they'd approve. After all, I'm not some stranger and they know I'm a nice guy."

Gavin's arguments made sense and were nearly impossible to re-fute. This left me with two options: admit that I was way more inter-ested in sneaking around than in being his official girlfriend, or resume kissing him—a distraction device. I chose option two. He was easily distractible and I felt my body respond as he pressed himself against me. I let him lower me to the bed, where we made out for a good twenty minutes. I even let Gavin get to second base, but when he tried to get to third, I pushed his hand away and sat up.

"I think I heard something," I whispered.

Gavin breathed deeply. "It's nothing."

"No, there were footsteps."

Then, to my horror, there was a knock. I lunged under the bed and hid.

"Yes," Gavin answered in a strangled voice. The door opened.

"Hey. Sorry to interrupt. I just wanted some Advil. Skylar, do you know where it is?"

Jo Beth's voice was flat, as if there was nothing strange about speak-ing to me while I hid under the bed. She crouched down. "Skylar, come out from there. I need your help."

The humiliation was so intense I thought I might spontaneously combust, but I crawled out. "Sorry. I was worried you were Dad."

Jo Beth's eyes were so glazed, I felt a spurt of alarm. Why wasn't she taunting me?

"Can you get me that Advil?"

I brushed the dust off my pants legs and out of my hair. "Sure. Of course."

"Or maybe something stronger? Do you know where Mom keeps her meds? I looked in her medicine cabinet and it was empty."

Gavin and I exchanged a look. His raised eyebrow annoyed me. *How dare you,* I thought. *Don't pass judgment on my sister.*

"Come on," I said to Jo Beth. "We'll find what you need."

I didn't give Gavin a second glance as I closed the door to his room behind me.

Chapter 12

Jo Beth

It was only days after Christmas, but Jo Beth felt this urgent need to return to South America. The feeling nagged at her like she'd left the stove on in her apartment, even though in Santiago Jo Beth lodged in a brightly painted hostel and the only stove was in the communal kitchen adjacent to the deck and lounge area. So, she knew her anxiety just stemmed from her new life calling her back to Brazil. "I met this really great girl named Magda and she and I have started a business," Jo Beth told Skylar. "It's such a great investment opportunity. We'll run day-trips to the coastal towns and do adventure tours along the Rio Maipo Gorge."

Jo Beth could almost hear the alarm bells going off in Skylar's head. *Great investment opportunity* and *really great girl*. Skylar probably thought that Jo Beth's new BFF was soaking her for a ton of money, because—well, Jo Beth was pretty loaded. When she'd won the silver, she'd scored a lot of big endorsements and Dallas's dad had found her a savvy financial advisor. Thanks to some well-timed investments in Apple, Jo Beth would never have to work another day in her life, not if she didn't want to.

But she did want to work. Jo Beth needed something to fill the skiing-shaped hole left inside her and running adventure tours with Magda seemed like the perfect solution. Jo Beth had met Magda in a trendy Santiago nightclub and they'd formed an instant bond. Now Jo Beth told Skylar about how she and Magda went shopping at the Central Market together; how they had a blast drinking together at La Piojera; how they had gone salsa dancing at Ile Habana. And how it was Magda who had come up with the idea to start a business together. Jo Beth showed Skylar all the goofy selfies that she and Magda had posed for during their various adventures. Magda was laughing in each; her shiny black hair was always sleek; her dark, almond-shaped eyes were always wide with wonder.

"She looks like the sort of girl who never worries about following rules or keeping up her GPA," Skylar commented.

Jo Beth gave her a sideways scowl. "What's that supposed to mean?"

Skylar's words seemed to just burst from her lips. "*She* could offer you *real* advice if you ever have guy problems and I'm sure she understands all your dirty jokes. I bet she tells even dirtier ones herself. How can I possibly compete?"

Jo Beth just shrugged. "It's not a competition."

"What is it, then? Are you two, like, involved?"

There it is, thought Jo Beth. After all her anti-romance indoctrination attempts, she'd known that someday Skylar would wonder if Jo Beth actually preferred women.

"What if we are?"

"I'd feel better," Skylar answered. "I get that one day you'll have a significant other; what I can't deal with is being replaced as your best friend."

Jo Beth scooted on the couch, closer to Skylar, and ruffled her hair. "That will never happen, Sky. You're my favorite. I love you best of all."

They dropped the subject and soon Jo Beth returned to Santiago, where Magda made it her mission to get Jo Beth to go skiing with her at Portillo, a resort a couple of hours from the city. "I can't believe you haven't been there yet." she said. "It's only the best skiing imaginable." Jo Beth couldn't say no, but there was a pit in her stomach the morning they drove up to Portillo. Magda was oblivious, navigating the curvy mountain roads, sipping coffee, and singing to the radio. "We're going to have an incredible time," she said, between bellowing out lyrics to Spanish pop songs. "And we can crash at my friend Mitch's place. Wait until you see the swimming pool deck!"

Jo Beth just nodded and stared out the window. The snow-covered mountains were set against a bright blue sky and a distant, bright yellow hotel sat nestled in the hilltops. Soon enough they arrived and Magda pulled into the resort parking. The whole place was small and seemed untouched, like you had to be a member of a secret society to even know about it.

Magda and Jo Beth got their lift tickets, put on their gear, and took the lift up the mountain.

"This slope will blow your mind." Magda cried. "Come on! Follow me!"

A year ago, no way would Jo Beth have let someone else take the lead, but now she was happy to have Magda in front. Jo Beth kept her eyes on Magda's purple parka rather than on the sharp rocks that were more plentiful than the patches of snow along the slope. Images of Tenderhook Ridge's stony ravine, the one that had been her undoing, flashed behind Jo Beth's eyes. She felt the mountain air pressing her down, like it wanted her to fall again.

They reached a narrow path along a low cliff. It overlooked a glacial lake and when she looked down, Jo Beth trembled with dizziness. She figured there ought to have been a sign at the beginning of this slope, *For Skinny People Only*, maybe with an image of an obese skier and an x through it. Because seriously, if she moved half a foot to her left she'd push up against the cutting edges of the mountain. If she moved half a foot to her right, she'd topple over a thin wire fence and then she'd tumble about one hundred feet into the frozen glacial lake beneath.

Would she crash through the ice, or would she just bounce, like she was on a cold, slick trampoline?

No. The ice would crack and Jo Beth would sink—skis and all—into the frozen depths. With this knowledge came a weight on her chest and her knees buckled. Was her still-weak ligament acting up? But both her knees were threatening her, so no. No. It was all due to her nerves, to her craziness.

Jo Beth took a deep breath and told herself to get a grip.

"Have you ever seen anything more beautiful?" Magda cried.

"Amazing!" Jo Beth yelled back, surprised she could find her voice.

She dared to look to her right. The frozen water was so clear that the craggy mountain on the opposite side of the lake was reflected, almost like there was a second mountain growing beneath the water, into the bottom of the earth. She'd seen a lot of mountains and she'd skied thousands of slopes, but if she could reach past her anxiety she'd have to admit that no, she'd never seen anything more beautiful.

It was literally breathtaking.

Jo Beth closed her eyes for a couple of seconds, felt the wind at her back and velocity pulling her forward. *You're safe*, she told herself. When she reopened her eyes, there was Magda's purple parka, still ahead of her. And although Jo Beth was now navigating the narrow slope with ease, she thought, *I can do better. Heck, even Skylar could do better.* Soon the slope widened, they were away from the glacial lake, and the whole mountain stretched before them in a steep, precarious, wonderful mess. Jo Beth pulled ahead of Magda. "Race you to the bottom!" she cried.

Jo Beth was going too fast to hear whether or not Magda answered. It didn't matter. Jo Beth still won.

The only hotel in Portillo was a bright yellow building, which looked as if it been airlifted and magically placed into the tiny groove between two enormous, snow-capped mountains. Jo Beth marveled how civilization could exist around so many steep slopes and glacial lakes, but there it was: a locally-run resort whose one dining room was large and cafeteria-like, where guests and staff ate together, family style. But dinner wasn't until late, so Jo Beth and Magda went swimming first, in the outdoor pool, a little oasis smack in the center of rugged ice and rock.

"I'm heading straight for the hot tub," Magda said, as they reached the triangular shaped swim deck. The hot tub was in the corner, its bubbles casting out steam over layers of snow beyond the fence.

"Okay. I'm swimming first."

Jo Beth pulled off her robe and the frosty, brittle air stung her skin. Before she could think better of it, she dove head first into the deep end of the pool, letting herself descend into the waters depths, like she'd imagined herself sinking earlier into that glacial lake. But here the water was warm, protective, nurturing even, its security cause for celebration. She reversed course, kicked her legs, and pulled herself back up to the surface. Once Jo Beth's head was out, she took a deep breath and reveled in the beauty of the sky, the mountains, and the joy of living. She'd missed feeling like this.

Then there was a huge splash.

Someone had dived into the pool and landed dangerously close. A couple of extra inches to his left, and he'd have anchored atop of Jo Beth. She'd have sunk, against her will this time, unable to breathe from the weight of him.

"Sorry," he said, the instant his face rose to the surface. "I didn't mean to get so close to you."

"No worries," she replied, and started to breast stroke away.

He swam after her. "I'm Mitch," he said. "You know? Magda's friend who works here?"

Jo Beth pivoted in the water and faced him. Huge dark eyes framed by thick lashes. Black, curly hair and brownish skin. A wide, innocent smile that suggested he was barely aware of the beauty of his long, lean, muscular body. But even though he was mostly submerged, Jo Beth could tell he was gorgeous.

"I was trying to find a good way to introduce myself," he said. "But I guess I blew it."

He spoke with a slight accent; Jo Beth couldn't tell where from. "Are you American?" she asked. "I mean—North American? From the U.S.?"

He nodded while treading water. "Magda and I went to the same high school in Miami. She and I moved to Santiago together, for school. But after we broke up I got a job teaching skiing here at Patillo."

"Oh." Jo Beth wondered why Magda hadn't mentioned that it was her ex-boyfriend who had gotten them the room, why she hadn't mentioned an ex-boyfriend, period. "Well, thanks for helping us out."

He laughed. "Magda hasn't told you about me, has she?"

"No."

"That's so like her. Out of sight, out of mind. She's always been like that."

"But you must still be friends, right?"

"Oh, sure. Our breakup was mutual. It was just time to go our separate ways, yeah?"

The slight lilt to his voice was vaguely European. Jo Beth wondered if when you're constantly surrounded by tourists, you take on an amalgam of accents, like a linguistic Velveeta cheese. She smiled at him and then swam to the edge of the pool. Again, he followed. "How long have you worked here?" she asked.

"Three years. Originally it was supposed to be a break, until I figured out my next step. But I love it so much that I haven't been able to leave."

They had each grasped onto the edge of the pool, making it easier to look at each other, to take each other in. His face was so sweet that it made Jo Beth imagine a dozen dorky school photographs. One per year for a dozen years, where he would age slightly each time but there would always be a lock of hair sticking out or a mismatched button, and from kindergarten to senior year, the innocence would never leave his eyes or his smile. She could see the little boy he was once, the little boy he must still be to his mother. Yet looking at his body, Jo Beth could see he was obviously a man.

She realized it was her turn to say something. "I wish I could find something that I love that much."

He cocked his head. "But haven't you? What about skiing? I remember seeing your Olympic win on TV. Quite amazing."

"It was just the silver."

"Still. Quite amazing."

He looked at her like he meant it, like she was the only woman who'd ever truly impressed him. *Don't get taken in*, she told herself. *Flings are one thing, but you can't believe their lies.*

Mitch craned his neck, looking around. "Where is Magda?"

Jo Beth pointed to the hot tub. "Over there."

"Should we go give her a hard time? I can't believe she's never told you about me. Oh, the stories you've missed out on."

She laughed despite herself. "Then I guess we'd better make up for lost time."

That night they drank wine and ate tapas. By 2:00 a.m., Magda had fallen asleep on Mitch's bed while Mitch and Jo Beth stayed up, whisper-laughing, sprawled out on his tiny living room floor and sipping the dregs from the last of the Pinot noir. "What do you see yourself doing when you're old?" he asked.

"Huh?"

Jo Beth was sitting, but Mitch lay down, stretching his long limbs, and arching his neck. He gazed up at her. "I think about it a lot," he said. "One day I'll be an old man. And just like the world's ultimate path is to keep expanding from dark energy until all matter is ripped apart, my body's cells will keep reproducing and changing, but ulti-mately, they'll self-destruct, you know?"

She laughed. "Did you just smoke some weed? If so, where's my share?"

"Sorry, this is just how I think. But do you get what I mean?"

Jo Beth wasn't sure that she did, but she shrugged her shoulders like she totally followed him. Mitch continued. "Maybe my body will be too banged up for skiing, maybe I'll be too tired for travel, but I'm still going to do stuff."

"Like what? Golf?"

He sniffed dismissively. "Probably not golf. I made a list, actually." Mitch started counting off on his fingers. "Gourmet cooking class. Leatherworking. Chess tournaments. Learn magic..."

"Wait, you mean real magic? Like Harry Potter?"

Mitch's laugh was deep and chortle-like. "No. Like David Blaine—you know—illusions."

Jo Beth did her best to sound unimpressed. "Is that all?"

He shook his head. "I'll get some really big tattoos—maybe even learn to do them myself." His eyes shone with enthusiasm.

"But you already have a tattoo." Jo Beth pointed to the tiny pi symbol on his bicep. "What's that about?"

He shrugged. "I liked the irony of making something that's endless so small. They say you shouldn't get tattoos because when you're old, you won't want them anymore. But what if you wait to get them until you're *actually old*? Then that argument's dead."

Her fingers crept to the base of his head. It had become impossible not to stroke his curls. "I hear what you're saying, but life is short. Maybe you shouldn't wait several decades to get going on all this stuff."

"But I want to travel and ski while I'm still young and that takes time."

"I suppose." She let her fingers skim his forehead and that simple action made her heart pound. "But when I make a to-do list, I can't wait. It has to happen right away."

"Oh!" His face lit up. "I forgot the most important thing. I'm going to go back to school, for cognitive studies."

"You're like my sister. She's smart too. She's convinced that her life depends upon getting into Cornell."

"Then I hope they accept her. But what about you?"

"What about me?"

Mitch sat up and met her eyes with an abrupt intensity. "What's on your to-do list?"

Jo Beth was suddenly so flushed that she had to look away. She spoke to the floor. "See the world; learn to paint; make up for all the crappy mistakes I've made." Glancing back at him, she shrugged. "It's not an extraordinary list."

"What about love? Is that on your list?"

Moonlight shone through his one window, casting his face in light and shadow, and though they'd only just met, Jo Beth could no longer remember what not knowing Mitch felt like. "No," she told him. "I like to make my goals attainable."

"Too bad," he said, inching towards her, taking her face in his hands, and tilting his head so their lips could meet. "But then again, if nothing ever felt impossible, there would be no surprise."

Jo Beth let Mitch kiss her and it was sweet, like bubblegum that's still soft and flavorful. More importantly, by kissing him, some crucial defect in her personality, one she hadn't even been aware of, felt suddenly and miraculously fixed. As she wrapped her arms around him she became a nicer person, balanced and generous all at once. "You don't feel impossible," she murmured between kisses. "Even though you are a huge surprise."

He laughed. "Please keep calling me huge."

Jo Beth giggled. When had she ever felt so light, like she had to clutch his shoulders or she might just drift away? That sensation never left her, not the next morning when she had to tell Magda that she'd fallen for her ex, and not in the weeks that followed, when Jo Beth spent all of her time with Mitch, falling in love like she was a heroine from one of Skylar's Brontë novels.

For underneath the giddiness was a dark desperation, the knowledge that if she clung too hard, she'd reach past the bubble's walls, and then it all would pop.

Chapter 13
Skylar

On March 11th I turned eighteen. My mom made my favorite meal, chicken Parmesan, and Gavin came for dinner. After we'd stuffed ourselves on pasta, Mom brought out the cake. I nearly salivated when I saw that it was coconut, with light pink cherry frosting.

"I'm going to be too fat to ski, Mom."

"Never," said my father. "Your metabolism is like your mother's. Besides, I forbid you to be one of those girls who's obsessed with her weight."

"I know, but if I ski next year for Vista College..."

Mom placed a slice of cake on a plate and set it in front of me. "You're getting into Cornell," she said. "I have a feeling."

I wanted to ask if she had any sort of feeling about a scholarship, but I held my tongue. Mom and Dad were solidly middle class, existing in this upper-crust town that had the same diversity as a loaf of Wonder Bread. No college was going to give me a free ride, especially not if they knew who my sister was. But Jo Beth hadn't offered to help with my tuition and I didn't know how to ask.

I took a bite of cake and savored the divine taste of butter, sugar, and euphoria. "Oh my God, Mom! This is the best cake you've ever made and that's saying a lot."

Mom pointed to Gavin. "It was his recipe. Amazing, right?"

Gavin's cheeks turned as pink as the frosting. "I actually think it could be tweaked a little..."

"No. Don't change a thing." I reached over to squeeze his shoulder. "Thank you, Gavin. It's absolutely delicious."

"Don't thank me yet," he replied. "You haven't even opened your present." Gavin reached a hand underneath the table, into his jean pocket, and pulled out a tiny box, which he gave to me. "Here," he said, flicking his bangs out of his eyes. "Happy birthday."

Judging from the size of the box, it had to be jewelry.

Oh God.

He was giving me jewelry, and in front of my parents, which only quadrupled the awkwardness factor. Hopefully the ring or necklace, or whatever it was, wasn't heart-shaped. My throat went dry and my panic must have been clearly telegraphed, because Gavin smirked. "Don't worry, Sky. You're going to like what's in the box."

I lifted the lid. Inside, nestled on a bed of cotton, was a silver book-shaped charm with *Jane Eyre—Brontë* engraved on the cover. Well, Gavin knew me well enough to know that *Jane Eyre* was my most favorite book, that I identified with Jane, who believed you could be conventional and still be wrong.

"It's a key chain," Gavin said. "You'll understand, once you open your next present."

"Huh?"

I looked from face to face in confusion. Dad took a deep breath and handed me a manila envelope, which he'd stashed next to him all through dinner. "It's from your sister," he said in a gravelly voice. He used his free hand to scratch at his beard, signaling his disapproval. I opened the envelope and pulled out the papers. There was a note on top.

Happy birthday to the best little sister in the world! Sky, you have goals and dreams that I don't understand, but never forget how much you have going for you at home. This is going to shock you, but I think you could be as good at skiing as I am, maybe even better. You just don't push yourself enough. That's why I want you to have my condo. You can train and you'll have a place of your own while you go to Vista College. Who knows, maybe the Olympics will be in your future!

Love always,

Jo Beth

Underneath the notes were some legal documents that I tried to make sense of, until Mom spoke up. "She's set up a trust, Honey. You will get the condo when you turn twenty-one. Until then you can live there, but none of it will legally be yours for another three years."

"But...why?"

"She was going to give it to you now," Dad said. "But after we talked, she decided it was better to wait. Your sister has an agenda, Sky. She's decided that what's best for you is to stay here and focus on your skiing."

This was all wrong. My tongue felt so thick, I was surprised my speech didn't come out slurred. "That's not what I meant. Why is she giving it to me at all? Won't she want the condo for herself someday?"

An uncomfortable look passed between my mother and father. "I don't know," my mother finally said. "Jo Beth can be erratic. But more than anything, she loves you, and that's why she's also decided to draft a will. Should anything happen to her, you will receive everything—all her stocks, all her money—everything."

"But she's only twenty-one! Why is she thinking about a will?"

Dad shrugged. "When you're worth as much she is..."

His voice trailed off, but Dad didn't need to finish his statement. We all knew what he was thinking. Jo Beth never planned on returning. She would spend the rest of her life in or around Santiago. And for whatever reason, she wanted to be prepared for the worst to happen.

Later, Gavin and I went for a walk. A few sunny days had melted all the snow, but nighttime brought freezing temps, turning the afternoon's puddles to patches of ice. I hit one the wrong way with the tip of my boot and went sliding. Gavin quickly grabbed my elbow and steadied me, saving me from what could have been an ugly fall.

"Thanks." I promptly pulled my arm out of his grasp.

"Don't be mad," he said.

"I just don't get why you knew about the condo and the will before I did."

He tipped his head back and looked up at the stars. "I didn't know about the will at all. As for the condo, I just thought you got to live there by yourself for as long as you wanted."

"Yeah? I still say that you and my mom are too close."

"Come on, Sky." He looked at me with eyes like the frozen puddles I'd just skidded over. "I asked her what I should get you for your birthday and she said, 'get her a keychain.' Then she just spilled." He stepped on a slippery patch over a slope in the sidewalk, and the impact of his boot made a satisfying crunching sound. "She probably thought I'd understand, since my grandpa left me his cabin and I know what it's like to own property at such a young age." Gavin had been super close to his grandfather; he was the one who'd taught him to cook, and Gavin's favorite childhood memories had taken place at his grandfather's cabin in the woods. When his grandfather died from cancer a few years ago he'd left the cabin to Gavin. I'd visited the cabin a few times and found it charming with its rickety, homemade furniture, like the family's cottage that the monster from *Frankenstein* spies upon. While we were there Gavin would always cook me a gourmet meal and afterwards he'd try and make out with me. Sometimes I'd let him. "Anyway," Gavin continued, "your mom made me promise that I wouldn't ruin the surprise, and honestly, I don't see what difference it makes."

I filled my lungs with alpine air. Beyond me, the mountain was lit by tiny lights. My parent's house was miles from the ski resort, but when we were at Jo Beth's condo—my condo soon—we'd be closer to those lights.

I stepped in next to Gavin and slid my hand into the pocket of his wool coat. Gavin was the only guy I knew who didn't wear a ski jacket. "Do you think I ought to stay here and ski, instead of going away to school?"

Gavin stopped walking, so I did too. Inside his pocket, his fingers closed over mine. "I can't answer that."

"Why not?"

"Because what I want you to do and what I think you ought to do are all confused inside my brain." He used his free hand to trace a path among the freckles over my nose and cheeks. Then he leaned in and let his lips do the same thing. Baby kisses against my face, a hand squeezing my fingers, an arm around my waist, his chest heaving against mine. "You should just kiss me for real," I murmured.

"You're bossy," he replied.

I made my lips find his and my free arm wrapped itself around his shoulders. For a moment I was just a girl who sort-of loved her sort-of boyfriend, trying to decide between leaving him for school or staying with him for skiing. But soon my anxiety crashed the party and thoughts of Jo Beth took over.

I pulled away.

"We should get back," I said. "My parents will wonder what took us so long."

That night, sleep would not come. My mind was too full of questions. Was Jo Beth in trouble? And if so, did it have anything to do with this new boyfriend she'd emailed me about, Mitch? After I'd been lying in bed for an hour I surrendered to insomnia, powered on my computer, and re-read Jo Beth's most recent email, which was already weeks old.

Sky,

I'm down in Santiago for the day to do some shopping and I stopped at a cyber café so I could email you. I have so much to tell you! I guess Mitch and I are moving sort of fast, because I'm pretty much living with him now! But everyone at Portillo is like family and I can't get enough of Mitch. I wish you could meet him. I never knew there'd be someone for me, someone I could spend my days with and not feel restless, someone I could talk to, someone who would understand me and love me for who I am.

You have to come to Portillo. I'll pay. Maybe this summer? Graduation gift? Say yes!!

Love always,

Jo Beth

I'd already responded, saying I'd love to visit if it didn't interfere with my college plans, whatever they turned out to be. And, of course, I'd need Mom and Dad's approval, but otherwise, it was a solid yes.

Now I wrote back again.

Jo Beth,

Today's my birthday and I got your generous gift. Thank you!

Then I stopped. I wanted to sound gracious but I also wanted answers. Why was she trying to control my life by forcing me into the skiing career she'd given up on? Why was she so sure she'd never come home? And why was she thinking about wills—about death—when, if I took her emails at face-value, she ought to have been thinking about love, marriage, and maybe even motherhood?

I resumed typing.

You're too good to me. I can't wait to see you, Jo. It's been way too long.

My questions would have to wait. I would get no answers from an email. I needed to see my sister, face to face. After all, I had learned the same lesson from her as I had from Charlotte Brontë in *Jane Eyre*. It's silly to believe people can be content with calm. Jo Beth especially needed action and drama, and she was always willing to invent her own, unless some drama came along and found her first. Had drama found Jo Beth and had it taken human form? Was its name Mitch?

Meeting him was the only way to find out.

Chapter 14

Jo Beth

"I'm bored."

"Then go skiing," Mitch rolled over in bed and put the pillow on top of his head. In twenty minutes, his alarm would ring and then it would be time for him to get up and teach ski school. But Jo Beth had been awake for hours and there was no reason for her to go back to sleep. She had nothing she needed rest for. Besides, if she got tired she could take a nap in the afternoon, and that was the problem.

She stretched out her foot and kicked him gently in each ankle. "Mitch, I need to go back down to Santiago next week."

"Why?" he said, his voice muffled by the pillow.

"Because I've been neglecting Adventuras Tours and I think Magda is mad at me. She and I were supposed to do this business together."

"If Magda was mad at you, you'd know it. She's not the type of girl to hold it in."

Jo Beth repressed a frustrated groan, hating that Mitch had ever been intimate with her business partner/best friend. But it was easier to shift her body and push herself up against him than to voice her insecurities. "I'll hate to leave you."

Mitch's breath was hot against her ear. "Then I'll convince you to stay." He reached over and shut off his alarm, a pre-emptive action so that eight minutes later, they wouldn't be disturbed by a beep-beep-beeping. Then Mitch distracted her, briefly making her forget that she had nothing else to do for the whole rest of the day.

An hour later, after he'd showered and dressed, he was pulling on his boots and putting on his coat. "You could always get a job here with the ski school, you know."

"But I don't speak enough Spanish."

"Still, they'd have you for sure. A star like you—I'm surprised they haven't begged you already. In a parallel universe, I bet they have."

Mitch had already explained the parallel universe theory, telling her how time was like a ribbon and every choice they made could create an alternative multiverse where infinite possibilities were played out. But Jo Beth wasn't interested in a parallel universe, for she was stuck in this one, where her options felt limited. She sat in bed, watching Mitch prepare to confront the day, while she would stay in this tiny apartment indefinitely. "I'd make a terrible ski instructor. I couldn't deal with all the fat tourists who are just after a good photo op for next year's Christmas letter."

He gave her his schoolboy grin. "You're thinking of home in Colorado. It's not really like that here."

She pulled up her knees and rested her chin against them. "Maybe. But I don't want my job to be about skiing."

"Why not? You've got talent and fame. Why shouldn't you build a career around skiing? Lots of people would kill to have what you have." She silently snapped at him, sending him a look of laser-focus indignation, but Mitch ignored her attitude. "Do you even need a career? I mean, how much are you worth?"

It wasn't the first time he'd ask her this, and Jo Beth couldn't tell if he was simply curious about her money since he didn't have any of his own, or if his intentions were more selfish. "Well," she said, jokily evading the question, "my parents think I'm priceless."

He laughed. "And I agree!" He secured his ski hat over his thick black curls, came over, brushed a lock of her hair away from her face, and planted a kiss on her freckled cheek. "You're right. You should call Magda. Go back to working with her."

Did he just say that so she'd invest more of her money into the business that Magda had insisted upon starting? What if this whole thing was a setup, what if Mitch and Magda were in collusion? "Yeah..."

He stood up straight. "I'd better go or I'll be late for my first client. Have a good day."

"You too."

When Mitch shut the door behind him she fell back in bed. Staring at the ceiling, she knew it was crazy to think this way. Mitch was a good guy and he just wanted what was best for her. No, she was simply imbalanced. After all, here she was, a ski star at one of the best resorts in the world, and she didn't care to go skiing. That was insane. Yet she couldn't motivate herself to go outside and conquer some slopes. She knew she needed to call Magda, but Jo Beth had broken the don't-fall-for-your-best-friend's-ex code, and while Magda pretended to be cool about it, Jo Beth realized the growing silence between them was personal. Jo Beth had abandoned their friendship and their business, and for what? A guy. Magda had every right to hate her.

Jo Beth hated herself.

This was nothing new. She had hated herself back in Black Diamond when she'd betrayed Skylar. She had hated herself as she travelled around South America, aimlessly looking for a new identity, as if she could buy one at a street stand and wear it like an Alpaca sweater. She had even hated herself as she fell in love with Mitch, thereby breaking every rule she'd ever established for Skylar and for herself. But he was such a charming, handsome guy.

Screw it, Jo Beth thought. Having a purpose was more important. She'd call Magda, do some groveling, and get their business and herself back on track.

Chapter 15

Skylar

Cornell rejected me.

I wasn't prepared for that moment of finding out, of opening that thin envelope, of telling myself that maybe there's still a chance, that perhaps their acceptance letter comes first and the thick packet of information will come the next day. *Thank you for your application. Unfortunately, space is limited and we cannot grant you admittance at this time...* the words blurred together and my heart fell, like a thick ball of ice through a fresh powder of snow.

All my years of hard work, my dreams of escaping this homogenous ski town, of being more than a girl with sticks attached to her feet, evaporated as quickly as the tears began to pour. I dropped the letter onto the table, raced to my room, and shut the door behind me. Then I buried my head beneath my pillow and sobbed.

Mom was at the bakery but Dad was home, working in his studio. He must have come in for a snack, saw the abandoned rejection letter, and heard me crying. Because after a while there was a soft knock on my bedroom door.

"Sky, I'm coming in," he announced in his easygoing voice. I didn't respond. He entered, sat down next to me on my bed, and enfolded me into his arms. I could smell the turpentine scent that he always carried. "I'm sorry, Honey."

I pressed my face against his shoulder and his soft flannel shirt absorbed my tears. "I really wanted to go there," I murmured. "But they don't want me."

He hugged me harder. "Rejection sucks," he said. Then, with a sigh, he loosened his arms and pulled away, so he could look me in the eye. "But, unfortunately, it's a life lesson few of us escape. And honestly, I feel bad for the people who do escape it. They don't ever learn how to create their own opportunities."

I wiped my eyes with the back of my palm. "What do you mean?"

He contemplated for a moment, letting his eyes scan the ceiling. "If I'd been accepted into a prestigious art program and found an agent, I'd have lived a different sort of life. But instead I've worked hard to create something that's my own and I like the life I have." He kissed my forehead right at the hairline. "Meanwhile, your sister has had everything come easy and now she's at a loss."

The tears just wouldn't stop flowing. "I'd still rather go to Cornell."

"I know. But you'll study literature somewhere else. Or you'll figure out new goals." He gave me a soft, "atta girl" punch in the shoulder. "And you won't give up, which is why I know that, ultimately, you're going to be okay."

"So, you're saying I should stay here, ski for Vista College, and figure out a new plan?"

He shrugged. "Would it be so bad, living at your sister's condo and starring on the ski team? I mean, you love to ski."

"Yeah, but it's not what I want to do with my life, Dad. I'm not Jo Beth."

"Thank goodness for that." Dad got up, but before he left my room, he looked down at me and smiled. "There are plenty of ways to leave Black Diamond, Sky. You don't need Cornell to get out of here. Just make sure that when you do go, you're not leaving yourself behind."

What does that even mean? I thought, as Dad exited my room.

Unfortunately, I would have plenty of time to figure it out. In the weeks that followed, I received another rejection letter from Brown and an acceptance letter from Penn, but without an offer of financial aid. Of course, I thought about asking Jo Beth for tuition money; I could sell the condo or get an advance on funds she'd already promised me. But I didn't feel entitled to any of it and the very idea of her bequeathing me her fortune made my skin crawl. I wanted Jo Beth, not her money, so I settled on a ski scholarship with Vista College. They were giving me a free ride and I'd take every single literature class they offered—all six of them—and work on transferring to a better literature program by my junior year.

But for now, the only way that I'd be leaving Black Diamond was on my spring break trip, which was also my graduation gift, to South America.

It wasn't the first time I'd ever left Colorado, or the U.S. for that matter. One-time Mom and Dad had taken us to Mexico for a beach vacation, and there'd been camping road trips to Wyoming. And of course, we'd gone to cheer for Jo Beth when she'd competed in the Olympics. Yet when my Santiago-bound plane took off, I sat there, strapped in and awestruck as I looked out the window; the sky stretched and the ground became nothing but shadow.

Maybe my life *was* full of possibility. Maybe I just needed to adopt the right attitude. After all, this was the twenty-first century and unlike all the literary heroines whom I admired, the main thing holding me back was my mindset. In fiction, there were halo-wearing submissive gals and there were the self-assured live-wires, but either way, they all had very limited options. Either find a man and become a good wife, or commit suicide after being naughty and exhausting all other possibilities. But times had changed since Madame Bovary had found the rat poison or since Edna from *The Awakening* had wandered into the Gulf of Mexico, and I wondered what I might discover if I refused to limit myself.

I slept during the flight so I wouldn't be jet-lagged. It kind of worked. When Jo Beth picked me up at the airport she was all hugs and enthusiasm, talking a mile a minute, showing off her Spanish, and walking so fast I could barely keep up. But I did keep up; I kept up that night when she insisted we hit Santiago's night clubs, I kept up the next day when we explored historic Valparaiso, and I kept up the day after that, when we went hiking in the Andes.

She kept me busy and Jo Beth was the consummate tour guide. There was never a dull moment, which meant there was never a time to relax and talk. Besides, Magda was always along. On the fourth day, Mitch showed up, and we all took a bike tour through the Santa Rita vineyards. We pedaled down wide dirt paths atop sturdy green bicycles, which were heavy enough that they became difficult to steer. Every so often we'd stop, park our bikes, walk through a vineyard, and taste different wines. By lunchtime I was exhausted, dehydrated, and a little light-headed.

We had a picnic of goat cheese, grapes, and pan amasado, which was the best bread I'd ever eaten. More importantly, I chugged water, bottle after bottle, and Jo Beth insisted that I shouldn't stop. "I packed plenty," she told me.

"She thinks of everything," Magda said. She was stretched out on the blanket, rubbing her left ankle. "I don't know how we'd even be in business without your sister."

"Don't say that." Mitch's sun-lit voice contradicted his bossy command. "As soon as the ski season resumes in June, I get her back with me, at Portillo."

"So she can teach ski school? Please." Magda smirked and turned toward my sister. "Tell Mitch you're staying down in the city."

Jo Beth shrugged. "I don't know yet."

"Yes, you do, Jo Beth. You know." He spoke like they shared a secret language, or like she was dyslexic and he was her special, backwards newspaper, written in their own private code. And I could see his effect on my sister.

She wavered, nearly trembling in the gentle summer breeze. "Yeah, but our business is doing so well..." Jo Beth reached for my water bottle and I handed it over. She took a swig before continuing, and we all waited, expectant for whatever she was about to say. "I mean, I want to be up at Portillo with you, but I also want to be in Santiago, running day trips."

"Because our day trips are way cooler than teaching ski school," said Magda.

"Portillo happens to be the coolest ski resort in the world," Mitch countered. "You can't get 'cooler' than that."

Magda laughed and extended her leg toward Mitch. "My ankle is sore. Rub it for me?" Mitch instantly placed her ankle in his lap and began kneading with both of his thumbs.

"After all that wine and water, I have to pee like a madwoman." Jo Beth got up and spoke only to me. "Come on, Sky. Let's go find a hidden spot where we can do our business."

"Okay." I stood, stepped over the blanket and the food, and joined my sister. Jo Beth was smiling, her freckled cheeks rosy, wisps of her brown hair bleached blonde by the sunlight. She was the picture of health and vitality, yet it seemed almost too good to be true, as if her appearance had been photo-shopped.

As we walked away, Mitch and Magda murmured and laughed. The ease between them was natural yet unnatural, like incestuous siblings. Jo Beth took my arm and pulled.

"What do you think of Mitch?" she asked.

"He's cute." And he was; the guy could turn some heads. Imagine a mixed-raced, younger, curly-haired, and slightly better-groomed Brad Pitt. That was Mitch.

"I wish he wasn't so busy with school," Jo Beth said. "His fellow-ship is taking all his time."

"What's it in again?"

"Cognitive studies."

"Wow. Impressive. And he has to live on campus?"

"Yeah."

We both fell silent; there was the crunch of twigs underneath our feet and a soft wind ruffled the grape leaves. After several moments, I asked, "So you miss him?"

"I do…" Jo Beth let her voice trail off, ending at a humble, sad pitch.

"What's wrong, Jo?"

She let go of my arm and squared her shoulders. When she spoke, she returned to her usual tone: the strong and loud one. "I can't tell if Mitch and Magda are fooling around."

"I thought Magda was your best friend. Do you really think she'd do that to you?"

Jo Beth barked out a laugh. "You're so naïve, Sky."

"But…"

"Mitch belonged to Magda first. It doesn't matter that they were long broken up by the time Mitch and I met. Magda still thinks that I stole him from her."

"Okay." I pushed a protruding branch from the vineyard out of our path. "What about Mitch? Don't you trust him?"

Jo Beth's footsteps came to an abrupt halt, so I stopped too. We stood, freckled face to freckled face, each brushing wispy brown hair from our eyes, each blinking away the sun while staring the other one down.

Jo Beth's chin quivered. "I'm scared, Sky."

"Of what?"

She took three deep breaths. "Mitch and Magda. I'm scared of them both."

"But... why?"

"I think they're up to something. They're always speaking in Spanish, quickly, so I can't keep up. And the other day I found some papers..." She looked away from me, off into the distance, at the rows and rows of grape vines that will one day be plucked, smashed, and made into wine. "That's why I signed my condo over to you. The less I have in my name, the better. It's also why I'm working with Magda. You know, that whole 'keep your enemies close' thing."

"You don't have to do that. You can just leave. You don't need either of them, Jo."

At the sound of her name, Jo Beth snapped out of her reverie. She shook her head slightly and rolled her eyes. "Don't be insane," she told me, laughter filling her voice. "I'm in love. There's no way I'm leaving Mitch. And my business with Magda totally rocks. I'm not leaving that either." She playfully hit me, because *clearly* what I'd said was so ridiculous that it warranted some false physical punishment. "Come on. I really do have to pee." Jo Beth stepped off the path and into the vines, to find some place to crouch and relieve herself. I followed.

I always followed.

Chapter 16
Jo Beth

Jo Beth and Magda took their customers on adrenaline-filled day trips and the season passed quickly, in constant bursts of color. They clung to bright orange rafts as they faced down the rapids of the Maipo River, they zip lined over the deep green trees along the Cajon del Maipo, and they paraglided across the turquoise sea. For Jo Beth, it was as good a rush as skiing, but without the anxiety. Life would have felt almost peaceful in its excitement, except for the explosive arguments she had with Magda. Jo Beth had never met anyone who could hold her own in a conflict the way that Magda could. The two of them were well and truly matched.

"We need to upgrade," Magda told Jo Beth "We can't compete without the best equipment possible."

"We just bought new equipment," Jo Beth responded. "I'm not spending thousands more on one of your whims."

"Then you're okay with failing?" Magda's voice grated like copper against steel. "Jo, if you're not careful, you'll be nothing but a burnout, and no one will respect you."

Jo Beth ignored the verbal slap's sting. "So? At least I'm not mooching off someone else's money."

"You're too cautious and you're too cheap!"

"And you're a bitch."

Magda responded with a delighted smile. Too late, Jo Beth remembered that Magda liked being called a bitch, which made Jo Beth entirely unoriginal for calling her one. Later, Jo Beth told Mitch all about it.

"I can't believe your friendship has lasted this long," Mitch said. "Magda knows how to play dirty. It's why I couldn't stay with her."

"But I invented playing dirty," Jo Beth replied.

"That's what you think." He smiled, and as always, it was like his cheeks had been smooshed down with a halo. "But you're wrong. The two of you have begun mirroring each other, repeating each other's patterns, and making it impossible to tell who's in back and who's in front." They were in bed, and he laid his arm across her stomach. "You don't have to put up with her. Come back to Portillo with me for the ski season."

She snuggled against him and pulled the covers up to her chin. When the sun went down across the mountains it turned cool, sometimes dipping down thirty degrees past the warmest moment of the day. It wasn't yet winter but the wind rattled their window and Jo Beth burrowed her face into the curve of Mitch's neck, trying to feel safe. When it was just him and her, she believed that he could protect her, that they could protect each other.

"I'll come with you to Portillo," she said. "I think it will be good for Magda and me to take a break."

Yet Magda was always around. She'd apologize for their latest conflict and then insert herself into the daily life Jo Beth shared with Mitch. Often, she would show up unannounced and always she would find Mitch before she found Jo Beth.

"Magda's staying with us tonight," Mitch would say. He said it a lot.

She was constantly sleeping on their couch after a day of hitting the slopes, and when the three of them ate dinner, she and Mitch would fall into Spanish, their conversation flying over Jo Beth's head. "Speak English!" she'd demand. "You're both from Florida."

Mitch always laughed in response. "Sorry, Hon. I've spent so much time speaking Spanish I guess it's become second nature." Then they'd return to their native language.

Jo Beth had packed her bags several times, had written more than one goodbye note that she'd placed on Mitch's pillow for him to find after he returned from a day of teaching ski school, but some invisible force always made her turn around, rip up the note, and berate herself for thinking she could hitchhike out of Portillo. Where would she go once she was back in the city? Besides, she'd still be the seriously flawed Jo Beth no matter where she went. She would still feel guilty for betraying her sister all those months ago and she'd still have nothing more than athletic skill to put on her resume. Skiing was all she had left and it was time to get back to it.

Most afternoons, it was her skis against the snow. She burned tracks down the white mountain, inhaling the icy air and blinking behind her goggles. In winter, the hours were stretched-out and dusky. She could lose her sense of time, as if emerging from a darkened movie theater in the middle of the day, surprised to find that it was still light outside. Because of this, somehow it became possible to forget her worries, to forget the sinking feeling she had every evening, until right before she opened the door to their studio apartment. Would she find Mitch and Magda together, naked and in bed, giving in to their most primitive, animal instincts? One time, the porn movie in her head was particularly aggressive; it kept playing outrageous Mitch-and-Magda-sex-scenes, and no matter how many times Jo Beth tried to press pause, it kept going. Then, right before she opened the door, she heard laughter. Magda was squealing.

"No!" she cried, clearly implying 'yes.' "You can't do that!"

"Oh, I think I can." More laughter from them both.

She stood outside, listening, almost hoping for some tangible evidence that she could hurl back into their faces.

"Mitch, that's so unfair!"

"Who ever said that I play fair?"

Blood was pounding in Jo Beth's ears and she could see the blood, their blood, blood that she would draw.

She turned the knob and entered. Magda and Mitch were sprawled on the floor, a stack of playing cards between them. Magda was wearing one of those off-the-shoulder sweatshirts with nothing underneath, and the way she sat gave Mitch a perfect view of her bare chest. Mitch had on a button-down flannel shirt with the top three buttons undone. Both wore tussled hair, satisfied smiles, and an air of gratification.

When they looked up and saw her, they didn't even bother to act self-conscious. "Hey, Hon," Mitch said. "We're playing gin rummy, but if you want to play, we can switch to hearts."

She stormed over and stomped on the cards that lay on the floor. She kicked and ground her heel into a queen's face, which was a poor substitute for digging her heel into Magda's face, but oh well. She spun around. "Shouldn't you be running day trips in Santiago? What's the deal, Mags? Incapable of doing anything by yourself?"

"You know this is the off season," Magda snipped.

"What I know is that you're screwing my boyfriend."

"Jo!" Mitch yelled. She turned toward him.

"Never mind," she said. "She can have you."

Jo Beth crossed over to their one closet and with shaking hands, pulled down her duffel. "I'm done," she said. "I can't stand living here, dying of boredom, while you two are fucking each other."

"You've got it all wrong," Magda said. Jo Beth had to ignore Magda; otherwise she would be lunging forward and strangling her.

Mitch got up, took two large steps to get to Jo Beth, and tried to take the duffel bag from her hands. She yanked it back and resisted the urge to whip it across his face, to mark his beautiful complexion with canvas burns and zipper scrapes. "If you try to stop me, I'll scream."

He spoke to Magda. "Do you mind giving us some privacy?"

Magda instantly jolted up, put on her boots, and grabbed her coat. "Sure thing."

"Sorry," Mitch said to her.

"If you apologize to her again, I'll kill you both."

They shrank back at the severity of Jo Beth's words, or maybe it was the utter seriousness with which she spoke them. Whatever. She had made her point and Magda silently left their apartment without a second glance.

"What is wrong with you?" Mitch demanded.

"I think I made myself pretty clear."

"There's nothing going on between Magda and me!"

"I'm not an idiot, Mitch!" She turned back towards the closet, grabbing shirts, sweaters, and jeans to stuff into her bag.

"You're imagining things, Jo. I'd never cheat on you. Please believe me."

"Why should I?"

"Because I love you! And because...." He sighed. "Look, don't freak out, but around this time of the month, don't you get a little paranoid?"

She froze at his suggestion. Normally the very implication would make her livid but her brain was racing too fast to register any more anger.

She couldn't remember the last time she'd had her period.

Chapter 17
Skylar

Sky,

Guess what?

I'M PREGNANT!!!!!!!!!

I bet you're scratching your head right now, wondering if I'm cut out to be a mother. I wouldn't blame you for that. But after I got over the initial shock, I realized that I really want this baby really bad. Mitch is super excited too. We couldn't be happier.

Oh, BTW, don't tell Mom and Dad.

You know Mom; she'd probably fly over here and try to convince me to come home. But I know what's best for me and being here with Mitch is what's best. He's going to make an excellent dad.

Love you!!!!

-Jo Beth

I shut my laptop and shut my eyes. Jo Beth was pregnant. The news felt like waking up and looking outside on an unkind, sleety morning, knowing I'd spend my day all cold and wet. As it was, I should try to appreciate the orangey autumnal weather. It was still warm outside, yet in the mountains, September can burn out quickly. Soon enough it would be winter and I was silly to squander the opportunity for fresh air and sunshine. But on this beautiful Friday afternoon I sat inside, feeling flat and uninspired.

My freshman year at Vista College had begun. I'd gotten through orientation and the first week of classes. And while I was grateful for my athletic scholarship and to be living in Jo Beth's condo, coming home to an empty silence every evening made my heart heavy. I knew it was unfair to blame Jo Beth for this. But instead of emailing her back, I got out *Turn of the Screw*, which was the first bit of reading required for my British Lit course.

I splayed out on the living room couch, my eyes creeping towards the window and its view of the Rockies. I would force myself to stay inside and read, but I cared little for the characters, Miles and Flora. Creepy children are such a literary cliché and even if Henry James was the first to use the device, it still seemed overrated. Besides, a confusing ending doesn't add to a novel's depth, just to its frustration level.

When I heard a knock, I dropped my book and jolted up, grateful for the distraction. I looked through the front door's peephole to see Gavin standing there.

"Wanna go for a hike?" he said, the moment I opened the door.

"Yeah, okay, let me get my shoes."

I went towards my front closet and he followed, letting himself inside. "How was your day?"

"Fine. Jo Beth is pregnant."

I was turned away from him, searching for my Merrells, so I didn't see his reaction but heard him say "Wow."

"Yeah. Don't tell my Mom."

"Okay." Gavin leaned against the wall in my entryway while I laced up. I saw him crease his brow and glance up at the ceiling, concentrating hard. "Is this good news?"

"What do you think?"

"That you're worried?"

He rotated his head down and to the side, so that our gazes met. Somehow, his dark brown eyes voiced all the unspoken words between us. But I'd elaborate anyway. "She sounded way too chipper in her email," I told him. "She's trying too hard to be happy."

"She's probably really scared."

"Yeah... I mean, she's having Mitch's baby, and she'll be stuck up in Portillo, away from a hospital, away from her family and friends, except for Magda, who I can't stand..."

"Why can't you stand Magda?"

I finished tying my boot and stood up straight. "I don't trust her. Jo Beth doesn't trust her either. I think she only stays friends with her because of Mitch. The whole thing is just disturbing, so yeah, I'm definitely worried."

He reached out his hand. "Then come with me," he said. "Some fresh air and exercise will make you feel better."

I felt a smile warm my face. "I want to climb up rocks."

He smiled back. "Then we'll climb up rocks."

Gavin was right about fresh air and exercise. Hiking cleared out all the gunk clogging my heart and brain. Later, we ordered a pizza and sat on my patio, drinking from a bottle of wine that Jo Beth had left behind in her pantry.

"You know who else I don't like," I said, as if our conversation from before had been going on for hours. "I don't like Mitch."

Gavin washed down his pizza crust with a swig of wine. "I thought you said he was nice."

"Oh, he's nice. *Too* nice. The guy wants to be everything to everyone. He's one of *those*." Gavin laughed and I turned indignant. "What's so funny?"

"How would you know, Skylar?"

"What do you mean?"

He cleared his throat. "You talk like you're familiar with all sorts of men, like you can classify them or something, when really your experience is pretty limited."

Blood rushed to my cheeks. I hated how embarrassed I felt, knowing that Gavin understood me in ways that I didn't want to be understood. On some subjects, it's better to remain a mystery. I stood, scraping my patio chair against the pavement. "Time for you to go, Gavin."

"Oh, come on." He held his glass of wine in one hand and a new slice of pizza in the other. "I'm still eating."

I felt like Scarlet O'Hara, dismissing one of her beaus on an irrational whim, but I grabbed away both his pizza and his wine. "You're done."

"Look, I'm sorry. I didn't mean it. I'm sure you're very experienced."

The laughter in his voice only further incited me. "You think you know me so well, but you have no idea. Maybe I've been with all sorts of guys. Just because I won't give it up for you, doesn't mean there haven't been others."

His face fell and I knew that I'd hurt him. Good.

"Fine, I'll go," he said.

Gavin stormed out, barely remembering to grab his keys. I didn't have time to change my mind, to apologize, to tell him that I was wrong and he was right.

Was that regret breathing down my neck? Yet, in the emptiness of the condo I felt none of the restlessness I'd felt this afternoon. I went inside, retrieved my laptop, and came back out onto the patio where I set up my computer on the wobbly metal table that went with the chairs. I would enjoy the rest of the wine and pizza out here while I did some writing. I'd probably suffered from post-traumatic writer's stress after the Neal Morgan/Facebook poetry incident, but I hadn't stopped writing altogether. In fact, I'd switched from poetry to novels: a gothic romance, to be more specific. I was letting the Brontë sisters inspire me.

I looked back over my most recent scene, where the romantic tension between the main characters had begun to sizzle.

Patrick looked up as I came close "You needed something?" he asked.

"Yes, I wish to put in my notice."

"Mary, where will you go?"

"That is none of your concern," I said.

He did not speak, but I noticed the restless twitch of his arm and a swift, erratic blinking of his eyes. Otherwise, neither his face nor body betrayed emotion. "I can't keep you here," he stated solemnly. "If you wish to go, then go you shall."

My voice was strangled with unshed tears. "It's not what I wish but what I must do."

I stopped typing and took a sip of wine. Gavin was right. I knew nothing about men. When it came to how they thought, responded, and loved, I was flying in the dark. Yet for me, writing was a form of wish fulfillment, so I resumed.

He closed his eyes as if praying. A moment later when he raised his gaze, it was with such love and longing that my breath escaped me. I had to be in his arms. He enfolded me into a rough embrace. We kissed and...

I sighed. And what?

I couldn't let my novel become a typical, bodice-ripper romance. It needed depth. Right now, it was little more than a superficial Jane Eyre knock-off.

We kissed and I pulled the small pocket knife that I'd hidden in the folds of my dress. In one swift motion, I plunged it into his neck. Patrick floundered like a fish, choking on his blood, on his confusion, on his fear. Betrayal etched across his face as he muttered his very last word.

"Why?"

I realized that I had no answer for Patrick. There was no legitimate reason for why Mary would kill him and yet she just had. Maybe she was going all Heathcliff, thinking that the murdered do haunt their murderers. But why would Mary prefer a dead Patrick to a living one? I leaned back in my chair, letting my eyes roam away from my computer screen and up to the starry sky. It occurred to me that for every pinprick of light there could be a complete world full of living beings with wants and needs, just like how for every writer, there's an infinite amount of possible characters who could take on a life of their own. By letting Mary kill, I'd also let her live, and even though I'd just created a blizzard-sized plot hole, I couldn't press delete. It wasn't my right.

Homicide was too satisfying to erase.

Chapter 18

Jo Beth

Pregnancy was a revelation to Jo Beth, because she suddenly had more than herself to think about. Abortion was never an option, not once she'd imagined the baby as a newer version of Skylar: a tiny little being whom Jo Beth would care for, and she'd do so without making all the bad mistakes she'd made before. This baby would be Jo Beth's fresh start. Yet that didn't automatically make everything all good with Mitch and Magda.

"We weren't doing anything," Mitch kept insisting. "I'm not into her. I love you."

"Okay," Jo Beth answered. "I feel bad about yelling at Magda. I guess I was just really hormonal."

"Don't beat yourself up about it," Mitch said. "But maybe you should apologize."

"Do you think she'd talk to me?" Jo Beth stilled her trembling chin, sniffed, and widened her eyes until they watered.

Mitch pulled her in for a hug. He'd just come in from outside and she could smell the fresh air on him. "I'm sure she'd talk to you."

"But what if she won't? Except for you, Magda is my only real friend on this entire continent. I need her on my side but I'm worried I've ruined things forever."

After the big blowout, Magda had stopped coming up to Patillo and Mitch knew enough not to call her. Now Jo Beth needed him to believe that getting in touch was his idea.

"I'll shoot her a text," he said. "Maybe the three of us can have lunch next week, when we go down to Santiago for your pre-natal appointment."

"Really? That would be so great. Thank you, Mitch."

They met at *Tiramisu*, a popular lunch spot surrounded by trees. Magda ordered a salad, Mitch ordered a steak, and Jo Beth ordered a pizza, because the only food that didn't make her feel like puking were carbs, carbs, and more carbs.

"So how far along are you?" Magda asked.

Mitch answered, his voice padded with pride. "Eight weeks." His smile glowed even brighter than usual as he spoke. "The doctor said everything looks great: the beginnings of what should be a very healthy pregnancy."

Magda's grin seemed so fake that Jo Beth could almost taste the saccharine. "That's great," Magda said to Jo Beth. "But what about your moods?"

Her skin prickled at Magda's question. "What about my moods?"

Magda stabbed a cherry tomato with the tine of her fork and bit into it, speaking as she chewed. "You can't be on your anti-depressants while pregnant, can you?"

"There is some risk to the baby, so yeah, I'm staying off of them."

"She'll be fine." Mitch reached over and squeezed Jo Beth's shoulder.

Magda tilted her head to the side, an attempt to seem empathetic. "Mitch, I think you should be realistic. Pregnant women have more estrogen rushing through their body in one day than non-pregnant women do in an entire year. Add in going off her meds..."

"Okay, enough." Jo Beth's irritation had become a vise, squeezing the air out of her lungs. Yet she couldn't succumb to acting out. Magda was just trying to rile her. "Magda, I appreciate your concern; really, I do. But this lunch was supposed to be about reconciliations and apologies." Jo Beth placed her pizza crust on her plate and stared across the table at Magda. "I am so, so sorry for losing my shit that day. I mean, I understand why you're worried after I acted so crazy, but all I can say is, now that I'm aware of my condition, it will be easier to control my emotions."

"I hope so."

"Will you forgive me?" Jo Beth asked.

Magda barely blinked those big, brown eyes. It was like she'd never once doubted that she deserved an apology. "Yes, of course I will, Jo Beth."

Jo Beth flashed a relieved smile and reached underneath the table for the bottle she'd stowed in her bag. Luckily for her, in Chile, it's completely cool to bring your own wine to restaurants. "Great. Because look what I brought!"

Magda's face lit up when she saw it was her favorite type of Cabernet, way too expensive to drink very often.

"Babe, you shouldn't have done that," Mitch said. "Especially since you can't have any of it."

"Of course I can," Jo Beth told him. "A little bit won't hurt, and besides, we're celebrating."

Jo Beth got up and took the bottle to the bar, where she could pay for corkage and ask for glasses. After the bartender poured three glasses-worth, Jo Beth asked for a glass of water. When his back was turned, she took the little bag of powder from her bag, poured a little into two of the glasses, and dumped the rest of the bag into the bottle. "Would you like help carrying this back to the table?" the bartender asked as he handed her the water.

"No, no. You're busy. I can handle it." Jo Beth made two trips, making sure to swirl the wine with the powder as she walked. Hopefully it would dissolve without a hitch.

"A toast," Jo Beth said, once she'd sat down. "To friendship, love, and new life."

They clinked their glasses together and Mitch and Magda drank up. Jo Beth modestly sipped her own wine, aware that Mitch would be concerned about her alcohol intake, being pregnant and all.

"Hey, I was online the other day. Did you know they have skis for one-year-olds?" Mitch laughed. "We need to decide how soon we want to turn this kid into a skier."

"Perhaps we should let her learn to walk first." Jo Beth said.

"Don't be such a philistine," Mitch replied.

Magda smiled at his joke but spoke to Jo Beth. "You're assuming it's a girl."

"It had better be a girl," she responded.

The afternoon passed pleasurably enough. They finished their meals and ordered dessert. Over tiramisu (the restaurant's signature dish), Mitch and Magda polished off the last of the wine. They were both slightly tipsy when Jo Beth finally told them.

"By the way, that slightly different woodsy taste in the wine today was from the laxatives."

Mitch looked at Jo Beth with a blank face. "What do you mean?"

"I mean, I bought a jar of powdered Ex-Lax and put it in the wine."

"But—how?" asked Magda.

"Never mind how! Are you serious, Jo?" Beads of panic sweat were already lining Mitch's forehead.

"I'm totally serious."

He placed his hand over his stomach, like he could already feel the laxative's effects. "But, why?"

"Why? Because you two are obviously still attracted to each other. Whether you're cheating on me is kind of irrelevant. The attraction has to stop."

Jo Beth leaned over and reached into the pocket of Mitch's jacket, which he'd draped over the back of his chair. She took out the car keys, held them up and jangled them. "I'm driving back now. I suggest you stay over with Magda, where the two of you will spend the night puking and shitting, over and over and over. While you do, I hope you both think of me, and good luck having just one bathroom between the two of you."

"You're joking," Magda said. "You wouldn't really poison us with laxatives."

"I think "poison" is sort of hyperbolic," Jo Beth laughed. "But, of course I would put laxatives in your wine. Because from now on, neither of you will be able to look at the other without remembering how it felt to have your colon explode. It will always stay with you: the smell, the sounds, the stomach cramps..."

"Jo, if you're for real, I'll never forgive you." Mitch said.

"You'll never forgive me for a prank?" Jo Beth made a face of pretend shock. "Gosh Mitch, have a sense of humor. It's not like I cheated on you." She stood and grabbed her bag. "Besides, I'm having your baby, and the pain I'll experience during labor will be a million times worse than what you're about to go through. I'm sure you'll find a way to forgive the mother of your child." She spoke to Magda. "I don't care if you forgive me."

Their mouths hung open and their skin tinged green. Jo figured that the combination of alcohol and Ex-Lax must be starting to work its magic. Never mind; from here on out, Jo Beth would have to imagine their pain. It was time to make her exit, before they recovered from their shock and began to yell.

"See ya," Jo Beth said.

It was easy to walk away.

Chapter 19

Skylar

*S*kylar,

Being pregnant sucks. I thought the nausea would go away, but after three months it's only gotten worse. I try to keep my eyes on the prize, tell myself that soon I'll have a BABY and all the puking, mood swings, and exhaustion will have been worth it. Because eventually I'll have an amazing family of my own.

Mitch is adorable. He can't stop talking about baby names, and how he's going to teach it baby sign language, and how he's going to order a pair of baby skis. Great, right? I probably shouldn't admit this, even to you, but his excitement annoys me. Sometimes I look at him and wonder who he is. Do I even know the guy that I'm having a baby with?

I suppose it's natural to have this sort of anxiety?

Ski season must be underway in Colorado by now. I get mixed up sometimes, being south of the equator. Here in Santiago, Mitch is taking his summer classes and I'm back to running adventure tours with Magda. I don't go zip-lining or climbing like I did last summer, but I do whatever I can, whenever I'm feeling up to it.

Win some tournaments for me!

Love always,

Jo Beth.

It was morning when I read Jo Beth's email. I had a full day ahead: class, ski practice, and my literary club meeting that evening. But now I had bigger things to think about. In a way, this email was worse than the paranoid, *Mitch and Magda want to hurt me* sort of email that Jo Beth had been sending lately. Jo Beth's departure into subtlety made her sound bad, like Daisy Buchanan bad, like next she'd start insisting that the best thing a girl can be in this world is a beautiful little fool. And I was too far away to help.

I typed out a quick reply:

Jo Beth,

Have you seen a doctor about the nausea? Maybe there's a remedy.

Please don't push yourself with the adventure tours, and don't worry so much about Mitch. You don't have to stay with him, you know. You can come home any time. We could live together in your condo like the old days, and I'd help you with the baby.

Think about it.

Love you...

Sky

"You want Jo Beth to move back home?" Gavin stood over my shoulder, reading my email. I slapped my laptop shut.

"It's rude to spy on people."

"Sorry." He yawned and headed for the kitchen, where he started to brew a pot of coffee. I got up and stood in the doorway.

"How'd you sleep?" I asked.

"Oh, you know. I closed my eyes, tried to relax, let my mind drift a little..."

"Ha ha. Very funny." This wasn't the first time Gavin had made this joke, and I had never found it very clever.

"Okay, okay," he said, smiling. Gavin ran his hand through his hair, making it stick up slightly. "Fine. Your old bed is really comfortable..."

"That's good."

"... and I don't want to seem ungrateful, because I appreciate your letting me sleep here, but that bed would have been even better with you in it."

I wasn't sure whether to smile or to scowl. Gavin was always around; he'd come over nearly every evening and we'd watch TV or he'd read while I studied or wrote. Lots of times he would cook me dinner, but usually he left by nine because he had to be up at four. He kept a baker's hours, after all.

Today was his day off, so last night was different. We watched *Twilight* and agreed that Kristen Stewart was way too twitchy. Yet the romantic movie must have affected us both, because when it ended, Gavin used the remote to click it off and immediately lunged forward, pinning me down on the couch and pressing into me. We made out for a while, removing clothing that had always remained intact during our previous make out sessions.

I was panting when I pushed him away. "It's late," I said. "You should probably go."

Gavin smiled in his subtle, gentle way. His voice was subtle and gentle too. "Or, I could stay."

Part of me wanted to say yes. But I couldn't lose my virginity to Gavin; I'd only be proving him right when he realized how inexperienced and ignorant I was. I had to sleep with someone else first, before I slept with him.

"No, you should go."

"But it's snowing." Gavin pointed towards the window. I looked in the direction of his finger and saw that he was right. Big, powdery flakes were falling, like the earth had some serious dandruff.

"Wow! That's going to make great powder. I can't wait for skiing tomorrow!"

Gavin placed his fingers underneath my chin and lightly pushed my face toward him, so I was looking him in the eye. "Please, Sky? Let me stay."

He was shirtless, as was I. I couldn't imagine going out in the cold but I could imagine us crawling into bed, clinging to each other, creating our own brand of heat. I let him kiss me and then his hands were doing crazy nice things and I was about to say *yes, please stay*, when he stuck his tongue in my ear. Had Edward-the-vampire ever stuck his tongue in Bella's ear? I thought not. In fact, I doubted that in all the cheesy romance novels with covers that featured a shirtless man with a killer six-pack, that ever once had the hero shoved his tongue into his lady-love's ear.

I mean, in what world is that sexy?

I wriggled away, grabbed my shirt, covered myself, and stood. "Gavin, I have a busy day tomorrow, so I think I'll go to bed. If you don't want to drive home in the snow, you can sleep in my old bedroom."

His disheartened sigh was straight out of *The Old Man and the Sea*, but to be fair, Gavin had been shot down by me a million times already. "Sure."

Now, this morning, as I stood in my kitchen, watching him make coffee, seeing him comfortable in nothing but boxer shorts and a t-shirt, I realized that unlike Jo Beth with Mitch, I could be confident that with Gavin there would never be any surprises.

Yet, life without surprises was like a story without suspense.

"I have to get going," I said, completely evading his comment about last night, sure that he wouldn't press things. "Can you let yourself out?"

He nodded. "Sure. See you later?"

"Maybe."

Later at ski practice I raced down the mountain, flying around and over the moguls that I'd come to love, while in my mind anticipating the competition coming up this weekend. Our coach, Billy, thought I had a good chance of winning in several categories.

When I got to the bottom of the run he was there, stopwatch in hand. "Excellent, Skylar! That was your best time yet."

I removed my goggles and steadied my breathing. After finishing a run, it always took me a moment to return to earth. "Really? When I snagged an edge at the beginning of the course I worried that I'd slowed myself down."

"Nope." Billy showed me my time on his stopwatch. He was right. Not bad.

Then Billy and I competed for the broadest grin. "Have you thought about the Olympic trials?" he asked.

I stared at him, confused. "I'm not my sister."

"But you're an amazing skier in your own right. I think you have a fair shot at the team." Billy patted me on my shoulder, which had the effect of brushing snow off my parka. "Think about it," he said. "If you decide you're interested, we can talk more."

I did think about it. I thought about the Olympics all day, making Gavin, Jo Beth, and every other concern of mine melt like snow underneath a strong winter sun. But I could feel the puddles in my brain, dripping down and icing over, and nothing functioned right because there was too much going on. And to top things off, I had Literary Club that evening.

Literary Club met twice a month. Every two weeks we read a classic novel and then we'd each try to write something with a similar tone. This week's pick was *Catcher in the Rye*. Since I was determined to finish my novel, my writing exercises always became a chapter in the continuing story of Mary, the governess and secret serial killer who had a nasty habit of murdering the lord of each manor right after she fell in love with him. Thanks to the influence of Literary Club, each increment was written in a different style. One week, Mary sounded like George Elliot, the next week, she resembled Kurt Vonnegut. My heroine wasn't just a sociopath; she was also entirely schizophrenic.

And that evening, when it was my turn to read my chapter, I was as scattered as Salinger's Franny Glass in the midst of her existential meltdown. I suppose that was appropriate as I read my *Catcher in the Rye* knock-off, clearing my throat, trying to keep both my voice and hands from shaking.

"Yesterday at breakfast, Mrs. Hampstead served oatmeal, and it was the lumpiest, most tasteless glop I'd ever eaten. Ten times worse than what I was served as a child at the orphanage. It reminded me of Sunday mornings, knowing I would be made to sit in a hard-wooden pew for hours, underdressed in my thin coat, shivering beneath the drafty air and the reverend's watchful eye. I could barely stomach the glop, and then you came down. You sat, smiling and amiable as hell. You lapped up the oatmeal and praised Mrs. Hampstead on her cooking, and all the while you refused to meet my sad gaze. Could you sense the danger? Did you understand that I am the black widow?

It took you only a moment to finish breakfast, and then you disappeared behind those insincere walls and we were once more separated.

You drive me mad. I am so depressed I might literally go crazy. I hate goddam Chamberlin and every insincere molecule that comprises it. But most of all, I hate this urge to kill whatever or whoever it is that I love.

Because sure as sin, you're next.

I lowered my pages and waited for people to respond. There was a collective pause, and then Anna, the most outspoken member of our group, chimed in. "It's like J.D Salinger hijacked a Brontë novel."

I half smiled. "Is that good or bad? Because I was just trying to fit with the style."

Anna shrugged. "It's interesting. At least she has passion. But I'd be worried about maintaining a consistent voice."

I knew that would be the criticism, but how could I maintain a consistent voice when I hadn't even found my own voice yet? I constantly found myself thinking with leftover nuggets from classic authors and I understood that any cleverness I had was borrowed, just like my skiing notoriety was simply a castaway from Jo Beth.

"Do you have suggestions for how I can be consistent?" I asked.

"Get rid of all the adjectives and adverbs," said Kent, another member of our group. Deleting all the modifiers was always his answer for everything.

"Okay, but is Mary compelling, or do you just find her crazy?" I asked.

Anna's subtle little eye roll was not lost on me. "I mean, it's a romance novel. Aren't the heroines, by definition, crazy?"

"I don't know," I replied. "Is the search for true love ever marked by sanity, or will it always end in either a loss of self, or a loss of life?"

There was uncomfortable laughter, like I'd inadvertently insulted someone's religion, politics, or both. Then Anna took out her piece and just started reading. It was some literary mumbo jumbo about cats and the apocalypse and everyone loved it, yet they went ahead and dissected all its intricacies, because Anna wants to get it published by this fiction journal that nobody, except for the authors and the authors' mothers, will ever read.

After the meeting was over and I was in the safety of my car, I nearly banged my head against the steering wheel. What did I think would happen, that the group would love my piece, that they would get it, that they would get me? It didn't matter, not really, but if I can't even fit into the literary crowd here in Black Diamond, what chance did I have at Cornell? I put the key in the ignition and headed home. No; I headed to my *sister's* home. The place still belonged to Jo Beth, and most nights I could feel that the walls, floors, and furniture missed her. I missed her too.

When I walked through her door, glanced at my phone, and saw that Gavin had texted, wanting to come over, I texted back.

Not tonight.

If I couldn't be with Jo Beth, it was better to be alone.

Chapter 20
Jo Beth

Jo Beth could feel her sister's resolve from all the way past the equator. Every evening, Skylar would call as soon as she was done with ski practice and then she would voice her opinions, loud and clear.

"If you don't trust Mitch and Magda, you should leave," Skylar would tell Jo Beth. "Have your baby at home. Mom and Dad will be around, and I'll always be there to help with midnight feedings or diaper changes or whatever you need. We'll raise your baby together."

Several times Jo Beth said yes; she'd buy her ticket tomorrow and be home by the end of the week. Then she would go to tell Mitch, and he'd look at her with this unassuming twinkle in his eye, rub her belly, and whisper into her ear: *I need you. Don't go.* He'd say this before she'd even mentioned leaving, which only confounded her guilt. She'd remember how, weeks ago, he'd hung his head, pale and weak and still doubled over from stomach cramps.

"I drove you to this," he'd said. "I am so, so sorry that you doubt me, but I promise I will earn your trust. You'll come to see that for me, there is only you."

Then Magda apologized, so Jo Beth had two people telling her sorry after *she'd* made *them* overdose on laxatives. If Jo Beth was capable of erasing her emotions she wouldn't have bought their contrition. She wouldn't have believed a word or a sad smile from either of them. But besides her sister, Magda was the only real female friend Jo Beth had ever had and Mitch was the only man she'd ever loved.

So she stayed.

Things were okay for a while. Sure, half the time Jo Beth was sure that Mitch and Magda had it out for her, but the other half of the time she knew her paranoia simply came from hormones and a lack of meds. Then came the day that Magda and Jo Beth were running an adventure tour and Magda insisted that Jo Beth do the zip line, that it was safe and it would be good for her to get some adrenaline coursing through her veins. Except somehow her zip line wasn't properly attached. It happened at the beginning of the course and she only fell from six feet, but Jo Beth started bleeding and needed to be rushed to a hospital in Santiago. She didn't miscarry, but the doctors were gravely concerned. She would need to stay quiet for rest for the remainder of her pregnancy—another four months. That meant staying inside: no exercise, no walks, no fun.

"I will never forgive myself for this," Magda said. "I can't imagine—if anything had happened to your baby, my God, it's like the world would end." She kept crying and wringing her hands, pacing the floor of Jo Beth's hospital room. "Once we get you home, I'm going to take such good care of you. I'll wait on you hand and foot."

"It's not necessary, Magda."

"Yes, it is."

"You need to run the adventure tours."

Magda reached into her back jean pocket and pulled out a sheet of folded notebook paper. "No, look—Mitch and I have it all figured out. We've created a schedule."

She showed it to her; the hours when Mitch would be at home and the hours when Magda would be there instead. There were very few times when Jo Beth would be unsupervised, maybe an hour here or there, tops.

"Mitch and I *want* to take care of you. Please let us."

What choice did Jo Beth have? The doctors had absolutely ruled out travel, and neither her mother nor Skylar could drop everything, come to Santiago, and tend to her for the next four months. So, she let Magda take her back to her apartment, where there was now a cot set up in the living room. Before the accident, Mitch and Jo Beth had been staying in his student apartment, but the summer term was almost over and then he'd have to move out. Everyone decided it was best for Jo Beth to settle into one place where she wouldn't have to move around so much.

And she wondered what she'd done in a past life, or in this one, to deserve living such a unique form of hell.

"We'll never have any privacy," Jo Beth told Mitch.

"I know, but what can I do?" He ran a hand through his curls and reclined back onto Magda's couch, which sat opposite the cot now crammed into the tight living space.

"Find us a place where we can live! Once the baby is born, we'll need it anyway."

"But I thought you wanted to go back up to Portillo," he responded.

"I don't know what I want, but I can tell you what I don't want, and that's to be stuck in your ex-girlfriend's living room for the next four months."

Mitch nodded his head, his curly locks bouncing ever so slightly, as if they refused to match the solemnness in his eyes. "Okay, I'll find a place."

And he did try but somehow, despite his efforts, something always fell through. The potential landlord seemed shady, or the lease was too unreasonable, or it turned out the renters wanted double the original price. This went on for weeks, until it became obvious that there was no escape from the situation, at least not until the baby came. In the meantime, Jo Beth resigned herself to being a prisoner. Any resistance she practiced took place inside her mind.

"Do you want to go over this month's account activity?" Magda asked Jo Beth. She sat next to her on the cot, handed her some papers, and drew up her knees, which poked out of two matching holes in her jeans. Half an hour ago she'd come home after leading a hike through Cerro De Ramon and Jo Beth envied her pink cheeks and satisfied fatigue, the earned rewards of exertion.

Jo Beth took the pages and tried to make sense of all the columns of numbers. "Does this represent a loss or a gain?" she asked, pointing to one calculation.

"Oh, a gain." Magda laughed, and Jo Beth was struck with how white her roommate's teeth looked, how perfectly they contrasted with her brown skin. Did Mitch find that attractive?

"We're doing great," Magda continued. "Well, we did great. Remember, last month we advertised in Paste Magazine? That really brought in a lot of business."

"Did the ad pay for itself?"

"More. But not enough to pay for another ad."

Mitch came out from the bedroom dressed for work. He'd gotten a job as a bartender and his shift was about to start. "Can't you front the money for another ad?" he asked them both. Magda's place was small so there was no point in pretending he hadn't heard their conversation.

"That's up to Jo Beth," Magda said. "She's the one with money to invest."

Jo Beth bit her lip and turned her head toward the window. Dusk was falling. How she wished for a walk outside.

"Babe, we're not even paying rent," Mitch said. "Don't you think you could swing more for advertising?"

Mitch and Magda both seemed to think that Jo Beth was rich. Maybe she was, but that didn't make her Bill Gates. Jo Beth had always believed that her investment-made-wealth could disappear as easily as it had appeared, and spending any of it felt like playing with Monopoly money. Were Mitch and Magda just after her bank account?

"It's okay, Mitch. Jo Beth has already invested so much. I don't want her to do anything she doesn't feel comfortable with, especially with the baby coming." Magda ran her fingers through the strands of her long dark hair, which was tied back. Jo Beth expected that Magda had started the day with a neat bun, but as the hours passed, tendrils escaped, and now her hair was down as much as it was up.

Did Mitch find that sexy?

"I'm starving," Magda said. "What about you?"

"I'm trying not to eat too much," Jo Beth said. "I can't exercise and I'm scared I'll get big as a house."

"Not a chance," Magda replied, scooting her skinny butt into the kitchen.

Did Mitch just give her a second glance as she skipped by him? When Magda opened the refrigerator, leaned down, and inspected its contents, was he inspecting her contents in turn? Magda shut the refrigerator door and shook her head. "We have no food. How about I run out and pick something up? I'm really hungry for some empanadas."

"Sounds great." Mitch reached into his pocket, took out his wallet, and handed her some cash. This was annoying on more than one level. First, Jo Beth had given him that money, but now he got to seem generous by giving it to Magda. Second, Mitch was on his way out and wouldn't even be eating the food, so why was he deciding what they'd eat? Third, Jo Beth was gaining weight because she was pregnant and eating was the only part of her day that offered variety. She looked forward to dinner all day long, self-control was super hard, and the last thing she needed was more temptation.

But she couldn't avoid temptation, not unless she could avoid Mitch and Magda as well. Temptation was in their skin and it radiated out. It was a gas that poisoned Jo Beth's mind, making it futile to resist the dark thoughts that seeped into her brain. Mitch and Magda were sleeping together. Mitch and Magda were only after Jo Beth's money. Next thing she knew, Mitch and Magda would try to take her baby away.

No, that would never happen. Mitch and Magda would have to kill her first.

Chapter 21

Skylar

I woke up early and trudged downstairs to the basement to use the treadmill and lift some weights. After Billy, my coach, insisted that if I want to compete in the Olympics I should be in peak physical shape, I decided to adopt a daily morning workout into my routine. I kept my eyes up, away from the moving belt of the treadmill. Otherwise I'd get dizzy. Forty minutes running and then I sprinted for the last ten. But my mind wasn't as determined as my body and my thoughts sloshed around; what should I do about college, about Gavin, about Jo Beth?

After I finished running I did strength training, stomach crunches, and yoga stretches, listening to music from an iPod strapped to my arm. I had hoped the exercise would be meditative, that if I couldn't find answers to my most pressing questions, I'd at least come up with ideas for my novel and compose some brilliantly eloquent lines in my head. But when I finished my workout I was not racing upstairs to flip open my laptop. Sadly, there was no need to type out my ideas before they evaporated because they'd never materialized in the first place. Instead I hiked with heavy steps up toward the kitchen, where I'd resist temptation and skip the almond poppy seed muffins that Gavin had brought over. I'd eat an egg white omelet instead.

But first I decided to check my messages. When I looked at my cell phone, I realized I'd missed a call from Jo Beth. Her recorded voice sounded almost manic.

Sky,

Why won't you pick up? Mitch and Magda have been speaking in Spanish around me, like, all the time, and I think they're planning something. What if Magda wants to take my baby away? What if Mitch lets her? I can't deal with it anymore. Can you please, please call me?

I tried calling her back right away, but it went to voicemail. I called my mother instead.

"Mom," I said, as soon as she picked up, "Jo Beth sounds really bad. I think we need to do something."

"Oh, Honey." Mom's words sounded more like a whoosh of air than part of the English language. "I already talked to her. She must have called me right after she called you."

"So why didn't she pick up just now? Is she okay?" I paced around the living room, my eyes skimming over my notebooks and laptop that I left on the coffee table, and my favorite fleece pullover, which I'd draped over an armchair. I'd need to pack up all my stuff soon if I wanted to start my day.

"She's fine, Skylar. I calmed her down. She's going to try to get some sleep now, so don't disturb her and try not to worry."

Once I glanced at the clock I realized I didn't have time to worry. If I didn't get going, I'd be late for my first class. "Okay, Mom. But call me if anything else comes up, okay?"

"Sure, Sweetheart. Have a good day."

We hung up, but my mind stayed with Jo Beth. At practice I could barely focus. Why would Jo Beth think that Mitch and Magda were trying to take her baby? Had Jo Beth gone crazy from being cooped up, or were Mitch and Magda up to something? Snow fell, muting the colors and visibility of everything. I could only sort of see through my fogged-up ski goggles, and that seemed appropriate. I had no clarity outside or in.

The course was buried in powder but I knew every ski run in Black Diamond forwards and backwards. The bright orange fences that barricaded the forbidden zone were easy to ignore as they quickly became camouflaged in white. I thought about how I used to ski these runs with Jo Beth—all the crazy risks she used to take—so I didn't register any alarm or caution as I plowed into the prohibited area. Velocity was my only purpose and there was no turning back, no room for regret. I was straight-lining, breaking the laws of physics, when I hit a crack and suddenly, my skis were just two sticks suspended in the air.

I was flying.

A couple of seconds later, I was on the ground and Billy came running. To him, even though I had fallen eighty feet and arrived in a cushion of snow without a sprain or a break, I had still fallen.

"Are you insane?" Billy's face was red from shouting and fright. "Are you trying to get yourself killed?"

My ski coach couldn't seem to understand that I had risen to the laws of nature and fear is for the weak, and in that moment, I was closer to my sister than I'd been in years.

"No," I replied. "I'm just trying to live."

Later that evening I was still pumped. The dim lighting, soft classical music, and the glass of red wine didn't mellow me out. Gavin stood over the stove, stirring his homemade marinara with a small wooden spoon and I pretended not to notice him watching me as I sat on a stool by the island in the kitchen, leafing through an Olympics brochure. I could feel the angry path of a scratch that started at my cheekbone and extended down to my jaw, but I refused to admit to any discomfort or pain. Doing so would invite in Gavin's judgment and concern, and I knew I'd be ingesting them enough tonight as it was. They may as well have been ingredients in the spaghetti sauce.

I just talked as if his ears were receptive. "Billy pretended to be mad, but I think he secretly respected me. After practice today, he talked like there's no doubt I'd be in the Olympics. And seriously, being suspended in the air like that... well, now I understand how people become adrenaline junkies."

"I'm surprised you came out of the whole thing with only a scratch."

"You sound like my dad."

"Then I'll try to be less protective," Gavin gave me a twisty smile as he dipped the spoon into his sauce and came toward me. "Here, try this. See if it needs more garlic."

Halfheartedly, I let him feed me a small amount. We made flat eye contact and I shrugged. "I think you could go either way. I mean, it's fine, but is there such a thing as too much garlic?"

"I don't know." He raised an eyebrow. "I guess that depends; are you letting me sleep in your bed tonight?"

My eyes awkwardly glanced away from him and settled back on my Olympics brochure, which had a picture of a triumphant Bode Miller on the front.

"How long before dinner?" I kept my voice intentionally light, like I hadn't registered what he'd just said. "I might go downstairs and stretch. I still have a leg cramp."

"I can rub it for you later."

I leaned down and massaged my calf muscle. "Thanks, but I still want to stretch."

I glanced up to see Gavin's smile fade as he stepped away, walked back toward the stove, and spoke with his back to me. "I think we should talk." Ominous words if there ever were any. I stood without going anywhere, as if our situation required formality. "Did you hear what I said?" Gavin said. "About talking?"

His urgency, his obvious desperation, propelled words out of my mouth before I could trap them. "Can't you just be the guy for once?"

He dropped his spoon against the stove with a clang. "What? I'm not manly enough for you? I stay home in the kitchen while you go flying off a mountain, like you're trying to be your sister or something..."

"Wait." My defensiveness was instant and hot, a rash underneath my skin. "I do something spontaneous, something strong, and you think I'm just imitating Jo Beth?"

"Skiing past the safety barricades and off a cliff isn't strong, it's reckless, and it's not like you."

"Oh really? Maybe you don't know me as well as you think you do."

"Maybe I don't," he responded, "but it's not for lack of trying."

For a long, tense moment, Gavin stared at me, as if willing me to answer. I shifted my weight and looked toward the stairs to the basement, where I longed to escape from this conversation.

"I don't know what you want from me," I finally said.

"It's simple," he replied. "I want you to be safe. I want you to stay here in Black Diamond, and I want you to admit to me, to yourself, and to everyone else, that you and I are actually a couple."

My answer was spineless. "I don't know if I can do all that."

Gavin's face softened, maybe because he was as unprepared for my sudden vulnerability as I was. "Which part don't you think you can do?"

I could barely squeak out my response, for fear that it would hurt us both. "All of it."

Gavin nodded as if we'd just completed a business transaction. His shoulders rose and tensed as he turned off the stove with a flick. "I'm going. Just boil some noodles, then pour the sauce over them. It will taste good."

I gave Gavin a reticent smile meant to beg forgiveness, but he wouldn't look at me. "No, no," I said. "Stay. Please, I want you to."

He walked out of the kitchen, past me, and towards the front door. I followed and watched as he removed his wool coat from a hook and bundled up. My hands twitched from wanting to touch him, to soothe his anger, but my fingers were too timid to follow through.

He was clearly fuming. "Be honest, Sky. You'd rather have the night to yourself."

I pictured the evening ahead of me, should he leave. It would start with a cold blast of air as he opened the door, a slamming sound as he walked away, and then the emptiness and guilt as I poured his marinara sauce into the sink, a blood red stream trickling down the drain because I couldn't stomach eating his dinner without him. "That's not true," I said, trying to keep my voice close. "I just don't get why we have to turn into something serious, into something that we're not."

"Because I'm tired of being 'that guy'—the one you kill time with when you have nothing else to do."

I felt my face heat up "I admit that I'm anxious to get out of here and into the Olympics. But my restlessness isn't about you. I'm just sick of waiting for something to happen. You're still my favorite person to spend time with."

He paused, hand on the doorknob. I could see how he wanted to leave, how he wanted to stay even more. "Please don't go," I continued. "That sauce you made is delicious, and you don't have to add any more garlic. That way our breath won't stink too bad—you know, later on."

I stepped in closer to him and put my hand on the back of his neck. He relaxed under my touch.

"Fine, okay." Gavin whispered as he removed his jacket and we walked back into the kitchen together.

Later, I was in the bathroom, gargling with mouthwash. Green foam oozed down my chin and I used the sleeve of my oversized ski team jersey, which I wore as a nightshirt, to wipe it away. As I spat out the rest of the mouthwash I met my own eyes in the mirror.

Was that hesitation or fear lodged on my face?

I spat again, cupped my hand over my mouth, and breathed in and out through my nose, checking for signs of bad breath. There had been a lot of garlic in Gavin's sauce. But I was satisfied that I passed the halitosis test, so I fished in the drawer, digging past hair brushes, tweezers, and a bottle of ADVIL to finally find an unopened box of condoms, which I had previously shoved into the very back, out of sight.

Briefly I studied the box that I bought months ago as a precautionary measure. I ripped open the blue and gold packaging, which read *Trojan Ultra-Thin Pleasure Pack*, and clumsily pulled one out. How could this shiny silver square, which looked like it contained candy, make me so nervous? Skiing off a cliff was nothing compared to this. I wrapped my fingers around the bright foil package, making a fist, so I didn't have to see evidence of what I was about to do. I told myself that losing my virginity didn't make me Becky Sharp of *Vanity Fair* and that becoming a sexual person didn't turn me into an anti-heroine. I would instead be like Jo March, sleeping with her love, the professor, for the first time, somewhere off in the dusky void that existed away from well-lit pages underneath a reading lamp.

One more look in the mirror; this time it was a look of resolve. I studied the scratch on my cheek, made this afternoon by my ski pole when I'd landed in the snow, and lightly traced it down my cheek. "Gavin, I'm in the mood for more adventure," I whispered to my reflection, rehearsing. I closed my eyes, shook my head in disgust, and then faced my reflection once again.

"Let's take a chance tonight, okay?"

I gave my reflection the most provocative expression I could muster. My shoulders moved up and down, and then I walked out of the bathroom, determined to fly, not fall, off the cliff that I was launching myself from.

Chapter 22
Jo Beth

Jo Beth's pregnant body was all cramped up, making it impossible to sit comfortably on the sagging couch. Meanwhile, her unhinged emotions conspired to inflict the most amount of misery. From boredom to paranoia, Jo Beth felt her lunatic mind shrink as her body expanded. Skylar had tried to help by sending Jo Beth a Kindle loaded with books. Jo Beth knew if Skylar was apartment-bound for months, she'd want to pass the time reading, so it seemed natural that Skylar would wish the same for Jo Beth. Even though Jo Beth would never appreciate literature the way her sister did, she had enjoyed some of the books Skylar chose, like *Call of the Wild*. Jo Beth identified with Buck the sled dog and his yearning to shun society and become feral. After all, only the strong survive. But that book was super short and now she was on to *Valley of the Dolls*. Jo Beth puzzled over Skylar's choice on that one. It was about this group of Hollywood girlfriends who relied on drugs to numb the pain while they backstabbed each other and mourned losing their youth, beauty, husbands, and identities, all while living in an environment that was as vapid as each one of them had become.

And speaking of vapid, backstabbing girlfriends, Magda walked through the apartment door. Jo Beth found she was actually glad to see her, maybe because she brought evidence that the outside world still existed. Mud clung to Magda's ankles and was smeared along her neck.

"You must have been rafting today," Jo Beth said. "How'd it go?"

"Okay." Magda sighed and collapsed next to Jo Beth on the couch. If they'd been in Jo Beth's Colorado condo, on her beautiful cream-colored chenille couch, she'd have cringed. But they were still in Magda's grubby Santiago apartment, where it didn't matter that Magda was muddy because her furniture was already desperate for a good cleaning. "I missed you though. Our adventure business just isn't as much fun without you."

Jo Beth patted her protruding belly. "Not much I can do about that," she said.

"True." Magda pivoted toward her and leaned in, like they were still confidants. She hadn't taken such a friendly tone with Jo Beth for a while. "You know what I was thinking about today? Remember months ago, when that Barry Manilow fan wouldn't stop singing for the entire Cousiño Macul winery bike trip!?"

Jo Beth laughed. "Oh yeah! He kept belting the lyrics to 'Can't Smile Without You' over and over, until the guy from Omaha pushed him off his bike."

Magda's eyes danced as a smile sprawled across her face. "That's right! And the Omaha guy insisted that he'd pushed him over by accident, and the Barry Manilow guy was going to press charges until you talked him out of it. 'Let's all get along,' you said. 'It's what Barry would do.'" She squealed with laughter at the memory. "God, you can be so convincing when you want to be, you know?"

"Sure." But Jo Beth didn't know, not really. She could barely remember the part of her personality that easily handled tricky situations, the girl who could look conflict in the face and never flinch.

Magda sighed, letting out a slow stream of air. "Promise that you'll come back to Adventuras Tours, Jo. Once the baby is born we'll find a good nanny and you and I can work together again."

When Magda was like this, it felt possible for Jo Beth to stay and work on their business with her friend. She could recall the shared laughter, the risks they'd taken, the grand plans of helicopter tours, paragliding, and biking along the Andes. The sites she'd never thought she'd see became photos in her mind and a life outside this apartment was just out of reach. And a different Jo Beth, a very different one from who she'd become, was just out of reach too.

"I'd like that," Jo Beth replied, "But I can't promise, not yet. There's too much I still don't know about."

Magda started to reply but at the same time the door opened and Mitch entered. He squinted at them.

"Wow, it's so thick today. I can barely see you."

Jo Beth scrunched her forehead in confusion. "Huh?" Mitch wasn't near-sighted. Was he commenting on how dirty the apartment was?

"I need a shower." Magda, who seemed un-phased by Mitch's odd statement, rose, and headed toward the bathroom, speaking to Mitch over her shoulder. "¿Cómo estuvo tu día?"

"Estaba bien, excepto odio mi trabajo. Necesito un cambio," he replied.

Jo Beth's blood pressure instantly spiked. With her limited Spanish, she could barely decipher that Magda had asked him about his day and that he'd said he needs a change.

But she didn't need to translate the intimate tone. Magda spoke like Jo Beth wasn't even in the room, like she and Mitch were in bed together. "No te preocupes. El cambio está llegando," she said in a velvety voice. Then she disappeared into the bathroom, to shower.

Did Mitch wish that he was getting into the shower with her?

"What did she just say to you?" Jo Beth demanded.

He grinned and sat down, taking the spot that Magda had just vacated. "Nothing, just that change is coming." He placed his palm over Jo Beth's belly. "Which it definitely is." He was holding his notebook and he flipped it open. "I made a new list today. Want to see? It's called *Places to Travel with the Baby in her First Five Years.*"

But Jo Beth was too angry to sit next to him and listen to his stupid list, so she wordlessly hoisted herself up and made toward the kitchen to get some water.

"My God!" Mitch cried.

Jo Beth spun around to see his wide, shocked eyes staring at the floor. "What?" She demanded.

"The cracks!" he said.

Jo Beth knew her footsteps were heavy, but still, that didn't warrant Mitch's reaction. "What cracks?" Mitch said nothing, just kept his eyes glued to the path Jo Beth's feet had just taken. She looked down. Same old floor, covered with dust but entirely without cracks. "Mitch, what cracks?"

He snapped out of his reverie and glanced up, meeting her eyes. "Huh? Nothing. Sorry. Never mind."

Jo Beth put her hands on her hips. "Is this your way of saying I've gotten too fat, that I'm so heavy the floor is cracking beneath me?"

"No!" He jumped up from the couch and met her in the middle of the living room, where he leaned down and kissed her on the mouth. "Sorry, Hon. Don't listen to me, I just get into these weird moods sometimes and start talking nonsense. You're beautiful and that's what's real."

She let him kiss her again because she sort-of believed him. She wanted to believe him, anyway. If Mitch could love the new Jo Beth, the meeker, crazier, pudgier version of who she'd used to be, then she had to give him the benefit of the doubt. If only they could make love. But there was no privacy and besides, Jo Beth felt about as sexy as a potato. Speaking of potatoes, she was hungry. "I thought I'd sauté some potatoes and those beef tips for dinner. Okay?"

"Sure." Mitch smiled, obviously pleased with whatever, because unlike her, food had not become the very reason for his existence. It was all so unfair.

Twenty minutes later, Magda was out of the shower, food was prepared, and they all sat down for dinner. Jo Beth stabbed at her potato, willing herself not to scarf it down. How could she be so hungry?

"Después de que el bebé llegue podremos hacerlo." Magda said to Mitch.

"Tal vez. El tiempo dirá," he replied.

"What are you talking about?" Jo Beth demanded. "Something about the baby?"

"Sorry," Mitch said. "I keep forgetting. We'll talk in English now."

"But what were you saying?"

"Don't worry about it." Magda took a sip of wine. "Hey, there aren't any laxatives in here, are there?"

"That joke just never gets old, does it?" replied Jo Beth.

"You're lucky we can laugh about it." Mitch reached over and squeezed her shoulder.

Was that squeeze a little too hard, a little too aggressive? And why wouldn't they tell her what they'd said? Jo Beth knew it was something about being careful after the baby comes, but she wasn't sure of the context.

But every day, she grew more and more sure that she shouldn't trust them.

Chapter 23

Skylar

The weeks became a blur. I still studied and went to class, I still wrote, and I still spent time with Gavin, but that all was just noise, steps I took in normal footwear before I put my skis on so my real day could begin. I practiced whenever I could. I won all my competitions through Vista College Ski Team and then the skiing National Governing Board recruited me for Olympics training camp, which starts grooming athletes around two years in advance.

So, I said goodbye to Gavin as I left for Mammoth Mountain, California, to secure my spot in the next Olympics.

"I'll call you later?" he asked as he dropped me off at the airport.

"Yeah, of course. I'll make sure that my cell is charged."

Gavin leaned in for a kiss but before his lips reached mine I gave him a hug instead. I didn't feel any romantic yearning, just a fierce foreboding of homesickness. Leaving him was the riskiest proposition of my life. I buried my face in his shoulder and kept it there, taking in his scent of nutmeg and pine, until he unwrapped my arms from around his shoulders. "You're going to do great, you know," he said.

"Thank you."

I picked up my massive backpack and the bag with my ski gear, gave him a kiss on the cheek, and walked through the sliding doors of Denver International Airport. I didn't consider that Gavin might suffer from our separation, that he, more than I, would need reassurance, so I offered him none. I barely even looked back to see him standing with his hands shoved into the pockets of his wool coat, still and stoic, while the rest of the world moved in a revolving hustle.

I waved, but I don't think he saw, because he didn't wave back.

Once I got to camp it took all my energy and focus just to function. The training schedule was insane, with little time to sleep and less time to breathe. Athletes from all over the country were there to compete for just a few spots on the Olympic team and the stress was so bad I could barely eat, and when I did, I'd have to run the bathroom twenty minutes later. My only cure for angst was to work it out on the slopes. I would crouch down, tuck my arms into my body, and imagine myself a bullet shooting down the mountain. I barely ever stood up straight or did anything to break my speed. At night, when I closed my eyes, it would feel like I was still racing down the slope, which gave me the sense of uneasy perpetual motion. Despite this, I was exhausted enough to find sleep and morning usually came way too soon.

One day I woke to the buzzing of my cell phone. "Good morning, Sweetheart."

My stomach jumped. "Mom! It's so early. Is something going on?"

She exhaled. "I wanted to let you know that I'm flying to Santiago in a couple of hours."

"Huh?"

"Your sister called again last night and she didn't sound good. I think it's best if I fly out and see her."

I turned on the lamp that sat on my nightstand, rubbed my eyes, and tried to adjust to wakefulness. "What do you mean, 'she doesn't sound good'? What did she say?"

"More paranoid stuff about Mitch and Magda wanting to harm her and the baby."

As I sat up in bed, I was painfully reminded of my left hip muscle that I'd strained yesterday afternoon. Navigating moguls was going to be difficult today. "How do you know she's being paranoid?" I asked. "What if Mitch and Magda really do have it out for her?"

"I seriously doubt that's the case, Skylar."

"I've met them, Mom. You haven't. And you never want to believe Jo Beth about that stuff." My training, my plans, my Olympic dreams: they all burst into a cloud of forgotten dust. "I'll come to Santiago too."

"No."

"Mom, you know how worried I've been. Just give me time to pack."

"Are you insane? You would blow your shot at the Olympics because Jo Beth is going stir-crazy?"

It wasn't quite that simple. The intense competition, the constant anxiety, the everlasting aches and pains in muscles that I hadn't even known existed: it was all starting to get to me and I wasn't sure I could handle the pressure. Leaving now would give me an easy out.

Mom spoke with a measured tone. "Sky, honey, I'm not sure that Jo Beth wants to see you. You might do more harm than good."

The sucker-punch of her words knocked the wind right out of me. I waited, but she wasn't taking it back. "Think about it," she said. "You've never been in better shape and you have all these opportunities just waiting for you. Jo Beth feels trapped. She IS trapped; she can't go out, can't exercise, can't ski. You'll remind her of everything she's lost."

"But that's not my fault."

Mom's voice softened. "Of course, it's not your fault, Honey. However, you need to work on your training. Let me worry about your sister."

I nodded even though she couldn't see me. "Okay." Tears gathered behind my eyes but I sniffed them back. "I'll stay." I sniffed a little too loudly, for sure letting my mom know that she'd upset me. "Tell Jo Beth I love her."

Chapter 24

Jo Beth

She was on the couch again. Jo Beth was always on the couch, always looking around Magda's apartment, always trying not to hate her surroundings. At one point the scarves draped over lamps, the travel posters decorating the walls, and the satin pillows that dominated the room hadn't annoyed Jo Beth so much, yet now she wanted to throw them all out the window. But the window was small and the screen was nearly impossible to remove, so for now, Magda's possessions were safe. Jo Beth sighed. The couch wilted underneath her pregnancy weight as she tapped her fingers, wishing she could just vault away from herself, but vaulting with a pregnant belly was obviously out of the question.

Finally, from out in the hallway, she heard the voice she'd been waiting for, so she struggled up.

The front door opened and Mitch entered first, smiling and carrying Elizabeth's bags. Elizabeth came in behind him. Immediately Jo Beth extended her arms for a hug and walked towards her mother, forcing Mitch to step out of the way.

"Mom!"

"Sweetheart!"

Elizabeth caught Jo Beth in a tight embrace, squeezing her hard, as if to erase the time and distance that had come between them. When she pulled away she placed both hands on Jo Beth's protruding belly.

"You look so beautiful!" Elizabeth said as she sniffled. "Of course, I knew you were having a baby. But this is the first time it feels real. My baby is having a baby."

"Thanks for coming, Mom." Jo Beth led her to the droopy couch. "How was your flight?"

"Fine," she answered, "but I've never been able to sleep on planes."

"You must be exhausted."

Jo Beth glanced away from her mother's lovely face, which she had to admit, looked as worn out as the couch they sat upon. Mitch still stood by the door, absently gazing at them. It took him a second before he thought to put down Elizabeth's suitcase. Then he pasted on a smile before he spoke. "I offered to take her straight to the hotel, but she couldn't wait to see you." He walked toward the couch and sat on an adjacent armchair, first removing a Spanish novel and Magda's sweater, both of which had been resting there.

"He's right." Elizabeth patted Jo Beth's knee and then pivoted towards Mitch. "And I also couldn't wait to start getting to know you. We're family now, so we have a lot of catching up to do."

"I couldn't agree more," he answered. "Although, Jo Beth talks about you so much that I feel like I know you already."

Jo Beth shot him a look which he didn't receive. "I wouldn't say that I talk about her all the time," she said.

"Of course, you do." He spoke to Elizabeth. "I've heard so many stories: all the afternoons your family went skiing together and how you'd end the day at your bakery, where you'd make Jo Beth and Skylar hot chocolate and scones. And how you put a little bit of chili powder in the cocoa and toffee chips in the scones…" He grinned at the thought. "Sounds perfect."

Elizabeth beamed. "I like to think that Jo Beth and Skylar had good childhoods."

Jo Beth had to chime in. "Yeah, but the way Mitch tells it I was Anne of Green Gables on skis. It wasn't like that."

He shook his head at her. "Compared to my childhood, yours was the friggin' Waltons." Mitch turned toward Elizabeth and recited his sad story. "My mom took off when I was twelve and my dad moved us from Minnesota to Florida, where we lived in a dingy apartment. He worked so much that I barely ever saw him."

"Oh, what a shame," she answered. "Growing up like that must have been hard."

"Mitch did okay," Jo Beth said.

Then the door opened and Magda entered. "Oh, hello," she said, in her affected, vaguely Spanish accent. "You must be Elizabeth."

Elizabeth practically gushed out her response. "And you must be Magda. It's so nice to finally meet you."

Jo Beth could see that her mother was drawn to Magda like a fly toward rotting syrup. But why should Elizabeth be different than anyone else?

Magda stepped over Mitch's feet and into the room, where she embraced Elizabeth and did the friendly peck on both cheeks thing. Elizabeth clearly wasn't expecting that, so it was awkward when she rose from the couch and Magda's kisses landed first on her forehead and then on her nose. After the moment passed, Magda seemed to realize that there was nowhere left to sit in the small living room, so she leant against the armrest of Mitch's chair. Both Mitch and Magda appeared totally comfortable with this intimacy. In fact, Jo Beth was sure that had a stranger walked in, he'd assume that Magda and Mitch were the couple.

"How was your flight?" Magda asked. "You must be exhausted."

Jo Beth rolled her eyes. "That's what I said."

She watched as her mother surrendered to a seesawing smile. "Yes, well, the jetlag is starting to get to me. The room is swaying just a little."

"Oh, it always does that," said Mitch. "But we should get you to your hotel." He stood, and as he did, his hand grazed Magda's thigh. "I can take you now, and pick you up after you've had a chance to nap. Magda and I have dinner planned. We're going to make you feijoada—

"—this stew with beans and pork. Brazil's most popular dish," Magda finished.

"Oh, that sounds wonderful," Elizabeth said. "You don't have to go to so much trouble for me though."

"It's no trouble," said Mitch. "We want to celebrate your arrival."

Magda batted her eyes in agreement. "I just wish the apartment was big enough that you could stay."

Elizabeth laughed and looked around at the tiny space that Jo Beth had been confined to for the last several months. "There's obviously no room for that." Then she rose from the couch slowly, as if her joints needed a good oiling.

"You're going already, Mom? You just got here."

"Don't worry, Jo. Your mom will be back."

Magda's voice sounded counterfeit and it matched the false look of sympathy she gave Jo Beth. Too bad she couldn't hit Magda, but Jo Beth knew her mother would be horrified by the violence. "Really?" Jo Beth said, packing her words with venom. "You've known her for thirty seconds and you're reassuring me on her whereabouts? Please. Just because I'm carrying a baby doesn't mean that I am one."

"Sorry," Magda said.

Sorry-not-sorry is more like it, Jo Beth thought.

Elizabeth swallowed hard, obviously sensing the tension. Jo Beth knew that the two things her mom avoided at all costs were burning caramel and conflict. To Elizabeth, both resulted in a sticky, smelly mess. Elizabeth seemed to hem and haw, but ultimately she decided to stay silent as she looked to Mitch, who was so used to Magda's and Jo Beth's bickering that it barely even registered.

"You ready to go?" he asked Elizabeth.

"I'm coming too!" Jo Beth nearly shouted.

Jo Beth surprised herself at how swiftly she rose from the couch, but that's the power of determination. Mitch, Magda, and Elizabeth all just stared at her, noiseless as she moved into the hallway and scrounged through the tiny, bursting closet for a pair of shoes that she hadn't had cause to wear for months. Mitch was the first to finally say something. "Babe, you know you can't leave the apartment. The doctor wants you on bed-rest. You're already moving around more than you ought to."

Where were those damn shoes? "I don't care. I want to be alone with my mom."

Elizabeth spoke next. "Sweetheart, why don't I stay a little longer? I'm not really that tired. I'll just hang out here for a while and Mitch can take me back after dinner."

Jo Beth wanted to scream her frustration; every single shoe in that closet belonged to Magda, whether they were the pair of size six waterproof Teevas or some delicate, strappy heels. She pushed all of them deeper into the closet. "I need to talk to you, Mom. Now." Jo Beth took her mother by the hand, and led her into the bedroom, which was taken up almost entirely by a "full" bed. It was even smaller than a queen, and lately it had been unmanageable for hugely pregnant Jo Beth to share it with Mitch, who was six foot one when slouching.

They'd started using the bed after Magda had volunteered to sleep on the cot in the living room. Otherwise, Mitch would have had no place to sleep, unless he shared the bed with Magda, and even Magda wasn't bold enough to suggest that. The bed was unmade with rumpled sheets and the room's curtains were drawn. But Jo Beth didn't care how unwelcoming or unkempt the room may have seemed; she shut the door and spoke in a fierce whisper. "You have to take me with you, Mom. It's not safe for me here. They're trying to hurt me."

Elizabeth sat on the edge of the bed, her attempt to control her response obvious. "Trying to hurt you, how?"

Jo Beth launched in, the accusations that she'd obsessed over for weeks just rolling from her tongue. "The accident wasn't an accident, Mom. Magda didn't secure my zip line on purpose. She wanted me to fall, and she wants to keep me here, bedridden, where I can be controlled. Mitch is in on it too. I just don't know why. Not yet. But I have to get out of here and you have to help me."

"Darling," her mom said evenly, "I know it's been difficult, stuck here all these months, especially when you're used to being so active. But I really don't think Mitch means you any harm. He loves you and he loves the baby."

"What are you basing that off, Mom? One conversation that you had with him during the ride from the airport?" Jo Beth took her by the shoulders. "This is not just pregnancy hormones or my chemically imbalanced brain. This is real. Leaving is the only safe option for me."

Elizabeth ran her fingers through her messy hair and pushed up her glasses to the top of her nose. "If you leave and start walking around, you'll most likely go into labor."

"So?" Jo Beth replied. "I'm almost full term."

Elizabeth's look was so rueful that she may as well have been wagging her finger at her daughter. "Not for another three weeks. Don't you want your baby to be as healthy as possible?"

"Yes, of course, Mom."

Elizabeth sighed. "So, I'll be here and I'll take care of you during the day, and if Mitch and Magda are truly trying to hurt you, then I'll know and we'll do something about it."

Jo Beth began to scratch the back of her neck but, actually, her whole body itched. "During the day doesn't count. They can hide it during the day. What really matters is at night." Jo Beth paused and peered into her mother's eyes. "Are you just humoring me, Mom?"

"No, of course not."

She'd lost her ability to read her mother, so Jo Beth decided to just play along. "Good, because I'm not making this up. They're always whispering and speaking Spanish, like they're pretending they're not American anymore. And yesterday Magda served me this pudding made with coconut milk."

Instead of a strong response, Elizabeth just gave Jo Beth a blank stare, and that made Jo Beth yell. "You know I'm allergic to coconuts!"

"Is it possible you're over-reacting?"

"Mom! Coconut milk makes me break out in hives! If I have enough of it, I get SERIOUSLY ILL!"

"Well, perhaps Magda didn't know that and she was just trying to be nice by making you pudding."

Of course, she would say that, Jo Beth thought. To her mother, food equaled love. "Magda was trying to poison me, Mom."

Elizabeth stood and led Jo Beth to the bed so she'd be the one sitting. "Darling, I think you're exhausted and overwhelmed, and with the hormones running through your system, well it's enough to drive anyone crazy."

"I'm the opposite of exhausted. All I ever do is rest. I've gone all *Yellow Wallpaper*."

"Huh?"

How could she not get the reference? After all, Skylar had gotten her love of reading from Elizabeth. "*The Yellow Wallpaper*? Skylar's favorite short story, about the woman who goes crazy because her husband forces her to rest? Skylar put it on my Kindle and I could totally relate. I'm ready to rip everything apart with my bare hands."

Elizabeth's mouth hung open but the corners of her lips seemed to tighten, as if they were trying to push words out. Then there was a knock.

"Jo Beth?" The bedroom door opened and Mitch peaked his head in. "Hey, sorry to interrupt."

Jo Beth stood from the bed and crossed her arms over her chest. "Don't pretend that you weren't eavesdropping."

Mitch entered the room and did a sideways shuffle to stand next to Jo Beth in the crowded space. He placed his large hands on her shoulders and she stiffened.

"You're going to give your mom the wrong impression." He turned toward Elizabeth without waiting for a response. "The bed-rest has been hard on her. Someone as active as Jo Beth, well, it's only natural that she goes a little crazy."

"I'm not crazy!"

"Then you know we're only keeping you here for the baby's well-being," he replied. "Come on, can't we have a nice evening and celebrate your mom's arrival?"

"How about I take a little nap here?" Elizabeth suggested. She gestured to the bed, in all its unmade, rumpled glory. "You can keep me company while Mitch and Magda cook dinner."

There was a long, uncomfortable pause. Jo Beth swallowed down her courage and anger. "Fine, if that's what you want, Mom. I certainly don't want to ruin the evening."

Obviously relieved, Elizabeth hugged her daughter. "We're the same, you know. I missed being on my meds during pregnancy. But I got through it and you will too. Pretty soon your baby will be here and you'll be so busy taking care of her, you'll forget the insanity that led up to her birth. I promise."

"Thanks, Mom."

Jo Beth met Mitch's eyes over her mother's shoulder as she hugged her. *I hate you*, she mouthed silently to him. But Mitch's face was unreadable and Jo Beth couldn't tell if he understood.

"Great," he said. "I'll go help Magda start dinner. Hope you're both hungry."

Chapter 25
Skylar

I was so consumed with training that I actually stopped worrying about Jo Beth for a while. One afternoon I completed a run in record time, going straight down and only extending my limbs when airborne. Once finished I removed my goggles and my helmet to face my new coach, Ellen. She was usually all business, with the look of someone who's spent thousands of days out in the cold and sun. I was hoping she'd praise me, but her words froze like watery snowflakes against a frigid surface.

"You have great speed," she said. "But I'm worried about your form. I don't want to push you along too soon."

"What are you talking about?" I demanded. "Now is the time. In another four years, I'll be pushing twenty-five. That's ancient for an athlete!"

"Don't be ridiculous!" Ellen's leathery face turned contemptuous. "You'll be twenty-three, several years away from peaking. Take care of yourself, don't be reckless, and four years from now will be the perfect time to try again for the Olympics."

I had been at camp for two weeks. It was the end of my trial period, time for them to decide if I had Olympic team potential or not. Well,

I guess I had my answer. As the realization sunk in, I was faced with a choice. I could be calm, gather up my skis, return to the red barn lodge, and soak in the hot tub with the other losers. Then, possibly, I could get drunk with Cody, a freestyler from Utah, who was super-cute but also a Mormon, which meant he was even less experienced than me. Most likely I'd wake the next morning with a hangover, but no serious regrets. But that's not what I did. Instead I left the race-lane arena and took the lift up the mountain to the private slopes, to the highest point I could reach. Ellen had told me not to be reckless so I would be reckless. I would make it from the tip top of the slopes to the very bottom in less time than anyone ever had, and I wouldn't let moguls, dry patches, jumps, or extremely narrow paths detour me. I'd be equal opportunity and slow down for nothing.

Olympic races aren't won on form, I muttered to myself. *The winner is simply the fastest skier in the race. That's it. Ellen doesn't know what she's talking about.*

I decided that my entire life amounted to a series of attempts by the universe to hold me back. Nobody was on my side. I'd show them; I'd show the world. In my twisted, self-pitying state, I figured that my only chance for redemption was to conquer the slopes in front of me, to set both a personal and world record at once.

Halfway down the mountain I snagged my ski on a patch of ice and fell. I went tumbling at a pretty high velocity, but the real problem was my left knee. It twisted like an awkward middle-schooler at her very first boy/girl dance. The result was hot, stabbing agony. When I finally stopped rolling, bouncing off rocks and bruising every soft spot on my body, somebody from the ski patrol came. It was the calendar boy, Frank. (Seriously. The ski patrol really did have a calendar and Frank really was on the cover, shirtless, in tight black ski pants and suspenders.) Even though I was ready to pass out from the pain, I recognized him instantly as he climbed off his emergency snowmobile: muscled limbs, dreamy blue eyes, toothpaste ad smile.

"What's the problem?" He asked in a light voice. "Are you hurt?"

Chapter 26

Jo Beth

The four of them ate stew and pretended like everything was fine, Elizabeth gushing over the tasty feijoada, how well seasoned the pork was, how they'd cooked the beans just perfectly.

"It was all Mitch," Magda said with false modesty.

"No, no, Magda's the one who taught me to make feijoada in the first place. I couldn't have done it without her help."

Jo Beth glared at them, thinking again how much they seemed a couple, how convenient it would be for them both if she just disappeared, leaving behind the baby and all its inheritance. But Elizabeth didn't seem to notice, though she wasn't oblivious to Jo Beth's angst. When it was time for Elizabeth to leave she gave Jo Beth an extra-long hug and Jo Beth clung to her mother like she'd never see her again. "I'll be over bright and early tomorrow morning," Elizabeth said, forced to wriggle from her daughter's grasp.

After Mitch finally escorted Elizabeth through the door, Magda started clanging around in the kitchen, doing dishes, creating an angry symphony of running water and reverberations, as she furiously scrubbed away. Jo Beth refused to be intimidated and strolled in for a second helping of dessert. The moment Jo Beth was within ten feet of her, Magda spun around and shot her a look of such poison that a rattlesnake would be jealous.

"What the hell is wrong with you?" she shouted.

"Nothing. I'm just peckish," Jo Beth calmly walked over to the counter, where the glass dish with the rest of the flan sat, but she had to nudge Magda out of the way to get to it. Magda was holding a large wooden spoon and before Jo Beth could duck away, Magda whipped it through the air so that its flat, wide end landed on Jo Beth's cheek in a cutting blow. The shudder of pain was so concentrated that Jo Beth dropped the glass dish in surprise and it landed in shards among her bare feet. Magda was wearing shoes, clunky heals that made her taller than Jo Beth, and she walked over the glass, crunching it into hundreds of hazardous pieces. And she still held that menacing spoon in her grip.

"You think I'm trying to hurt you, Jo Beth?" She laughed. "I ought to have, after you stole my boyfriend, sabotaged our business, fed me laxatives, and took over my apartment for months while I wait for your brat to be born. But I tried to be nice. I went out of my way to forgive you and make you comfortable." Her nostrils flared and her olive complexion reddened as she stood ominously close. "And instead of saying thank you, you tell your mom that I tried to poison you?"

Jo Beth squared her shoulders and lifted her chin. Maybe she was as vulnerable as she'd ever been, barefoot and pregnant in Magda's kitchen, but that didn't mean she had to take this crap. "I was just telling it like it is."

Magda whacked her with the spoon again, but this time the blow landed on her neck and for a moment Jo Beth couldn't breathe. Involuntarily she doubled down, planting her knees and palms into the floor, into the sharp debris of glass. As soon as Jo Beth could find her voice, she cried out in pain.

"Sorry," Magda said. "But you've had that coming for a while." Then she dropped the spoon and extended her hand. Jo Beth realized that accepting Magda's help was the only way she could move from crouching to standing without digging more glass into her skin, so she took her hand and Magda yanked her up. Once they stood, face to face, Magda leaned forward and kissed her briefly on the lips. "Don't worry," she whispered. "I won't kill you. Only crazy people are murderers." She placed her palm against Jo Beth's belly. "And I'm the sanest one here."

"I'll tell Mitch what you did and said."

Magda's thick brows narrowed as she squinted her almond-shaped eyes. "He won't buy it."

"Yes, he will! He'll take one look at my face, knees, and hands, and he'll believe every word."

Magda bent down and picked up the largest remaining piece of glass from the floor. With her eyes boring into Jo Beth's, she dragged the shard's sharpest edge right below her delicate cheek bone and dug in until it bled.

"Stop!" Jo Beth cried, snatching the glass from her grip. "That could scar. You're insane."

"No, you're insane, and everyone knows it. I'll tell them that you attacked me first. After your behavior tonight, your mother and Mitch won't doubt me."

Before Jo Beth could argue, there was noise from the hallway and the sound of Mitch entering through the apartment door. "Hello?" He called. "I'm back."

Magda gave Jo Beth a sneering smile before she answered him. "Mitch!" Her voice was frantic and loud. "Help!" She tromped over the broken glass to meet him at the entryway. "She's gone crazy, Mitch! You have to help!"

Mitch grunted his surprise and came rushing into the kitchen. "What the hell happened?" he cried. At that moment, his eyes moved down to Jo Beth's hands, and she realized she was still holding the bloodied piece of glass that Magda had used to cut herself.

Jo Beth rolled her eyes before answering Mitch. "This totally isn't what it looks like."

Chapter 27

Skylar

In a perfect world, I would have made a clever, ironic response and pretended that Frank wasn't way out of my league. But the throbbing in my knee was so bad that instead, I rolled over and vomited up my undigested lunch of chili and grapes, right at Frank's feet. Yet Frank's gorgeous, soft lips didn't turn down in disgust. He just scooped me up, put me on his snowmobile, and rode me down to the clinic at the base of the mountain, where a sports doctor saw me immediately. An hour later, after the doctor had examined me and the nurse had let me rinse with mouthwash, I hobbled out on crutches, cursing my luck and the prospect of weeks of recovery. My injury was just like Jo Beth's, the one that was my fault, the one that cost her a spot in the last Olympics. I guess karma really is a bitch.

Frank was there in the lobby, filling out a form attached to a clipboard. "How you doing?" he asked. "Did the doctor fix you up?"

"I think I'm beyond repair." I tried to smile and succeeded, because Frank was so beautiful that smiling wasn't difficult. "Thanks for helping me earlier, and I'm sorry if I got any puke on your snow boots."

When he laughed, his chin dimple appeared. "No worries. I've endured far worse." He looked me up and down. "How are you getting back to your room? Do you need a ride or something?"

There were no cars allowed in the ski village, so perhaps Frank was offering me a bus token? But the buses here were free. Actually, they were more like theme park trolleys, but as far as I knew, the nearest stop was sort of far away.

"I wouldn't mind a lift," I said. "Do the buses ever stop right outside the clinic, you know, when people have been injured?"

"That would make sense, but no." Frank was looking back at his clipboard and not at me, checking off little boxes and signing his name at the bottom. "No worries. I can take you on my scooter."

That would mean sitting behind Frank, wrapping my arms around his broad chest and tight abs. I swallowed roughly. "What about my crutches?" If Frank was holding onto the handlebars and I was holding onto Frank, well, toting crutches would be awkward.

"I'll take you first, and then come back for your crutches," he said. Now he looked up, right at me, and our eyes met. I felt a zing even more powerful than the pain in my knee.

Forget common sense. Frank was so gorgeous, all I needed was one moment of eye contact to believe we shared a strong connection. Did every female experience that with him? Realistically, I knew that I was merely attractive enough to be inoffensive, so that deep-connection-thing I felt probably wasn't mutual.

"Stay here," he said, and then he pointed toward the glass door that lead to outside. "I'll pull around."

He was off, without waiting for me to say yes, and moments later I saw him pull up to the curb. He parked his scooter in the loading zone, hopped off, bounded through the doors, and before I could even protest, he scooped me into his arms once more and carried me outside.

But why would I protest? This was as much fun as a girl with dashed Olympic dreams and a busted knee could hope for. Soon we were both on his scooter, my arms wrapped pleasantly around his six-pack, as we zoomed through the tiny avenues of the ski village like we belonged in an Italian villa. I didn't notice that Frank had never asked me where I needed to be dropped off until we pulled up to an apartment building on the very edge of the resort, one where I knew most of the employees lived.

"No, I stay over in the skier dorms," I said. "Sorry. I should have mentioned that."

"This is where I live." Frank parked and helped me down, keeping his arms around me and supporting my weight. "I thought you could use a drink. You've had a rough day."

"You thought I'd like a drink at your apartment?" I croaked out a laugh. "I don't know much about this sort of thing, but shouldn't we at least start somewhere public?"

He gave me a sideways grin. "This isn't a ploy. You can relax on my couch and elevate and ice your knee while I serve you vodka tonics. But if you want me to take you back to your dorm, where your fellow skiers will celebrate that their competition just decreased by one, I'll do that."

Frank was right, and he didn't even know that I'd been cut from the trials before I fell. The last thing I wanted was to go back to the dorms.

"But, why?" I asked. "Why do you care about helping me or serving me vodka tonics?"

Another sideways grin. "Because you're cute."

If he was ugly or even ordinary, his behavior would have been kind of pervy. But my entire body flushed. "Let's go upstairs," I told him.

He carried me up to his apartment, settled me on his couch with a pillow under my knee, and served me ice-cold vodka tonics as promised. Frank sat on an adjacent arm chair, sipping his own drink. "Tell me how this happened," he said.

I closed my eyes, shutting out the poster of a crouching, bare-legged female skier with a perfect behind that hung on his wall. "You mean how I fell?"

"Yeah," I heard him say.

"It's a long story." I opened my eyes and returned Franks' dreamy gaze. "Do you want the long version or the short one?"

He shrugged, muscles rippling as he leaned forward. "I have nowhere to be. Give me the long version."

I told him everything: how my competition with Jo Beth was more intense than even she realized, how I drove myself to succeed at skiing after my college dreams of Cornell were dashed, how lately I'd forget who I was when I wasn't on the slopes. "But I'm not going to the Olympics," I finished. "And I'll never be as good as my sister."

Frank squinted at me, cocking his head to the side. "You're what, nineteen years old?"

"Yeah."

"You've got plenty of time," he said.

"Jo Beth had already won the silver by my age."

Frank showed me his chin dimple again. "So? The brightest stars always burn out first."

The vodka had loosened my limbs and my tongue. I let my head rest against the couch cushion. "Great metaphor," I said. That was a lie; I actually thought it was incredibly cliché and not particularly true. But he was sweet to try to make me feel better. "Hey, Frank, what's your story? Why doesn't a guy like you have a girlfriend?"

"What makes you think I don't?" he asked.

I thought about it for a second. "I guess because you seem like you might want to kiss me," I answered.

He nodded solemnly. "*You guess I seem like I might want to kiss you?*" He laughed. "Way to be definitive, Skylar. I'm no expert, but if you want to get into Cornell's writing program, I'd work on strengthening your declarative statements." He moved from his chair and sat on the edge of the couch, facing me. "Does it matter, though?"

"Does what matter?"

"If I have a girlfriend?"

I swooned. Whether it was from Frank's hotness or from a lack of food combined with a lot of vodka and knee pain, I wasn't sure. But I wanted him touching me. "I guess not," I replied.

Frank leaned back, sizing me up. His confident magnetism was an elixir, erasing every single problem I thought I had from my brain. Those huge blue eyes staring at me, those sweet, parted pink lips, the steady rise and fall of his chest: they all combined into the most fabulous compliment I'd ever been paid, and his attention quickened my pulse. His large hands took my face and held it gently. He tilted his head, leaning in for a kiss I absolutely could not refuse. His lips were hard and searching yet his kisses were slow and drugging, and I was shocked at how soon my addiction set in. Then he took me in his arms and instinctively my body arched towards his. He must have carried me from the couch to his bed. He must have lightly removed my clothes, because I registered no pain or discomfort in the process of getting naked and lying beneath him. My only thoughts were *don't stop* and *I want more.*

I dug my fingers into his shoulders, which I swear were a mile wide and carved from bronze. He lifted my leg with the injured knee and elevated it against his perfectly formed rear end, but it didn't matter, because soon my body melted into his, delirium pulsed through me, and the bliss was so real, so explosive, I was unaware that I'd ever felt any pain.

Chapter 28
Jo Beth

Mitch used tweezers to not-so-gently remove all the glass from Jo Beth's skin. They sat in the bathroom, her atop the toilet with its lid down, and Mitch on the floor, his back leaning against the edge of the tub as he picked out the glass piece by piece, shard by shard, dropping each one into the wastebasket.

Occasionally he'd look up and his wide, dark eyes pooled with distress.

Jo Beth couldn't keep silent. "Mitch, I swear that she started it. Magda hit me with that spoon and then she cut herself to make it seem like it was my fault."

Mitch's chest heaved up and down. He kept his eyes on her knees. "Jo Beth, you have to stop."

"But I'm telling the truth."

"Jo Beth!" His inhale was sharp, like he'd just been hit. "Once the baby is born, we'll leave. I don't care where we go, but we'll figure something out. Until then, you have to keep it together."

"She's still in love with you, Mitch." Jo Beth could say this as loud as she wanted because Magda was out, having taken herself to the emergency room after Mitch said that her cut probably needed stitches.

Mitch vehemently shook his head. "No. It's not like that. *She* dumped *me.*"

"Wait, what?" Jo Beth felt her brain synapses coil tightly in confusion. "I thought you said that your breakup was mutual."

He dug the tweezers into the base of her ankle, right where some glass was lodged. Suddenly Jo Beth felt like he was playing that board game, Operation, and she was as real to him as the clownish cartoon character who needs gas bubbles removed from his stomach.

"No," Mitch replied. "She decided it was time, after I lost my ability to see through the blood-red cloud that surrounds her. That's what happened."

"Ouch!" Jo Beth yanked her foot away. His excavation attempts were just too vigorous. "What are you talking about? What blood-red cloud?"

Mitch grabbed her foot back and held it tight as he mined for more glass. "The one that surrounds Magda?" His tone was condescending and impatient, almost as bad as his nursing skills. "Don't tell me you don't see it."

"Mitch..."

He wouldn't look at her but stayed focused on his task.

"Mitch, you're honestly telling me that a blood-red cloud hovers around Magda?"

"Yeah." He sighed. "I realize that not everyone can see it, but I can. I've always been able to see things that other people can't. My ability is more a curse than a blessing."

The pressure behind Jo Beth's eyes was uncomfortable, just like the pricking of Mitch's tweezers. Could he possibly be for real? "Why haven't you ever mentioned this before?"

"Magda wanted it to be our secret," he said simply. "But things changed, she broke up with me, and it was fine. There was no tidal wave, no crisis, she didn't disappear, and we stayed friends." Mitch finally dislodged the last pieces of glass and after depositing them in the trash can, he dropped the tweezers like he was dropping a microphone. "And I love you, Jo. But you have to stop acting so crazy."

She had to stop acting so crazy? Jo Beth just nodded and gripped the edges of the toilet beneath her. How could one little statement from this man change everything?

"You know what? I'm tired. I think I'll go to bed." She stood and so did Mitch, and then she kissed him on the cheek. "Thanks for taking such good care of me."

Jo Beth went to bed and lay there until she heard Magda come in, and then there was the sound of their voices speaking in low, romantic tones. Were they kissing? Had they been intimate with each other this entire time? She was surprised to realize that she didn't even care. But when Jo Beth was sure they were too consumed with each other's company to worry about her, she got out her cell phone, hid under the covers so her voice would be muffled, and called Skylar. It was the middle of the night where she was, so Jo Beth thought for sure she'd answer, but it went straight to voicemail.

"Sky," Jo Beth whispered. "You have to believe me because Mom doesn't. Magda and Mitch have charmed her into believing that they're innocent. But I know the truth. Magda is an evil bitch and Mitch is crazy." She took a deep breath, trying not to feel claustrophobic underneath the covers. "I'm actually sort of relieved," she continued. "Maybe Mitch actually does love me. Maybe's it's not his fault that he's insane. I don't know how long he's been like this, maybe his whole life, but it explains everything. It explains why I can't trust him." She tried to keep her tears out of her voice. She had to stay strong. "Skylar, where are you? Why didn't you come? I have to get myself and my baby away from Mitch. Once she's born I'm going to leave and I'll need your help. Promise that you'll help me." She took a deep sniff. "We need to talk in person. I don't know how that will happen, but just know that I love you. You're my favorite and I love you best of all."

She pressed end, emerged from the covers, and sat up. Then she reached under the bed and removed the knife she'd kept beneath the mattress for over two weeks. Jo Beth gripped it in her sweaty hand, wondering if she was capable of murder, or if her subconscious just liked to pretend. Hell. She was pretty sure she was capable. The bigger question was whether she was up for the effort that murder required. Exhaustion slowly dripped through her, turning her muscles and mind to slush. She must have fallen asleep with the knife still in her grip, because after what seemed like hours, she woke to Mitch's face looming above hers.

"Why are you holding a knife?" His voice was sharp, like the blade she clutched.

"Huh?"

He took the knife from her and her breath caught. If he wanted to kill her, right here, right now, there was no stopping him. "Are you afraid of me, Jo Beth?"

She pushed him away and struggled into a sitting position. "No, Mitch. I'm not afraid of you. But I think we should break up."

"What?"

"As soon as I have the baby I'm going home with my mom."

Mitch closed his eyes and fell back against the bed. "You can't do that," he whispered.

She took the knife from his hand and he let it go without protest. "Yeah, I can."

His eyes rolled toward the ceiling. "So much water," he said, holding out his palms as if to catch a nonexistent flood. "Like the roof is crying."

"Mitch…" She placed her hand on his shoulder. He sat up abruptly and swiped back the knife. "Why can't we just be okay? Is that too much to ask?"

Suddenly Jo Beth was afraid, but not of Mitch. There was a flood, but it wasn't coming from the roof. It came from between her legs. "Mitch!" she cried. "Stop being delusional. My water just broke."

Chapter 29

Skylar

Chapter 29: Skylar

I was woken by a woman standing over me. She screamed and swore and ripped away the sheets, which had been the only thing covering my nakedness.

"What are you doing in my bed!" she yelled.

My head pounded and my mouth was dry as dirt. I couldn't think clearly enough to form a response. I looked around, the sunlight penetrating my skull, making my brain throb like a stubbed toe. I wasn't in my condo; I wasn't anywhere at all familiar. Then I saw a Ski Patrol stocking cap on the floor and I remembered.

"Where's Frank?" I managed to rasp.

"Huh!" This girl, this waifish blonde with multiple piercings and a Betty Boop tattoo on her thigh, put her hands on her hips, which were covered by a diner uniform with a short skirt and apron. "He's gotta be at work. That doesn't say much about you. Usually when he brings a whore here, he at least wakes her up before he goes." She rolled her eyes and simultaneously grimaced. "He must still be pissed at me for hooking up with Jimmy," she said this softly, as if talking to herself. Then, in an instant, remembered her anger and set her torch-like eyes back on me. "Get dressed and get out!"

I moved just a little and my knee sent out the urgent reminder that it was wounded. "I can't walk," I said, "and my crutches are back at the clinic."

"Not my problem!" she yelled. "You have three minutes to get out, or I'll call the police and have you arrested for prostitution."

"Um, I'm not actually a prostitute..."

"I DON'T GIVE A SHIT! GET OUT!!!"

Somehow I rolled out of bed, but crawling around with my naked butt in the air represented a new low. Finding my clothes and getting dressed improved matters slightly, but once I was out in the hallway, with the door slammed behind me, reality set in. I had no phone, no crutches, and no way home. I used the stair railing to hoist myself up, stood on my right leg and attempted to put weight on my left, but doing so made me yelp. So I sat and crawled down the stairs, toddler style, my massive hangover and my knee crowning me as the queen of pain. I thought about the chili and grapes that I'd puked up the day before. At least I never ate dinner last night, because it would surely be all over the stairwell by now if I had.

After what seemed like a month, I made it down the stairs. I hopped on one foot, pushed open the front door and managed to struggle outside where I stood, leaning against the building, until someone, anyone, came by who could maybe help. Around twenty minutes went by. Twenty minutes that seemed like twenty years, as I shivered in the icy wind, leaning against the building, trying not to put weight against my knee, trying not to think about who I was and how I'd gotten here.

You did it to yourself. Lyrics from one of Gavin's favorite songs rang through my head.

Gavin.

I was flooded with guilt at the mere idea of him. Why hadn't he entered my mind last night? How could I hook up with Frank without giving Gavin a second thought? No, forget about second thoughts. If I was being honest, I'd admit that Gavin had never even rated a first thought.

Finally, somebody came by on a scooter much like Frank's, and I convinced this stranger to give me a lift to the nearest bus stop. From there I got off at the stop closest to the clinic, where I sat on a bench, until I saw a fellow skier who I recognized from the dorms, and I convinced her to go to the clinic and retrieve my crutches. After that things got easier, but they were still no picnic. I was sick with shame, dehydrated and nauseous, and my knee forced my whole body to pound and ache. I didn't think things could get any worse, that I ever would feel such self-loathing, such pain, such an intense desire to disappear.

Chapter 30
Jo Beth

As Mitch and Magda drove Jo Beth to the hospital, her contractions were fast and hard, like a train slamming into a brick wall. She was conscious only of pain, of long, agonizing stretches that took her breath away. Once they arrived at the clinic doors, she was immediately wheeled into delivery, totally skipping the waiting game of walking up and down corridors and trying to spur labor. There was no time for an epidural. Even with Jo Beth's limited Spanish, she understood when the doctor said that her only option was to push. She imagined herself back on the ski slope where she won the silver, only this time she would tune out the bells. This time she would win. She channeled every last bit of energy, every last bit of strength, and with all the hope and faith she never knew she had, she pushed. Jo Beth pushed until she was here.

Bijou. Her precious, beautiful, gold-medal-girl.

"She's perfect," said Mitch. After Bijou and Jo Beth were both cleaned up, he sat on the bed next to Jo Beth, admiring how the baby's five tiny fingers already knew how to coil around his very large index finger.

"I think she has your hair," Magda said to Mitch. Magda had insisted on coming to the hospital with them and Jo Beth had been too out of it to protest. Now the three of them were together in Jo Beth's hospital room, like the three points of a dysfunctional triangle.

Then Elizabeth arrived.

"Let me see her!" she exclaimed immediately. In one hand, she carried flowers and in the other a tin of what had to be baked goods. She placed both down on the bedside table and then extended her arms to hold Bijou.

"Isn't she beautiful, Mom?" Jo Beth handed over her baby, never feeling prouder of anything, ever, in her entire life.

"She certainly is." Elizabeth's smile was wide and Jo Beth recognized that loving look in her eyes. She'd given that same look to Skylar and her thousands of times. After a moment of gushing and cooing, Elizabeth glanced away from the baby and focused on Jo Beth. "And, how are you?" she asked. "How are you feeling?"

"I'm starving," Jo Beth said. She also had the beginnings of a powerful headache, but she figured that was because she was dehydrated. She turned to Mitch. "Can you find the nurse? I thought she said she was bringing me breakfast."

"I'll go get you something," said Magda. She stood and went toward the door, but paused before exiting. "Congratulations, Jo Beth. And I'm sorry about before."

Magda smiled so Jo Beth smiled back. There seemed no point in holding a grudge.

"What's she sorry about?" Elizabeth asked, after Magda had left.

"It doesn't even matter anymore," Jo Beth said. "Today is a whole new world."

There was more cooing over the baby, and fierce fascination about how she puckered her lips and how she tried, unsuccessfully, to force her fist into her mouth. Magda brought breakfast, and Jo Beth practically gulped down the eggs and toast. "Is there anything else to eat?" she asked.

"Here, have a lemon bar," Elizabeth said. "I forgot to bring them out last night."

"You baked these? Thanks, Mom! You know how much I love lemon bars." Jo Beth ate three before she started to feel full, but even then, she still had room for a fourth.

She was holding Bijou, trying to nurse her, but the baby wouldn't latch on, when suddenly Jo Beth's patience ran out. The pain behind her eyes had quadrupled in an instant. Horrendous, crushing spasms burned inside her brain. "Take her!" Jo Beth yelled to Mitch, worried that if he didn't, she might inadvertently harm her daughter. Mitch took Bijou. Jo Beth sensed Elizabeth watching her, realizing that her eyes had rolled back so that only the whites showed, that her head fell forward as if her neck had been broken.

"Jo Beth!" Elizabeth cried, rushing to her daughter's side. "Call the doctor!" she screamed to no one, to anyone.

Magda ran into the hall. "Necesitamos un doctor!" she cried.

People came running, and they wheeled Jo Beth somewhere—to surgery, maybe? She wasn't sure, because for the second time in several hours, she'd entered a dark tunnel of inescapable agony and she couldn't turn back. The whole new world she'd only just spoken about became the end of the world, for her at least.

But as she unwillingly released her grasp on her very existence, it occurred to Jo Beth that at least it wasn't the end of the world for Skylar. And for Bijou, the world had only just begun.

Chapter 31
Skylar

Finally, I entered my dorm, found my phone lying on the night-stand, and saw that Jo Beth had called. So had my mother, twice.

First came Jo Beth's desperate plea. Then there was a joyful message from my mother: "Your niece is here! Bijou is seven pounds, six ounces, and mother and baby are doing great."

But there was still another message waiting for me from Mom. I didn't know why, but dread froze the soft, dense part of my bones as I waited for it to play. Somehow a sixth sense kicked in, and I knew without knowing that after I'd heard that second message, my life would change irreparably. Mom's voice was tearful yet separate from the person I knew her to be. "Skylar. Call me as soon as you get this. Something happened. Something happened to Jo Beth."

This morning, I had been naive to think I'd known pain. My knee, the sting of defeat, and my hobbling walk of shame: they had all amounted to just a pebble in a beach full of quicksand. Now I was to be sucked in. Maybe someday I'd find my way out and see daylight again, but even then, nothing would ever look the same.

Chapter 32
Mitch

There was always something I couldn't explain and there was always something to feel bad about. Well, maybe not always, but the phenomenon didn't begin with Jo Beth. It began in middle school, specifically in math class. With math, you couldn't have an opinion and you couldn't have faith. What if I didn't believe that two plus two *always* equaled four or that the sine function's maximum and minimum values *must* stay consistent to find a solution? At twelve years old, I'd already learned that solutions came from a belief in the inconsistent and in the faith that irregularities occurred every moment of every day.

Speaking of irregularities, Amanda Butler had made me promise to call her. Amanda wore pink flip flops to school, to show off her toes, which were always painted purple. This was a dress code violation but the teachers were too scared to lecture her. She floated through the halls of Sanford Middle School, always elevated an inch off the floor, so her flip-flops never got dirty and her toenail polish never chipped.

"Hey Mitch," she'd said to me one day. With all the familiarity in her voice, it was like we'd been friends for years.

"Hi," I mumbled, scared that my voice would turn all Peter Brady and I'd squeak instead of grunt.

"Whatcha doing later? Walk me home?"

"Definitely."

It didn't matter that she lived in the opposite direction of my house, or that I'd be skipping band practice. Amanda wanted me, so I was there. On the way home, we talked about our favorite vegetables. Amanda said she liked broccoli with cheese, but I preferred Brussel sprouts. "What about eggplant?" she asked. "That's also a good one."

I looked into her eyes and saw that they had changed to a deep purple, just like eggplant, just like her toenail polish, just like the Vikings jersey that my dad still kept in the closet after having moved from Minnesota to Florida. "Eggplant is great," I told her. "I love it with spaghetti sauce and cheese."

She laughed. "You mean eggplant Parmesan?"

"Yeah. That's what I mean."

When we reached her door I handed her books to her. "Thanks for carrying them for me. You're the sweetest." She stepped in close and stood on her tippy toes, making an L shape with her feet and flip flops. Then she kissed me, once on the cheek and once on the lips.

One plus one equaled a million.

We were a couple for almost ten days. Then, one night I was supposed to call her but I had math homework. In middle school, ten days equaled several years, at least when it came to romantic relationships, and I'd gotten comfortable enough to take her for granted. Besides, I'd noticed how other girls were now looking at me. If Amanda had chosen me, I must be valuable.

My phone rang at 9:30.

"Mitch," my dad said. "It's for you."

I could hear the scowl in his voice. I shoved my math book closed, wandered out into the hall, and he handed me the phone. "It's after your bedtime. Make it quick."

"Hello?"

She was already laughing. "You have got to get your own cell."

"Yeah…" My dad just stood there, glaring. "Um, sorry I didn't call you but I just got busy. Can we talk tomorrow?"

"Tonight," she answered. "Meet me at Plymouth beach in two hours."

"I can't," I said.

"You can. You will. Just sneak out."

I swallowed, my throat suddenly sore, and looked away from Dad, who stood there being imposing. He'd never lost his Minnesota lumberjack look though we'd been living in South Beach for years.

"Sure," I told her, because I wanted the conversation to end. "Talk to you then."

I hung up.

"You're too young to have a girlfriend, Mitch," said my dad.

"Yeah, I think you're right."

I brushed my teeth and went to bed, but seventy-five minutes later I stealthily traipsed over our shag carpet and out into the hallway of our apartment complex. Plymouth beach was not far from where I lived; it was adjacent to a public park and playground, and Dad and I would picnic there when it wasn't too hot out. I arrived first, so I lay down on the sand and looked up at the stars, summoning my courage to make out with Amanda. All I had to do was kiss her and the rest would just follow naturally. That's what I told myself, but the longer Amanda took to arrive, the more nervous I became.

Finally, a pair of pink flip flops was in my line of vision. I sat up.

"I've been waiting for you," I said.

"I know."

When she didn't sit down next to me, I stood. "Amanda, I love you." I took her hand and tilted my head down to kiss her but she giggled and took a step back. The tide was coming in and the waves kissed the inch of pink foam that separated her feet from the sand.

"Mitch, it's time we go our own ways. I didn't want to have to tell you at school and I thought you should have a chance to digest the information before we see each other tomorrow in math class." In the moonlight, her eyes shone like dark ocean waves, so blue they were almost black. I couldn't speak. No words would come so I just stepped closer to her again. This time my effort to kiss her would work and we wouldn't have just broken up. She put her hands against my chest and pushed me back. "I mean it, Mitch. Our relationship has run its course. Time to move on."

After a week and a half?

Her words echoed what my mother had said to me, right before Dad and I had moved out of our Minneapolis home. "Why can't you come with us?" I'd asked.

"Your dad and I aren't getting along anymore," she'd answered.

"Then I'll stay here with you."

She'd shaken her head. "No. I have things I need to do, Mitch. This life doesn't fit me anymore. I need to move on before it's too late."

But dad and I were the ones who'd moved, from the polar vortex to the land of endless summer. I'd wake up every day sweating and the heat would linger underneath my skin no matter how high the air conditioner ran.

"You don't get to do that," I told Amanda now. "You can't just end things whenever you feel like it."

"Of course I can."

Then the ocean jerked back like it was having a seizure. For a moment, the water receded into a jet-black funnel, just like Amanda's eyes, but immediately it shot back up, erupting into a massive tidal wave. A tidal wave in Florida is a huge irregularity; oceanographers had declared the possibility all but impossible. But I was drenched by water that reached as high as the moon. Salt filled my mouth and I gagged. I tried to swim, struggling against the waves, but my feet sank into the sand and I couldn't move from the spot where I had stood when Amanda Butler broke my heart.

I'm not sure how much time passed before the tidal wave receded, but I do know that it swallowed Amanda whole. One moment she was standing on the beach with me and the next she was gone. I walked home, changed out of my wet clothes, and went to bed.

The next day at school, the principal came to our class. He cleared his throat, pushed his index finger against his glasses so that they rested further up his nose, and let his hand skim his balding head. "Class, I'm afraid I have bad news. Amanda Butler is missing. Her parents called this morning and said she was not in her bed when they went to wake her. There is no trace of her and we could use your help. Have any of you seen or heard from Amanda in the past twelve hours?"

I sat on my hand to keep from raising it. On the board, Ms. Palmer had written an equation, one I had spent hours the night before trying to figure out. I had worked on this equation when I could have been calling Amanda. At the time, I was sure that I knew the values of x and of y, but now the numbers crashed like waves before my eyes and I realized that they had absolutely no value.

None at all.

Fast forward fifteen years. I was no longer a child, no longer too young for a girlfriend, no longer too young for a wife. I had become a father but still I was a bereft young boy, confused and alone, stuck on land while a tidal wave swept away everything that mattered most.

Chapter 33
Skylar

"No, I don't understand. I will *never* understand." I paced the length of my dad's studio, which was really a garage full of oil paintings and sculptures. Dad could never commit to a single medium, and his drive to be an artist with his "own space" had caused him and my mom to spend countless mornings scraping the ice and snow off their cars after parking by the curb.

Dad sat at his easel, smudging grey and black paint over a large, white canvas. "What don't you get, Sky? He's the baby's father and we're lucky he's bringing her here at all. I think the least we can do is welcome Mitch into the family."

I'd been looking at one of my dad's framed pieces: an abstract snowstorm with flicks of blue and pink, camouflaging what must be our house, but I suppose nobody would recognize the blurry brown blob as home except for me, Mom, Dad, and Jo Beth. Yet Jo Beth would never recognize anything, not ever again.

I turned my angry eyes toward my father. "The least we can do is report Mitch and Magda to the police."

Dad took a measured, pained sigh. "Don't be like that, okay? It doesn't help."

"Dad, they're responsible!"

"Your mother was there and she says that they're not." Dad cast his gaze toward the ceiling, as if that would stop more of his tears from coming. Drip, drip, drip. He'd been crying constantly, like a stubbornly leaking pipe that can't be fixed. I envied him. My anger was too aggressive to let my tears see the light of day.

"Mom's not always right."

"But she's right about this." Dad lowered his voice into his most serious of tones. "It was a severe allergic reaction brought about by an amniotic fluid embolism. Clear and simple."

Did Dad even know what that meant? Maybe it helped him to say the supposed cause of Jo Beth's death out loud, but it didn't help me to hear it. "But what about the marks on her face and the cuts on her hands and feet? And what about Jo Beth's voicemail?"

That voicemail. That terrible voicemail was a tattoo on my conscious. *Why didn't you come, Skylar?* Every time I closed my eyes I heard those words as if for the first time, and they screamed at me from the cell phone in my mind. After I got the horrendous news that Jo Beth had died three hours after her labor, I immediately left the training camp and flew home, where Gavin and Dad were waiting for me, their tearful hugs encircling me like a straitjacket. I didn't deserve their kindness, but I also didn't comprehend the full extent of my guilt and negligence until I thought back to all the warning signs, to all the moments when Jo Beth might have accepted my help yet I did nothing.

"You know she wasn't in her right mind," Dad said. "We have to trust your mother on that. Mom's gone through the same...challenges as Jo Beth, so she could recognize the signs in her own daughter. Jo Beth was suffering."

"No, Dad. I did some research. Turns out there are poisons that can cause the same reaction as amniotic embolisms. Mom told me that Jo

Beth ate breakfast after her labor. It would have been so easy for Mitch or Magda to just slip a little bit of hydrofluoric acid into her orange juice. Because soon after her heart just *stopped* and everyone assumed it was because of a complication during labor—my God, it's the perfect murder!"

Dad closed his eyes and took steady breaths, like it took all his focus not to just spontaneously combust. "What's their motive, Sky?"

"Jo Beth's money."

Dad laughed sardonically, opened his eyes, and gave me a tearful glare. "Mitch would have already married Jo Beth if he was after her money. And where are they going to get hydrofluoric acid? You can't just walk into Walgreens and buy it."

"I don't know, but Dad, I wish you'd take me seriously on this. Mitch is dangerous. We've got to protect little Bijou. As soon as they get here, we need to order him to leave."

"Skylar!" Dad threw his paintbrush to the floor, startling me with his raised voice. Dad rarely yelled. "We will do no such thing! Mitch and Bijou are all we have left of Jo Beth, so your mother and I will let him stay with us if he wants. And I won't have you spouting off any more of this paranoid nonsense. Mitch is Bijou's father and you can't legally take her from him."

My guilt and my sense of obligation clawed at me with sharp, dirty talons. I knew I should concede before the scratches grew too deep.

"Then they'll stay with me," I said with a sigh. "That makes the most sense. Technically, the condo still belongs to Jo Beth, so technically it belongs to Bijou. We can set up a nursery and make it her home."

Dad pressed his lips together and I knew he was trying to settle on an emotion before his mouth went slack. He looked like he'd aged ten years in the last ten minutes. "Your mother wants the baby with us."

"I know, but Jo Beth said she wanted Bijou to be with me. It was her last wish before she died." I didn't say that if Mitch was staying at the condo, I'd be able to watch him. Dad had probably already jumped aboard my train of thought.

"Well, we'll leave it up to Mitch to decide where he'd rather stay," said Dad. He narrowed his eyes at me. "But if you try anything, if you say anything to him about your conspiracy theories, I swear to God, Skylar—"

My car keys were resting atop an art supplies cabinet and I grabbed them. "I'm going shopping for baby stuff right now. I'll have everything ready by this evening, when they get here."

He sighed. "Do you know anything about taking care of a newborn?"

"No, but I'll figure it out." Now I struggled with the stupid crutches that were still necessary for me to get around. Shopping would be a challenge.

Maybe I should call Gavin.

Chapter 34

Gavin

One of the first times that Gavin and Skylar had ever hung out, she told him that he belonged in the English countryside instead of a Colorado ski town. "Dressed in your wool pea coat, walking around with that notebook of yours, you're like a benevolent, sober version of *Lucky Jim*."

He'd never read *Lucky Jim*, but after Skylar told him that, he instantly checked it out from the library. The novel is about this lower-middle class guy, Jim Dixon, who gets a job teaching history at a British university, but he's terrible at participating in the social rigmarole of campus life. He gets drunk a lot, falls for the girlfriend of another professor's son, and constantly one-ups himself in rebellious acts against pretension. When Gavin was done reading it, he wasn't sure if he should be flattered or insulted. Sure, Jim had his charms, but he was an acquired taste. Like curry. Gavin would rather be universally loved by women, like Mr. Darcy. Like a flourless chocolate torte.

Still, he didn't take offense. That would just get in the way of his ultimate goal, which was to make Skylar his. He couldn't pinpoint what it was about her that obsessed him, but he did firmly believe in the rarity of love. All the novels that Skylar read professed the same theory: It is only the lucky who truly know love, who can sacrifice their own well-being to benefit someone else. Gavin would sacrifice himself and all he wanted in return was a piece of her heart.

Gavin thought back to a year and a half ago, to what he considered their fourth date. He'd taken her to his grandfather's cabin in the woods. It was an overcast Sunday afternoon, and they had snowshoed over hills and amongst tall trees before reaching the cabin, where he cooked a French beef stew, spiced with a rare Dijon he'd had to drive to Denver to buy. The memory was so vivid he could replay all the details like they were happening that instant.

Skylar's eyes had widened in delight after she'd taken her first bite. "Wow!" she'd said. "Is this your own recipe?"

"No, it was my grandfather's." Gavin had gestured around the cabin. "The cabin was his too. He died eight years ago, but he left me this place. I also got my love for cooking from him."

Skylar had looked so pretty in the flickering candlelight of the cabin, her face like fresh cream, her hair like honey. "He sounds special. You two were really close?"

He'd nodded, holding back tears. "Sort of like you and your sister." Skylar then gave Gavin a crooked, questioning look, so he'd tried to explain. "You know; he was the person who understood me best, who loved me best of all. I like to come here because it makes me feel like he's still around."

"Yeah, I understand."

They had been sitting on the rickety old couch, holding their bowls of stew while eating, but he'd placed his bowl on the rustic coffee table that his grandpa had made himself, using two-by-fours as the base and some thick iron pipes as legs. "You must miss her a lot," Gavin had said.

His heart had skipped a beat as a sad smile invaded Skylar's face.

This was back when she'd believed that her sister being a continent away was the worst thing that could happen. He'd urged her then to tell him stories about their happy times together and she'd complied.

One day I'll make you as happy as she does, he'd thought to himself. *One day I'll be the person who loves you best, who understands you best.*

Now he knew his time had come.

Chapter 35
Mitch

The first time I saw Jo Beth in the swimming pool at Portillo, I felt the earth shake beneath my feet. I looked around to see if anyone else was experiencing the tremor but quickly determined that they weren't. It was just me, being overcome by Jo Beth's beauty. She was like a seal with her wet hair slicked back, able to move so fluidly, as if her limbs were blessed with a super-power. The more I got to know her, the more I realized how spot-on my first impression was. Jo Beth was more than just human; she was divine.

That tremor never went away. Jo Beth was always inadvertently cracking floors beneath her feet. I didn't mind. The world could open up and swallow us both whole, as long as we fell together. But when she said she was leaving me, it wasn't the floors that ripped apart; it was the ceiling, sending forth a gush of water like a baptism. I worried it would drown her like the tidal wave that had taken Amanda so many years ago. Luckily, it didn't work out that way. And yet, it hadn't worked out at all.

We had her cremated. My beautiful Jo Beth was reduced to ashes and confined to a jar, which now rested on my lap while Elizabeth held Bijou. I stared out the airplane window, looking at the icy white peaks below. What if I opened that window and threw out what was left of Jo Beth, so she became one with the snow and mountains? She'd probably morph back into her original form, like she'd just been through that molecular transporter on *Star Trek*. Her skis would instantly attach to her feet and she'd be in her personal version of heaven. I clutched at the window and tried to lift it, but it wouldn't budge.

"Are you okay?" asked Elizabeth.

I nodded. "I hate these airplane windows that won't open."

She took a moment to answer, shushing the baby instead. "Well, there's obviously no way we can open windows on an airplane, but I see what you mean. It's sort of a reminder that we're trapped."

I looked at Elizabeth, at how she sat next to me, holding Bijou with such ease and grace. She'd been so young when she had Jo Beth, and now she was pretty much the same age as all those women who wait until later in life to have babies. Plus, Elizabeth's freckles and her athletic frame made her pass for a millennial. With the family resemblance, everyone would just assume that she's Bijou's mother.

"If you want to take a nap, I'm fine taking care of Bijou." Elizabeth said this in a hush, as if already anticipating my sleepy state.

"No thank you," I answered. "Every time I close my eyes I dream of Jo Beth." The dream was always the same and if Jo Beth was trying to make a point, well, message received. She was storming my subconscious, looking for some way to dwell inside, lodged between my sorrow and my self-reproach.

Elizabeth's breath caught and she took a sharp inhale. I placed my hand on her shoulder. "Sorry," I said. "It hurts just to her hear name, doesn't it?"

A limp smile was her only answer.

"Can I hold her for a while?" I asked, gesturing toward Bijou.

"Yeah, of course." Elizabeth handed me the baby and I took her, careful to support her head. Once she was nestled against my chest, I took in that baby smell of talcum powder and fabric softener. It combined with some intangible drug-like effect on my senses.

"Joseph texted me," Elizabeth said. "He says that Skylar is fixing up a nursery in the condo, you know, the one Jo Beth bought? So, you can choose where you and Bijou would like to stay. Of course, you're welcome at our house and I could help with middle of the night feedings and with taking care of her...." Elizabeth's voice trailed off but I got the impression she wanted to snatch Bijou from my arms. I thought about my own mother; it would probably be months before she'd meet Bijou. Maybe that was for the best. Nothing made sense right now. My life was just a bunch of mismatched puzzles pieces that only fit together in a crooked, forced sort of way.

"I think we'll stay at Jo Beth's condo." I had to look away when Elizabeth's face fell. "I mean, I'm sure we'll rely on your help far too much, but I like the idea of Bijou staying in the home that Jo Beth bought."

Right now, Bijou was only capable of sleeping, sucking on a bottle, and pooping. She certainly would hold no appreciation for her dead mother's condo. I don't know why I was compelled to stay there, why I would turn away from the one person who was desperate to care for my newborn baby.

I guess my desperation was just as fierce.

Chapter 36
Skylar

Was I coldblooded?

My heart should have been a wreck, rendering me incapable of action or rational thought. I waited for my breakdown, for the moment when the world came crashing in and I finally grasped that I now had to live my entire life without ever seeing Jo Beth again. But until that moment arrived, I would focus my energies on getting the condo ready for Mitch and Bijou's arrival. Gavin set up the crib while I sorted through shelves and drawers, removing any of Jo Beth's possessions that I found.

"Do you really need to throw away all her old stuff?" Gavin asked, as I shoved tubes of lipstick, half-empty bottles of lotion, pairs of worn down Smartwool socks, and past issues of *Skiing Magazine* into a large white garbage bag.

"I'm trying to be nice. Mitch might get upset if he sees her things just lying around. Besides, this is what you do when someone dies."

Gavin cursed under his breath. I looked over and realized he'd done something wrong with the crib and now he was unscrewing his work. "I don't understand why you care about Mitch's feelings." Gavin grimaced and strained to loosen one of the crib's railing "Only hours ago, you were accusing him of murder."

"Exactly. I need to keep my eye on him, for Jo Beth's sake. And for Bijou."

I pulled a slim volume of poetry from Jo Beth's bookshelf. Was this mine? I didn't recognize it. When I flipped the book open, I discovered it was by various 20th century female poets. From some crevice in my mind, I retrieved a memory: "I can be literary too, Skylar," Jo Beth had told me one afternoon while we sat on the ski lift. "I've decided to start reading poetry so I can talk about it with you."

I had said *great, yes, do that*, but I didn't seriously think she would. And Jo Beth had never brought it up again.

"She never told me about this book," I murmured.

"Huh?"

"Nothing." I slid the book back onto the shelf. Suddenly my body felt liquid, like my bones and muscles might transform to warm saltwater, but I dog-paddled the sensation away. I glanced at the clock. "Let's hurry up. They should be here soon and I'd rather not be home when they arrive."

"Why?"

"Because it's awkward."

Gavin's nod of understanding didn't register on his face. "Where are you going? It's not like you can hit the slopes."

"There's more to me than skiing!" I'd been snapping at Gavin a lot lately. Here he was, trying to offer me love and support during this difficult time and I was too awful to forgive him for that. I couldn't, not until I was ready to forgive myself for betraying him. I softened my tone. "I'm going to the library."

"Oh. Okay..." Gavin knew that I wasn't enrolled in any classes this term. Earlier this winter, I'd anticipated that I'd be too busy training for the Olympics to register.

"I'm going to research correspondence courses, something to tide me over until I have a better plan for next fall."

"Can't you do that at home on your computer?"

"You're missing the point. I need to get out of here. I need a distraction. Why don't you understand?"

He stood and walked over to me. "I do understand." He tilted his face down, towards mine, and gave me a soft kiss on the mouth. Part of me wanted to collapse into his arms, but the other part wanted to run away. And if Gavin sensed my ambivalence, hopefully he attributed it to all the awful events of the last week and not to any personal insult on his behalf. Luckily, Gavin gave me a smile like snow melting in the sun. "Why don't you get out of here? I can finish up."

I should refuse; I should stay; if I ceased my perpetual motion, I might implode and that would be really, really messy. "Thank you." I used my crutches to awkwardly exit down the stairs, through the front door, and into my car. Once I got to the library it didn't take me long to browse the online courses offered through Oxford University and find something on the Brontës. Their admission policy for extension students was lax, so I just filled out a couple of digital forms and charged a few hundred bucks to my credit card, and then, voila! I was a student in an Oxford literature course. I literally could not wait to begin. My local library had all the books I needed, so I immediately read through several of the Brontës' poems, plus the beginning of *The Tenant of Wildfell Hall*.

The distraction was such a relief that I lost track of time and was surprised when, hours later, a soft, patient voice came on over the intercom, announcing that they'd be closing in fifteen minutes.

I looked at the clock and realized it was a quarter to nine. Then I looked at my phone and realized there were several new messages from both my mom and from my dad, all to the tune of *where the hell are you?* One glance out the large, paneled picture window and I realized that the sun had set hours ago. Now people were making their way through the circular main room for last-minute checkouts at one of the many self-service computers that sat along the walls. I grabbed every Brontë book that I didn't already own and awkwardly carried them to a checkout station. This was no easy feat with my crutches

"Here, let me help you!" A fellow patron swooped in when I dropped a book. I didn't refuse her assistance, though my stomach fizzled like a flattened balloon. Should I tell her that I didn't deserve any goodwill?

"Thank you," I said, after she helped me check out my books.

"Do you need help carrying them to your car?"

Truth was I did, though I hated to admit it. "That would be great."

She followed me, carrying my books. This lady in her mom jeans and middle-aged woman haircut was probably the same age as my mother, though she seemed older. Would my mom seem older too, now that tragedy had transformed her? Would either of my parents ever feel whole again? And what about my niece? Would she ever feel whole at all, without having a mother to protect her? I didn't have answers, but I knew one thing: there was no more room for mistakes. I must protect everyone I loved at all costs. I vowed that whatever ache and anguish Jo Beth had gone through, Mitch would experience the same, and I'd be the one to unleash such misery upon him.

Later, I opened the front door of Jo Beth's condo to find dark, empty silence. Mom and Dad must have given up on me and headed back. Relief crisscrossed through me when I realized there'd be no forced family reunion and no heavy group crying session—at least for now. At first, I thought I might have hit the jackpot, that maybe Mitch was already asleep, but then I heard movement from upstairs, the back and forth squeak of floorboards. I assumed that Mitch was rocking Bijou in the chair I'd had delivered this morning. It took me awhile to get up to the nursery and once there, I hovered outside the door until I heard a low, nearly inaudible voice say, "Is that you, Skylar? Come in."

I entered the nursery and found Mitch sitting in the oak, hand-carved chair that I'd just bought. He was rocking a little bundle swaddled in pink whose head rested atop his shoulder. Mitch's skin looked especially dark against his white button-down shirt and faded blue jeans. His hair was slightly shorter than I'd remembered and his eyes were drooping. But when he smiled he did so with his whole face: a tired, sad, friendly smile.

"Hi." I knew my lame greeting didn't take up enough space in this tiny room that, twenty-four hours ago, was just a huge closet that held ski-wear and sporting goods.

Still holding Bijou, Mitch got up from the rocking chair. Instantly he was coming toward me and I was too paralyzed to turn away or step back, so I let him kiss me on the cheek. He had to lean down to do so, not like Gavin, who was only a couple of inches taller than me. The effect of his kiss was also different than anything I'd ever experienced with Gavin, probably because my hatred for Mitch was a living, breathing force of nature. But when his lips contacted my skin, I flushed so hot that I worried I'd break out in a sweat.

"You poor thing," he said, and it took me a moment to realize he was referring to my crutches. "You should sit." Mitch gestured toward the rocking chair he'd just abandoned.

"Oh, no, that's okay. I just came in to say hello."

"Don't you want to hold your niece?" He sounded almost playful, as if taunting me with a secret.

With a start, I realized just how much I did want to hold her. In fact, I needed to have Jo Beth's baby in my arms like I needed to be soothed after a dreadful nightmare. I went toward the chair and sat, and Mitch wordlessly put Bijou in my arms. Her eyes were closed but her lids fluttered and she puckered her tiny lips, trying to suckle. Dark curls, just like Mitch's, covered her head but her skin was light, like Jo Beth's. Other than that, she was just a blob, completely un-extraordinary, yet I instantly fell in love. "Hello, Bijou," I whispered. "I'm your aunt Skylar."

"What do you think of the name 'Bijou'?" Mitch's voice startled me and my head snapped up.

"I don't know," I said, which was my honest answer.

"I kinda think that 'Bijou Blue' sounds like a porn-star name, but your sister insisted." He laughed and hiccupped at the same time. "I gave up a long time ago, trying to change Jo Beth's mind about anything."

"You could name her something else. There's nothing stopping you now." I cringed a little at how harsh that sounded, but Mitch didn't seem phased.

"Sure there is. I can't go against what Jo Beth wants." The smile fell from his face as his eyes grew watery. "Anyway, the more I think about it, the more I like it. 'Bijou Blue' is really kind of beautiful."

Our gazes met, which was accidental on my part, but Mitch's eyes widened at the connection. His dark cheeks colored ever so slightly, but then returned to his normal brown, and I wondered if seeing me hold his daughter was surreal for him, since I looked so much like Jo Beth.

I stared at Bijou's downy head and he looked away, at the bare walls which still needed some sort of nursery décor, and for a few seconds we were both silent. Then we both talked at once.

I could barely form words but said, "I hope the flight wasn't too awful." His voice was louder and came out in a burst. "I am so sorry about everything, Skylar."

I chanced looking at him again. "What do you mean?"

He leaned against the dresser, which wobbled beneath his weight. "I don't blame you for blaming me," he said. "My job was to protect Jo Beth and I failed miserably." He sniffed loudly before rubbing his eyes. "I should have known from the beginning how out of my league I was. I didn't deserve Jo Beth, and I don't deserve Bijou either, but you understand that I can't abandon her, right?"

"Umm..." my voice was soft. "Has anyone suggested that you abandon her?"

He shook his head and kept his eyes down. "I can't leave her. If I do, my life will be worthless. I'll be worthless too."

It took me a second before I could respond. "I suppose you're at a crossroads, aren't you?" He looked up and our eyes met, and again I felt that full-body flush, like when he'd kissed my cheek just a minute ago.

Mitch nodded. "I'll try not to get in your way while I figure out my next step, where I want to make a home for Bijou and myself."

"Okay."

Mitch would eventually leave with Bijou. The thought made me hold her more tightly to my chest.

"You don't know what it means to me, that you're letting us stay here."

I loosened my grip on the baby and pressed my lips to her forehead before answering. "You don't need to thank me," I said. "It's what Jo Beth would have wanted."

Chapter 37
Gavin

Gavin lay in bed, alone.

It had been months since he'd stayed at his parents' home. He didn't really have a place of his own, not unless you counted his Grandpa's cabin. He did stay there sometimes but it was so remote, making his commute to the bakery four times longer than it needed to be. He would stay with Skylar whenever she let him, but now, with Mitch and the baby there, he doubted his regular invitation still stood. Other times he'd crash with Joseph and Elizabeth, who lately were more like parents to him than his own parents were, but he knew he had to leave them alone to grieve.

That left Gavin with only one option. He'd been putting it off, because he hadn't wanted to face his mom and dad's questions and criticisms. *Why aren't you going to college, Gavin? Do you really believe you can make a good living as a baker, Gavin? Are you turning into the person you want to be?* The person he wanted to be was the man who Skylar loved, pure and simple. But maybe he wasn't enough for her. That doubt clung to him, like how flour stuck to the walls of the bakery no matter how often they swept and scrubbed.

"Honey, I just want to know that you have a plan," his mom had said that night when they sat in the breakfast nook sharing tea and a couple of pumpkin bars from the batch he'd brought with him. "Yum!" His mom's smile after swallowing down that pumpkin bar was probably the best compliment she'd ever given him. "Gavin, these are delicious."

"Thanks Mom. I came up with the recipe myself. It's one of my specialties."

But then the conversation inevitably turned and his mother asked him all those questions he couldn't answer, his sense of inadequacy building with each word she uttered. *When are you going to continue your education, Gavin?* He didn't know. *Do you really want to be a baker for the rest of your life?* Possibly. *Don't you have any higher aspirations?* God yes.

Now, alone in bed where he'd spent countless miserable hours staring at the ceiling and wishing for escape, he knew his mom was right. He needed a plan. Skylar was never going to settle for someone like him. He was almost like her brother as he worked for the family business and let her take him for granted.

Okay, I need a plan, he whispered into the night. *What's it going to be?*

Chapter 38
Mitch

"She's crying."

"Huh?" I couldn't orient myself or find my bearings as I woke in this foreign room to a foreign sound.

"Bijou is crying. You have to get her because I can't."

I fumbled around, patting my hands along the nightstand, trying to locate a lamp and switch it on. Finally, I gave up, got myself into sitting position, and put my feet on the floor. The trek to the nursery was short and lit by a nightlight, so that part was easy.

When I got there, I found Skylar standing on one leg over the bassinette, her crutches resting against the wall. She awkwardly leaned down in preparation for lifting Bijou up. Meanwhile, Bijou had switched from crying to angry screaming.

"Let me get her," I said, and I handed Skylar her crutches so she could move out of the way. Then I picked up Bijou and held her, but that did nothing to stop her wailing.

"Do you think she's hungry?" Skylar asked.

"Yeah."

Skylar sat down in the rocking chair. "I can hold her while you go and prepare a bottle."

"Okay." I was unsure of the way down to the kitchen, and how I'd find the stuff to get a bottle ready once I was there. But I handed Skylar the baby and walked off like I knew what I was doing.

Actually, the kitchen was where I'd expected it to be, and when I flicked on the light there was Jo Beth, standing in the middle of the room like she'd been waiting for me.

"There's the formula and the bottles," she said, pointing to the counter where a bunch of baby stuff had been left out, probably by Elizabeth, so it could be found easily in the middle of the night. "Don't forget to use warm water for the formula. Warm, but not hot."

Was it possible to be this tired? I hadn't slept on the plane and the hours before our trip were filled with life and death, but not with sleep. Every part of my body was heavy and it was incredible to imagine that I'd ever feel light again. "You woke me upstairs?" I said to Jo Beth.

"Yeah," she replied. "Now are you going to make the bottle?"

I walked toward the counter where the baby stuff rested and I opened the can of formula. I let a sigh from deep inside escape while I dropped the milky white powder into the bottle.

"What's your problem?" Jo Beth demanded.

"Nothing, I'm just tired."

"So?" She floated over to my side and hovered next to me, her hands defiantly on her nonexistent hips. "Do you have any appreciation for the effort it took me to get here? I bet you don't."

"How could I?" I went to the sink, turned on the water, and stuck my finger into the stream of cold until it turned suitably warm. "I have no idea how you got here and I'm betting you're not allowed to tell me."

"You know I've never given a crap about rules. But you're right; I can't tell you because you wouldn't get it."

There was no arguing her point. If I couldn't understand simple concepts, like how the universe could be created by a single burst of energy from a miniscule volume of space, or how it possibly rose like a phoenix from the dust of another, dearly departed universe, how could I ever comprehend Jo Beth's existence or her journey to find Bijou and me?

"Okay," I said simply.

Now it was Jo Beth's turn to sigh, which she did as I tightened the lid onto the body of the bottle and shook it. Was she angry because I wasn't arguing with her?

"Test the temperature on your wrist." Jo Beth said.

"Why?"

"To make sure it's not too hot."

"But how hot is too hot?"

"It shouldn't hurt."

I looked at her; even as a ghost she was beautiful. "Can you feel pain anymore?"

Her eyelids pulled down for a moment, and then she silently shook her head no.

"But you can remember pain?" I asked.

"Of course."

"I'm sorry if I contributed to your pain, Jo."

She shook her head again. "Our daughter is crying. You should get upstairs."

The bottle was ready, so I turned toward the stairs, toward the sound of little Bijou's wails. But first I looked back at Jo Beth. "Will I see you again?"

She shrugged her ghostly shoulders. "Who knows?"

"What if I can't live with that uncertainty?"

"You have too. Everyone does."

I almost pointed out that she doesn't have to live with uncertainty, that she doesn't have to live with anything, not anymore. But I kept my mouth shut for fear of being insensitive and climbed the stairs to find Skylar rocking Bijou.

"I can take over," I said.

"Okay."

We did the awkward dance of switching places, which included our handing the baby back and forth while she retrieved her crutches, and at one point Skylar had to lean on my shoulder while I held Bijou. Skylar looked so much like a younger, less angry Jo Beth, and she even held the same soapy scent.

"Thank you," I said. I wanted to tell Skylar to stay, to sit with me, to not leave me alone. But right before those pleas escaped my mouth, I bit my tongue and managed not to beg. I put the bottle in Bijou's mouth and instantly her screams stopped. Then the only sound in the room came from her sucking that rubber nipple.

"You were hungry, huh little girl?" I rocked Bijou, feeling that pull of devotion that they say always happens to mothers, but not necessarily to fathers. This delicate, strong creature, with her paper-thin eyelids, silky hair, and strong grip around my index finger: I knew that if necessary, I'd kill for her.

I could live with any other uncertainty, but Bijou had to be okay.

Chapter 39
Skylar

I didn't sleep well. After I woke from Bijou's crying, I couldn't seem to get comfortable because the image of Mitch's face as he held his daughter was stamped behind my eyes. Casting his adoring gaze down while his protective arms held her to his chest, he was the very picture of paternal affection and yes, this conflicted with the murderer I knew him to be. My muddled emotions kept me awake. I was still tossing and turning at 6:00 a.m., when my phone buzzed with a text.

Come to the bakery for coffee? I need to talk to you.

Gavin. Compunction made me twitch. Had he figured out my betrayal? I wasn't ready to face him but if I waited until I was ready, I'd never get it over with.

Sure. I'll be there in about an hour.

I crutched my way out of bed and into the bathroom, where I took a bath instead of a shower because standing and balancing on a wet surface was too difficult. As I lay in the warm water, I thought about my night with ski patrol calendar-boy Frank, back when I was sure that losing my shot at the Olympic team was the worst catastrophe the world could offer. Now look at me. But here's the thing about self-pity: it spontaneously reproduces itself. I couldn't cry over my sad, sad story, or else the narrative would never, ever change. I had to remain clear-headed if I wanted to be in control and I remembered this as I finished my bath, got dressed, and tried to leave the condo without making enough noise to wake Mitch and Bijou. Somehow, I was successful at all three, and though I realized my pride only made me more pathetic, I still enjoyed my triumph.

When I got to the bakery I saw Gavin through the windows, laying out a tray of muffins, and my heart staggered. I knew I didn't deserve him but I also felt incapable of letting him go.

I used my crutches to swing my way up to the bakery entrance. Gavin looked up in time to see me approach and he opened the door for me. "Hi!" he said, and the warmth he packed into that one little syllable communicated that I hadn't been called here for a confrontation. Gavin was still in the dark about my dark side; he was the Plantation Owner to my Moll Flanders.

"I made your favorite scones."

"Raspberry white chocolate?"

"You know it." He gestured toward a little table, where a plate with a scone and a steaming cup of coffee already sat. "Let's sit and talk. I only have a few minutes before the morning rush begins."

I let Gavin help me into a chair and then he leaned my crutches against the wall. He sat opposite me, drumming his thick fingers against the table and flicking his light brown bangs out of his eyes. "So how was last night?" he asked.

"You mean with Mitch and Bijou?"

"Yes," Gavin answered.

"Okay. I mean, I don't trust him, but he was polite enough."

"Did Bijou cry all night?"

"No. I only heard her once."

Gavin's mouth set into something like a frown and a serious crease formed between his eyes. "Do you think this situation is going to be livable?"

"I'm not sure what you mean."

He let out a gusty breath. "Well, isn't it sort of weird? You and Mitch are both single and now you're living together and caring for a baby together, but the circumstances are so... unnatural?"

My defenses went up. "Unnatural?"

Gavin rubbed his forehead, signaling that what he was about to say was really, really difficult. "For better or worse, Jo Beth and Mitch loved each other, and whether you intend it or not, people might think you're trying to take her place...in every way possible."

I sucked on my bottom lip and gripped the table edge. "Wow. You must think I'm pretty stupid."

"No, I don't. That's just the point. I think you're the best, Skylar, and I think you deserve better than trying to fill Jo Beth's shoes." His eyes softened as his hands reached across the table to caress my fingers. "I want you to think about it. You've got your whole life ahead of you, and you have all this potential, and I hate to see you waste it on pursuing Jo Beth's dream and caring for Jo Beth's daughter, and—"

"And falling for Jo Beth's boyfriend?" I snatched my hands away and leaned as far back in my chair as possible. "Don't worry, Gavin. You don't have to compete with Mitch. I'm not even remotely attracted to him."

"That's not what this is about."

"Oh really?"

Gavin took a deep sniff. "Aren't you going to eat your scone?"

"I've lost my appetite."

"Fine." He got up, snatched my plate away and took it back behind the bakery counter. I stared out the window, and through the reflection I could see his gaze. "I just found out last night that I got a scholarship at Le Cordon Bleu."

Slowly I pivoted in my seat so I could face him. "Where is that?" I asked.

"There are branches all over but I'm going to the one in Chicago."

"Why?"

"Because I want to be somewhere with good job possibilities after I'm done with school. Chicago is perfect."

I picked up my coffee cup like I was going to take a sip, but really, I was just warming my hands. "So, this has been in the works for a while. Why didn't you tell me you were applying?"

"You didn't ask."

"Oh, Gavin." All at once, tears escaped and coursed down my cheeks and I couldn't explain why. I hadn't even cried yet over Jo Beth, so why was I crying now? "You would leave me?"

The moment he saw that he'd upset me, Gavin rushed over and captured me in a hug. I let him hold me, though I wasn't sure if I was sobbing about him or about everything else that had gone so terribly wrong.

He waited until I quieted down. I'm not sure how many minutes had passed, but finally he said softly into my hair, "You could come with me."

I pulled away. "To Chicago?"

"Yeah. There are tons of good universities there. I was thinking we could do some research, find out where the best literature programs are, and you could apply."

I wiped my face with the back of my hand and tried to get a grip. "But it's the Midwest. Where would I ski?"

Gavin attempted to laugh but it came out forced and distorted. "Maybe you could take up a different sport." With a pensive sigh, he leaned in, kissed my forehead, and then stood up. Looking out the window, he said, "I see a customer coming. We'll talk later?"

I nodded as the bell over the bakery door rang and somebody entered in from outside.

Chapter 40

Gavin

Gavin didn't worry about lying to Skylar. So what if he hadn't yet been accepted into Le Cordon Blue? He would be soon enough. As soon as his shift at the bakery was over, he went to his parent's home and downloaded all the application materials. His mom and dad would be happy he had a plan.

But at the same time, he knew it wasn't enough.

Already he could tell Skylar was conflicted. After all, she'd told him that she 'wasn't remotely' attracted to Mitch! What was that about? Less than forty-eight hours ago, she was sure Mitch had killed Jo Beth, and now she was analyzing whether she had feelings for him?

No. *Hell* no.

So, while plan "A" was to make himself more desirable by being slightly out of reach and having the promise of success, plan "B" was all about Mitch. He would dig up dirt, dirt he could use to set Skylar against him.

He drove over to Sky's after his shift at the bakery. "I'm going to the library to study for my Brontë class," she'd said before she left that morning. "I work better there. After that, I have a physical therapy appointment."

He parked by her curb when he knew she'd be gone, and he waited, hoping to catch a glimpse of the infamous Mitch. After about an hour he emerged, with the baby in one of those slings that was like a forward-facing backpack. Okay, so Mitch was tall and broad, and with a great head of hair. And when he placed his large hand over the baby's head, murmured something to her, and smiled a warm, wide smile, Gavin clenched the steering wheel in disgust. This guy was Mr. Darcy and flourless chocolate torte wrapped up in the flawless package of an intellectual-looking NBA player. Gavin doubted there was a woman alive who could resist him. But what the hell; why was Mitch smiling? His girlfriend was dead and his daughter was motherless.

Mitch was obviously an asshole.

Gavin waited until Mitch wouldn't notice and then he got out of the car and followed him, keeping a safe distance so his presence wouldn't be detected. He trailed Mitch as he walked into a busier part of town, where there were little shops that sold things like hand-made paper, wine, and specialty knitting supplies. Gavin hurried through puddles and over piles of slush, cursing his thin leather shoes, while Mitch's long legs traipsed easily and quickly over the wintry mess, his feet protected by Sorels. Mitch turned into a boutique grocery store that Gavin knew to be overpriced, stocked with European imports that offered exotic packaging but disappointing flavor.

Gavin followed him in and browsed the aisles while Mitch made his selections. "Excuse me," he said to a saleslady, "but can you recommend a good olive oil?"

She was happy to and she also gushed over the baby. Except for one moment when Mitch sort of tripped over his own feet, he stood so tall and proud that you'd never guess he'd just been punched by tragedy. That was only one of the reasons Gavin didn't trust him. Flirting with the salesgirl and buying over-rated food products to most likely use in an incompetent dinner attempt for Skylar: that all made Mitch seem shady, but it could maybe be forgiven. However, on the walk home, Gavin heard Mitch talking to himself. It was like he was having a conversation with a ghost.

It was like he was crazy.

Chapter 41
Mitch

I decided to make pasta with pesto sauce. I'd missed pesto. The only way I could have it in Brazil was to make it fresh and my efforts never produced a good result. But today I went on a walk and easily found everything I needed to make a passable pesto. Once we got back to the condo, Bijou and I spent the afternoon hanging out. She slept, she pooped, she cried, and she sucked on a bottle. As for me, I cooked and tried to rid myself of the spinning sensation I'd had ever since Jo Beth died. The earth no longer trembled, but with Jo Beth's absence, it quickly twisted around instead. I found myself suffering from vertigo, often grabbing the edge of the kitchen counter, or placing my palm against the wall to maintain my balance. Yet the instant Skylar hobbled in, I felt steady, as if my equilibrium had been regained.

It was dinner time and I could tell Skylar was hungry by her long, loud sniff of the garlic lingering in the air.

"I made pasta with pesto," I said. "Do you want some? There's plenty. I even added shrimp."

"How did you get the ingredients?"

"I put Bijou in the snuggly and we walked to that market down the street. This condo is in a great location. There's so much in the immediate area."

Skylar nodded at me like I'd said something profound. "Where's Bijou?"

I pointed to the living room, where Bijou had fallen asleep, safely strapped into her baby papasan chair. I could effortlessly see her from the kitchen. "So far, she's pretty easy to care for."

"Except for last night," Skylar answered.

"Yeah, but that's what babies do." I stirred the pasta, my stomach grumbling in anticipation. "But hey, I'm sorry she woke you. I'll try to wake up faster next time, so you don't feel like you need to get up."

Skylar used her crutches to come closer, but she stopped at the cabinets, balanced on one foot, and reached up to get two plates. "Don't worry about it. I'm happy to help with midnight feedings if you'll go downstairs and put together the bottles for me." She handed me the plates and gestured toward the bowl of pasta. "That smells really good."

I smiled and ladled a portion into both bowls, put them on the table, and then we sat. "I fixed that closet door that had come off its hinges," I said. "Hope you don't mind."

Skylar's cheeks turned pink. "The one in my room?"

"Yeah. But didn't it used to belong to Jo Beth?" Jo Beth had pointed it out to me this morning, taking me around the entire condo once Skylar was gone, and showing me what needed repair or improvement.

"She gave the condo to me," Skylar retorted. "Why wouldn't I use the master bedroom?"

I speared a piece of shrimp onto my fork and then twirled the green pasta noodles until they formed a cocoon around it. "No, you totally should. I was just thinking out loud." Skylar looked at me skeptically, so I continued. "Really. Jo Beth is proud of this place and she's proud of you. It makes sense for you to be in her room. She even said it's what she wants." I slid the shrimp and noodles into my mouth and began chewing, enjoying the burst of garlic and basil, so much so that I didn't immediately notice the stricken look on Skylar's face.

"You talk like she's still alive."

I swallowed my food and it instantly formed into a lump at the back of my throat. "Sorry."

Then I realized that while I could see Jo Beth, Skylar could not. I would have to be more delicate when talking about my encounters with her sister.

"I've had a rough day," she said, after several moments of just staring at her plate. Skylar looked so glum, like lifting her fork to her mouth was far too much for her.

"Because you miss Jo Beth?" It seemed like an obvious question, but sometimes it's the obvious questions that need asking.

"Yes, but there's other stuff going on too and the worst part is that I can't tell Jo Beth about any of it."

"Well, maybe you can tell me and that will be like telling her." I didn't add that perhaps I could act as messenger and relay the information to Jo Beth, that maybe I could get an answer from her, and then I could share it with Skylar. Because what if that didn't work out? The last thing Skylar needed was to have her hopes dashed.

Skylar started talking and it seemed as if her words were aimed at the walls as much as they were at me. "Last week I blew my shot at the Olympics. Then I hurt my knee, got drunk and had a slutty one-night-stand with a ski patrol guy, and now Gavin, who doesn't know that I cheated on him, wants me to move to Chicago with him so I can—I don't know—figure out who I'm going to be since I'm not going to be Jo Beth." She met my eyes and my heart parachuted.

"Do you want to go to Chicago?"

"I don't know. I don't know what I want. I used to want to go to Cornell and become a writer, but I blew that chance too."

I set down my fork, thinking that Skylar deserved my one-hundred percent focus. "I don't think you have to know what you want right now. It's probably better *not* to know, and if nothing else, all this indecision will make great material for you to write about someday."

Her face hardened, and when she spoke it was nearly in a hiss. "But I *should* know what type of person I want to be. More specifically, I should know that I *want* to be a good person. Right, Mitch?"

From the living room came the sound of Bijou's fussing and I anticipated that soon her whimpers would turn to cries. "You can be a good person and still make mistakes. Just look at Jo Beth."

"I can't look at Jo Beth. Jo Beth is dead!" At that, Skylar clamped her mouth shut. Only a half second later her head fell forward and she sobbed. "My sister is dead, Mitch. She's dead!"

Skylar's suffering seemed massive, like a black hole sucking up anything that happened to be in her proximity and turning it into anti-matter. Then Bijou's cries quickly escalated and equaled Skylar's in both volume and intensity, so I did the only thing that made any sense. I went and picked up Bijou, came back into the dining room, and inserted her into Skylar's arms. Skylar did not stop crying, but she held Bijou, and together, their wails formed a cacophony of need and despair that was more real, more immediate, than anything I'd ever heard. Their misery caused my own to overflow.

We didn't have to speak. Our shared grief was strong enough to connect us. In that moment, Skylar, Bijou, and I became a family.

But families don't always love each other, do they?

Chapter 42
Skylar

We had a funeral for Jo Beth and tons of people turned out. The press came too, though they hadn't been invited. Jo Beth probably would have been pleased that they showed up, but to me their presence offered an extra level of anxiety because I was to deliver the eulogy. I stood at the podium, shivering underneath a scratchy, black wool dress that failed to keep me warm. When my knees buckled and words failed me, I looked out across a room occupied mostly by strangers and my eyes settled on the hundreds of white carnations dotting every available space. We'd covered the funeral parlor with the most predictable of flowers, but I'd chosen them because I thought they looked like little fragrant snow balls.

Speak, Skylar, a voice inside my head told me. It was a voice that sounded like Jo Beth.

I can't, I silently plead, *because once this speech is over and once this funeral is over then you'll really be gone. Once we put you to rest, you really are dead.*

"*I may be dead*," the voice responded, "*but I'll never be at rest.*"

I focused my gaze on Mom and Dad, sitting in the front row, their hands gripped together. I couldn't add to their pain by refusing to talk.

With a heaving chest, I told my favorite stories about Jo Beth, about her courage, skiing skill, success, and her magnetic personality.

"Jo Beth was talented," I said, finishing up. "But it wasn't her talent that defined her. It was her passion. She loved fiercely and she fought fiercely too. From the first day I was conscious of anything, I was conscious that my sister loved me. It's her love and encouragement that's made me who I am today." My tears forced their way out; I was powerless to refuse, so I just let them flow. "The world will be a grey place without Jo Beth. The sun won't reflect off the snow as brightly as it used to. I know Jo Beth would have done anything for Bijou and all I can say is..." I could hear my voice splintering with sorrow, "...Jo Beth, I promise to be a great aunt to Bijou, just like you were a great sister to me."

Afterwards, Mitch approached me, holding Bijou. "That was lovely," he said.

"Do you really think so?"

His eyes gleamed but I couldn't tell if it was with tears or with happiness. "I think Jo Beth hated to be at her own funeral, until she heard your speech, and then she felt a whole lot better."

Weeks went by and Mitch and I established a routine. Soon I was off my crutches so I didn't need him to go downstairs in the middle of the night to fill a bottle with formula. We would take turns getting up with Bijou, but often we'd lose track of whose turn it was, and then both of us would get up. On those nights, we would sit while the rest of the world slept. While Bijou drank her bottle, Mitch and I drank in Bijou. I can't say that I trusted Mitch or that I no longer suspected him, but somehow I wedged those fears into a less prominent place of my psyche, like they occupied a parking spot a mile away from the main event. Meanwhile, I worked on my coursework, on my novel, and on physical therapy for my knee.

One afternoon I came home after a particularly grueling session to find Bijou napping in the nursery, but there was no sign of Mitch. I limped around, softly calling his name, until I found him on the top floor, which I had set up as an office with a desktop computer. Mitch sat at it, consumed by whatever was on the screen and oblivious to my presence.

"What are you doing?" This was more accusation than question, and my malevolence-filled voice made him start and turn around.

"Oh, hi." His Adam's apple rose and fell and he let his fingers run absently through his curls, while his other hand tapped listlessly against the desk. He was no longer looking at the computer screen but he wasn't looking at me either. I came closer and saw what had been the focus of his attention. It was my email account. He'd been reading an old correspondence between Jo Beth and me.

Hot rage occupied my limbs. "That's private! What gave you the right to read it?" I reached over and slammed my laptop shut, cursing myself for not signing out of my email account the last time I was online. How could I have been so stupid?

He wheeled his chair back. Now there was enough distance between us to look at each other. "I'm sorry. I just missed her and I felt desperate for a picture that I'd never seen, or to learn something new about her. But I should have asked you first."

"You're damn right you should have asked me first! This is a total violation!"

Mitch remained calm in the face of my storm. The way he just hung his head made my cyclone-like anger twirl, unable to touch down. "I apologize," he said. "And I wish I'd never read it. I mean, I had no idea that Jo Beth thought such things."

A beat passed, maybe two, where neither of us spoke. Then I pivoted back toward my computer. I lifted its lid and read:

Skylar,

I can't stand being cooped up in Magda's apartment one second longer. Mitch is still in love with her and she's still in love with him. Every day I grow more afraid of them and then I get these violent thoughts that are too awful to describe. Plus, I worry that I'll be a terrible mother. I think the baby will be better off if Mitch leaves me, which is probably what will happen. He and Magda will steal my baby and they'll be a family together.

I sighed. Jo Beth had sent me lots of emails over the course of her pregnancy and they all had one of three themes. One: she was happy and in love. Two: she was anxious to get out, frantic to return to her former self. Or three: like the email Mitch had just found, her ramblings were paranoid, lonely, and kind of creepy. No matter the theme, I had put all the emails into their own folder so I'd never accidentally delete them, but right now I had no desire to read any of them or remember what I'd been trying so hard to forget.

"Do you believe what she wrote in those emails?" Mitch asked. "Do you think I would hurt Jo Beth, take the baby, and leave?"

I let my eyes fixate on him, considering his question, wishing not to deflect it. After all, now was my chance. "Yes," I replied, and the pressure of my hostility suddenly popped like an angry zit.

Mitch gripped the armrests of the office chair. "Then why did you say that I should stay here?"

"So I could help take care of Bijou."

Unblinking brown eyes, inflated with reproach, sized me up. "Your mom would've done that."

"I also wanted to prove that you were guilty."

"Guilty of what?" he asked.

"Murdering my sister. Breaking her heart. Stealing her money. Sleeping with her best friend. Any or all of the above."

He stood and went to the window, casually, like he was interested in the afternoon's weather. "And once you proved this, what would happen next?"

"You'd be forced to leave and my parents and I would raise Bijou, without you. That's what Jo Beth wanted."

"You know what she wanted?" His back was to me, but I could see his arms were crossed. Did his stance indicate a guilty conscience, defiance, or just fear?

"Of course. I knew her better than anyone."

He turned toward me, his arms fell to his side and his expression turned cloudy, like a cumulus bursting with rain. "When did Jo Beth tell you that she wanted you to raise Bijou?"

"Hold on."

Sitting at my computer, I opened my dropbox, where I'd stored the very last voicemail from Jo Beth, and pressed play. "*Sky, you have to believe me because Mom doesn't...*" I watched his face as Jo Beth accused him of insanity, but he didn't flinch. He just squeezed his eyes shut and clamped his lips together, probably to ward away tears. "*Skylar, where are you? Why didn't you come?*" Now it was my turn to cry; I couldn't listen without being pelted by guilt. "*I have to get myself and my baby away from Mitch. Once she's born I'm going to leave and I'll need your help. Promise that you'll help me.*"

I pressed stop.

"I understand," Mitch said, sounding like a patient who'd just accepted his doctor's unfortunate prognosis. "Do you want me to go to jail, or do you just want to get Bijou away from me?"

I let my fingers glide over the keyboard, thinking about all the correspondences Jo Beth and I could no longer have, happy emails with good news, and sad ones wishing we were together. They were all gone and the horrible realization sunk in: not even making Mitch suffer would bring Jo Beth back. I inhaled heavily. It hurt to speak. "When my sister died, the world stopped making sense. I had to blame someone, so I blamed you instead of blaming myself. I wanted to make you miserable, because you made Jo Beth miserable. I would take Bijou away from you because you took Jo Beth from me. That would be my retribution. After that... I don't know. I guess I don't care if you go to jail or not."

"That's nice of you."

"I don't need your sarcasm."

"No really." He came over and leaned against the desk where I sat. "I deserve the worst punishment imaginable. Nobody is more irredeemable than me. I should be in hell right now. But don't worry..." He held out his hands in a limp, defeated gesture, as if the air around him was somehow made pathetic by his mere presence. "...I already am."

"I doubt that."

"Why?"

"Because as much as I blame you for Jo Beth's death, I blame myself even more. I'm the one who deserves to be in hell."

He didn't argue and at first, I thought he wouldn't answer at all. He just stared down at me, until finally in a whisper he asked, "Do you think I'm insane?"

"Why does it matter what I think?"

The eyes that examined me were passive but not still. His face held no flicker of challenge, nor a wish for a showdown. I got the feeling that if, at that moment, I whipped out a gun, he would remain rooted to his spot, but he might thrust out his chest to make it easier to shoot him in the heart.

When Jo Beth died, had a part of him died too? Did we have that in common?

"Never mind," I finally said. "Jo Beth always said that I was too romantic, that I'm just like all the heroines in all the classic novels I read, who are way too eager to forgive a guy for his 'many trespasses.'"

I'd used air quotes when I said, "many trespasses" but with an abrupt motion, my right index finger swung up and landed firmly on the keyboard's delete button, erasing Jo Beth's voicemail for good.

"Deleting it doesn't matter," Mitch said. "We'll both always remember what she said. That voicemail is like a living, self-regulating organism that will simply adapt to being erased."

"Okay...." I shook my head, unable to respond to his strange simile. "Look, I'll try to forget and I think you should too. We should start clean."

He rubbed his temples like he had a migraine. "Skylar, I wish I could explain what happened between Jo Beth and me. But I don't think I can. You're so pure, so convinced you know the difference between right and wrong, and maybe you do. Maybe you understand the things that will always confuse me. But nevertheless, I wouldn't even know where to start." He sighed and switched to massaging the back of his neck. "You loved her so much and she loved you back. No, go ahead and blame me for everything. It will make you feel better and I owe you that much."

I knew there was subtext to his little speech, but I wasn't picking up on the meaning. Slowly I rose from my chair, so we stood face to face. "What are you saying?"

His voice was soft, almost soothing. "I'm saying that I should go."

I felt like pushing him but I settled for putting my hands insolently against my hips. "You can't go! What about Bijou?"

"Obviously, she'll go too."

"You can't take her from me!" Those nights spent rocking her, the days spent encouraging her to lift her head during tummy time, or the moments of just sitting, propping her up against my knees so I could watch her face morph into a variety of expressions (which I knew were probably caused by gas and probably not smiles) all came rushing at me. I was already way more attached to her than I'd ever thought I'd be.

Mitch took in my face, my tone, my desperation. "Fine," he said, "then I'll stay with your parents. But I think some distance between you and me would be healthy."

"No!" I really needed something to push, so I chose the office chair. I sent its wheels spinning, slamming it into the desk. If my action shocked Mitch, he didn't let on and he didn't pull away when I grasped his forearm. "Look, I don't hate you. I doubt I even know you."

"But you thought you did. You thought you knew me just from Jo Beth's descriptions."

"So what?" I squeezed his wrist, liking how thick and sturdy it felt in my grasp. "I was eager to believe anything she had to say about you, especially if it was bad."

"Why?"

"Because I was jealous." My confession seemed to pull us closer together, though all at once I was aware of how tall Mitch stood over me, how his chest was almost twice the width of my torso. I released him and stepped away. "I wanted Jo Beth to myself and even though I should have been happy when she found you, I was eaten up inside."

Mitch's laugh was gloomy yet forgiving. "Wow. That's ironic, because I've always been jealous of you."

My raised eyebrows urged him to continue, which he did. "It was clear from the start that she'd never be as close to me as she was to you." His chin dropped and he was suddenly consumed with picking at what had to be a crusty spot of baby spit-up on the hem of his flannel shirt. "There were times when she scared me, when I knew I didn't understand and I didn't know how to make things better, and I thought, *if only Skylar was here*, and then I'd sort of hate you for being the one person who could help her."

"But in the end, I failed her."

"If that's true, then we both failed her."

We were silent then, and from downstairs came the sound of Bijou crying. "How long do you think she's been awake?" I asked.

"I don't know. But we should go down."

Mitch started for the stairs first and I followed. Once in her nursery we worked together: changing Bijou's diaper, giving her a bottle, and coaxing out a burp as she cried for over an hour. Then we ate dinner and watched TV, exhausted from the drama of the afternoon.

Mitch didn't mention leaving again.

Chapter 43

Gavin

"I need a job," Skylar said to Gavin.

She was watching him work, having stopped by the bakery unexpectedly just to say hello. He was so pleased at her unanticipated appearance that it took him a moment to grasp the weight of her words, that she wanted to create another needless tie to Black Diamond, one more obstacle that would prevent her from moving to Chicago with him.

"A job?" He stuttered. "But why? Why now?"

"Why not now?" she replied. "You have a job. My mom has a job. So does my dad. You're all productive citizens; you contribute something and you work for what you have. I don't do any of that. That's why I need a job."

"Oh, so you don't want to be like Mitch?" he retorted.

Skylar scrunched up her face and let her fingers glide over the handle of her teacup. "What does Mitch have to do with anything?"

"He's not productive. He doesn't contribute." Gavin tried to say this diplomatically but he knew it came out sounding petty.

"He's caring for a baby. I think that counts."

"Right." He finished straightening up the muffin display and pulled up a stool so he could sit across from Skylar. "But have you ever wondered about his sanity?"

"What are you talking about?"

"Exactly what it sounds like. I know you've had your suspicions—you've asked yourself if he had a hand in Jo Beth's death. Maybe he did. And maybe it's because..." Gavin tapped a finger three times against his head, "... something isn't quite right up there."

"Why would you say that?"

"No reason. Except..." He paused and took time for a long sigh. "The other day when I was over and you were in the other room, I heard him talking to himself."

"He was probably talking to Bijou."

"She was napping, and anyway it was like he was having a conversation with Jo Beth. Only she wasn't there. Obviously, she wasn't there."

Skylar squinted, concern overtaking skepticism. "What exactly did he say?"

"I don't know. Forget it." Gavin smiled, giving her a playful punch in the shoulder. He knew it would be impossible for her to forget, that she'd dwell on it for hours, days even. "What kind of job do you think you want to get?"

Chapter 44
Mitch

I was unprepared for Magda's call.

"I thought you were in the jungles of Brazil," I said, "and that you wouldn't have reception for several months."

"Don't sound so disappointed," she replied. "I got tired of camping and being homeless. Honestly, I got sort of homesick."

"For Santiago?"

Her laugh rang out from thousands of miles away. "No, dummy. For Florida. For my mom and dad. For you and Bijou."

I silently stumbled, my mind tripping over decent responses and settling on a completely lame one. "But Bijou and I are in Colorado."

Magda's patient tone was her own form of testiness. "I know. But plane trips between Denver and Miami are like, nothing."

It was morning and I was still in bed after a long, wakeful night with Bijou. I closed my eyes against the sun, which was peeking through the blinds insistently, promising strength as the day wore on. "Okay..."

"I'm going to see my parents first. Then maybe I'll come to Black Diamond. Or..." she paused for emphasis, "...or the two of you could come home to South Beach. I mean, you're not planning on living in Jo Beth's condo forever, are you?"

"I haven't thought that far."

She sighed. "Oh Mitch, I know you're hanging on to a lot of guilt but you have to let that go."

Her blood-red aura cloud was seeping out of the cell phone and surrounding me like a toxic gas, which, ironically, had the effect of a fairly pleasant high.

"Yeah, I know."

"We need to stick to our plan, Mitch."

"I know. I just didn't think it would be this soon. Jo Beth's family needs to be around Bijou."

"And I need to be around you." Her voice had become a soft rasp, reminding me of our most intimate moments, of other times when I had laid flat on my back in bed. Only then, she'd been close enough to touch.

"Call me when you're back in the States," I said.

"You know I will."

I pressed end on my cell phone and sat up. Blood rushed to my head, my vertigo came hurrying back, and there was Jo Beth on the edge of the bed, looking like she could slap me.

"How long have you been sitting there?" I asked.

"I heard the whole thing," she replied. "What the hell, Mitch? Why are you conspiring with the girl who wanted me dead?"

"No, look. It's not like that—"

Jo Beth floated so she was hovering right in my face. "Don't. I *know* that bitch had it out for me, and if you think she's coming anywhere near my daughter, then you're sorely mistaken."

"Mitch?" The voice behind my bedroom door belonged to Skylar. "Mitch, can I come in?"

"Sure."

Skylar entered but as soon as she saw me, quickly looked away. My dizziness vanished but I immediately became self-conscious, since I was dressed in nothing but boxer shorts. "Bijou is awake and I put her in the pack-n-play. I have to get going because I have my job interview."

"Oh yeah," I replied, taking in that she was dressed in a skirt and high heels, neither of which I'd ever seen her wear before. "You look nice. Good luck."

Skylar smoothed back her hair, which she'd put up in a bun. "I feel like a fraud, like I'm playing dress-up for career day."

I laughed. "Just try to relax. Nothing beats confidence, no matter what the situation."

Skylar bit her bottom lip and I caught that she was gazing at my bare chest for a moment too long. Her eyes darted up to meet my own, and although the room was dim, I believe I saw her blush. "Right," she murmured. "Are you getting up? Because I'm on my way out."

"I'll be right down."

Skylar nodded and then she exited my bedroom, wobbling on her high heels. Jo Beth, who was still hovering by my side, didn't have to speak. I already knew what she was thinking.

"Jo Beth," I sighed. "Don't even say it."

"If you go near her, Mitch—"

"I said don't say it!" Instantly I regretted yelling, and not just because Jo Beth had adopted that tearful, constipated expression that she sometimes got after I became mad. What if Skylar had heard me? She already doubted my sanity. "I have a new list," I whisper-shouted to Jo Beth. "It's called, *The Biggest, Most Stupid Mistakes I Could EVER Possibly Make*. Do you want to know what item number one is? It's 'sleeping with Jo Beth's sister.' Okay?"

"No! Not okay, Mitch!" She waved her phantom finger in my face. "You should have made that list a LONG time ago, and number one should have been, 'Letting Jo Beth Die!' But you blew it and now I'm forced to haunt you and make sure you don't ruin the lives of the people I love."

I inhaled slowly, hoping the intake of air would cool my boiling blood. "I wish I'd never met you," I said.

"Same here, only double. Now go downstairs and take care of our daughter."

I did as she said. After all, what choice did I have? My life had become intermittently plagued by natural, transitory actions which resulted in disasters of epic proportions. It was probably wise to follow the orders of a ghost, rather than listen to the voices inside my head.

Chapter 45
Skylar

My heels blistered and my toes were pinched. I wished desperately to be in my Sorels and jeans, but there was no turning back. I walked with painful steps into the cramped little office with one goal: establishing myself as an adult.

Everyone believed I was still a kid. I couldn't blame them, because I hadn't done anything to dissuade that notion. But when I'd said that maybe I should get a job, their dismissals irked me. "Are you sure that's what you want?" Gavin had asked, hoping that what I really wanted was to move with him to Chicago in the fall. "I don't know if office work is where your true talents lie," my mom had offered, but I kept up my nagging until she'd agree to set up an interview for me with an acquaintance of hers. Mitch didn't really respond at all when I told him about my interview, but for reasons I couldn't explain, not even to myself, I was anxious for him to see me as something more than Jo Beth's baby sister. I had to prove that I was mature enough to be trusted, resourceful enough to be respected, worthy enough to be admired.

Now Miranda Donahue sat at her desk, her slender back to me. She sipped coffee from the type of mug you'd call pottery. It looked heavy, brown, and ugly, not unlike one of the mugs my dad had passed down to me, made by an artist friend who owned a kiln. In Miranda's other hand she held a pen that she used to mark some document. She was seemingly oblivious to my presence. Even from several feet away I could see the large hearing aid nestled in her ear and I wondered if it was on.

The second hand on the industrial-size wall clock ticked endlessly away. I didn't want to insult her, but finally, I had to risk it. "Excuse me? Miranda?"

She spoke without turning to look at me. "I know you're here, Skylar. I'll be with you in a moment."

I shifted my weight, wondering how, on a scale of one to ten for awkward beginnings, I'd managed an eleven. After what felt like several minutes (but was probably just one) she put down her mug and her pen, swiveled in her chair, and faced me. I was startled by the amount of pink lipstick she wore; the cheery shade clashed with her pinched expression and severe brown bun.

"Have a seat." She didn't gesture to a particular chair, and the only ones besides hers were the boss's empty chair, which sat in its own space at a desk across the room, and one at the reception desk. What if this was a test, part of the interview itself? Maybe she was checking to see how I handled high-pressure situations, like real-life literary heroine Susanna Kayson from *Girl Interrupted*. Was she looking to see if I'd have trouble picking up on pictorial cues, almost hoping that my inability to choose a chair would help her feel stable and healthy in comparison?

Screw that. I hobbled towards the vacant, laminate-paneled reception desk, awkwardly maneuvered the chair out so it could face Miranda's desk, and sat. All the while her eagle eyes bored into me. She crossed her legs and arched an eyebrow. "Skylar, I have to admit

I'm surprised you're here. I couldn't exactly say no to your mother's request for an interview, but tell me, why do you want this job?"

Aren't you supposed to get offered a glass of water at job interviews? I had cotton mouth and it was hard to speak, so I overcompensated by speaking loudly. "Working here would be such a great opportunity! I really want to learn about the corporate world."

Miranda's smirk was more a frown than a thin-lipped smile. "You don't have to yell, Skylar. I'm not deaf."

"I didn't mean... that is, I know that you can hear me..." I lowered my voice into a murmur.

She cut me off with a loud sigh. "Why kitchen supplies? Do you have an interest in them, or do you just want this job to assert your independence?"

I suddenly saw myself as she must see me: a spoiled, entitled child who has never had to live in reality. My heart began to pound, loud enough that surely Miranda would be insulted by its volume.

"I love kitchen supplies," I answered.

"Really? Which ones in particular do you love?"

"Garlic presses? Cheese graters? Mason jars?" I thought Miranda would smile at the level of absurdity that this interview had quickly reached, but no. I took the plunge. "Look, Miranda. I'm thinking my chances at this job aren't great, so rather than making us both suffer through an awkward interview, I'll just cut to the chase. I'm a quick learner, I'm cheap, and I'm reliable. Please factor that into your decision."

I stood to go, but my bad knee lurched, my heel turned in these awful pumps, and I barreled forward. In an agonizing instant, I totally lost control of my limbs and then, to my horror, my face landed in Miranda's lap. There was a deadly moment when the world stopped and we both felt the ghastliness of my mouth being so close to her crotch. She gasped and bolted up, which made me fall back and become splayed out on the floor. Humor, however inappropriate, was my only defense. "God, Miranda. I'm sorry. I guess I should have bought you dinner first!"

My joke fell flat and she glared at me like I was a slug she wanted to stomp on. In my pencil-slim skirt and shoes that were foreign on my feet, it took me way too long to get up. Miranda offered no help.

"Sorry," I muttered, over and over. "I'm so sorry. I'll just go now."

Later I decided to make myself feel better by going cross-country skiing. It was still too soon to try downhill, but I didn't see the harm in tackling gentle slopes while getting some quality cardio exercise. I had just gathered up my skis, laced up my boots, and had gone through my front door when Gavin came strolling down my walkway. "Hey," he said. "I feel like I haven't seen you in forever."

We *had* been seeing less of each other; factoring Mitch and Bijou into the equation made it more difficult for Gavin and me to spend time together. "Yeah," I said. "Things have been sort of crazy lately."

"How did your job interview go?"

"Terrible. My face fell into her crotch."

"What?"

"I should never have worn heels."

The corners of Gavin's mouth crept up. His eyes tried not to twinkle.

"Don't look so happy," I said.

"Sorry," he said, stepping over puddles of wet snow to lean and give me a kiss. "I can't help it. And I never pretended that I wanted you to get this job."

"Whatever."

He looked me over—hat, mittens, boots, and skis. "Are you sure you're ready to ski?"

"I'll be fine."

"I could go with you. I just need to run home and get my gear."

I hesitated. The idea of quiet solitude, with pumping blood and an increased heart-rate, was what had made me want to go skiing in the first place. But I didn't want to hurt Gavin's feelings. I was trying to form a response that would let him down easy when the front door opened.

"Oh good, you haven't left yet." Mitch stepped out onto the icy front porch, with nothing but socks covering his feet. He was holding a fussy Bijou. "Have you seen her favorite pacifier? I can't find it anywhere."

"Isn't it by the bathroom sink?"

"No," Mitch said. "That's the one she doesn't like. Maybe I'll just drive to Target and get more of the type with a rounded nipple."

"And have her scream the entire time you're there?" I asked. "Do you want me to go instead?"

"What, right now?" Mitch squinted and looked at me, and then to Gavin, and then back to me. "Aren't you guys about to go out?"

"Yeah," said Gavin. "We're about to go cross-country skiing. I'm sure the nipples can wait."

Gavin didn't hide his contempt, instead he sounded like he was shooting down some outrageous demand made by Mitch, who responded by wrinkling his forehead and shifting his weight. "No, of course. You guys go. I'll figure it out."

He quickly went inside and I glared at Gavin. "That was really rude."

"What?"

"You know what." I turned towards my front door. "I have responsibilities now, Gavin. Sorry, but I need to go to Target."

Gavin didn't try to stop me like he might have done a few months ago, and I couldn't decide if I was relieved or chastised by his inaction. It didn't matter, because there were more pressing concerns to deal with.

I went inside. "Hey, Mitch," I called, as I shoved my skis into the closet and changed into normal walking shoes. "I can go to Target."

No answer. I walked upstairs and found Mitch in the nursery, pacing back and forth with Bijou in his arms. She had stopped crying and I saw her favorite pacifier in her mouth.

"Where did you find it?" I asked quietly.

"It was shoved between the mattress and the edge of her crib." He swayed back and forth and Bijou's heavy head slowly fell to rest against his shoulder. Mitch's face went all cubist on me, as he raised one bushy eyebrow and turned up only half his mouth. "Why aren't you skiing with Gavin?"

My hand floated out in a dismissive wave. "Don't worry about that. Sorry he was rude to you."

Mitch's smile turned broad, so now his eyes nearly closed and his dimples seemed a mile deep. "Poor Gavin." He softly laughed. "Why did you send him away?"

A moment ago the need for new pacifiers had seemed like a code-red emergency, but I knew if I told Mitch that, he'd only laugh at me harder. "I didn't know Gavin was stopping by," I explained. "And I sort of wanted to ski on my own. That's when I get my best ideas for writing."

"Sure." Mitch's grin relaxed into a sort of slack-jawed happiness, though I really didn't understand what he had to be so pleased about. "When are the two of you moving to Chicago?"

Why did that question make my windpipes tighten? It hurt to breathe out. "Who says I'm going?"

"Your mom."

"What? No. I never said that to her, or to anyone. I just said I'd think about it."

Mitch nodded. "Okay. I thought you'd decided, because, you know..."

"No. What?"

"Well, there are all these good schools in Chicago." The dim afternoon light turned everything beige and his dark frame became my only focal point. "You could study literature and writing like you ought to, and since you and Gavin are in love, it only makes sense."

It only makes sense? I dissected his statement, awkwardly shifting my weight, hovering in the nursery entrance, while my feet stayed exiled to the hallway. I thought about what Gavin had said, that Mitch talked to himself, that he was crazy, "I'm not in love with Gavin and I don't want to move to Chicago," As I said it, I realized for the first time it was how I felt. "I either want an East Coast school or I want to keep training for the Olympics."

"Oh." Mitch glided towards Bijou's crib, where he gently laid her down. Once she was settled he straightened himself and came towards me. I didn't move and he didn't stop until we stood face to face, close enough so I could feel his warm breath against my cheek and see the gentle rise and fall of his chest. "You should tell him," he whispered.

"I know. But I don't know how."

Mitch pressed his lips together and tilted his head to the side. His silence thickened the air and the fading afternoon light passed between us. The moment was more opulent than if we'd kissed, and it reminded me of the doomed, platonic relationship between Jake and Lady Brett in *The Sun Also Rises*. I was only thirteen when I'd read that book but now, six years later, I was finally starting to understand.

"You should tell him, Sky," Mitch finally murmured. "Don't break his heart any more than you have to."

Chapter 46
Gavin

Gavin could no longer lie to himself about the seriousness of the situation. For God's sake, his worst fears were coming true. If Skylar was willing to skip skiing to go buy pacifiers, then Mitch and Bijou were her top priority. It was so upsetting that he couldn't even savor the victory of Skylar's disastrous job interview. And besides, dropping hints and questioning Mitch's sanity wasn't keeping Sky from falling for him. Gavin needed something else, something bigger.

He needed Magda.

He waited a few days. He came over when he knew Mitch would be home too. Gavin and Skylar hung out, he made her lunch, and he even offered some bacon-cheese scones and salad to Mitch. Eventually, Mitch went upstairs to put Bijou down for her nap and Skylar went to the bathroom. Gavin grabbed his opportunity as he grabbed Mitch's phone, which had been left on the dining room table. It was so easy. There was no lock-screen code and Mitch's most recent text was from Magda. *I miss you and I'm so happy we talked the other day,* she'd written him. *Yeah, it was good hearing your voice,* he texted back. *I want to see you,* she'd replied.

He'd never answered her, so Gavin took the liberty of composing a little something.

Please come to Colorado as soon as you can. I need you. I'm waiting for you. Don't reply. Just get here ASAP.

As soon as the message was sent, Gavin deleted its history from Mitch's phone.

Chapter 47
Mitch

"I think death is merely a transition. Maybe we roam the earth as spirits, or maybe we float away to a new world, like to heaven or Atlantis. I'm unsure, but I'm not afraid to die. Death is simply a natural end that we all must come to eventually, and without it, there'd be no point to life."

"Who said there was a point to life?" Patrick stared into my soul as he loosened his ascot. "Perhaps Shakespeare got it right and we're merely players on a senseless stage."

"Then you don't believe in God? You don't subscribe to what they teach us in church?"

"I believe in you," he replied. "The rest of the world could disappear, but if you remained, there would be enough to believe in, enough purpose to fill my days." The fire crackled and wheezed, telling us it would soon go cold, but Patrick's hand against my own offered plenty of warmth. "Should you perish," he continued, "my faith would be destroyed. For how could I forgive a God that would make me love you, only to rip you from my grasp?"

I lowered the pages of Skylar's novel and put them on the coffee table. She was sitting across from me, alternating between reading some Brontë poems and typing on her laptop. The wall-mounted gas fireplace cast an orangey glow across her features, making her look at home in the warmth of the living room, while outside, night fell. Yet I could feel her eyes sporadically skipping toward me, to gauge my reaction as I read. That made it hard to concentrate.

"I like it," I said, "but I think it's best if I read the rest when we're not in the same room together."

She laughed, a nervous release that seemed to lessen the air pressure. "Am I that annoying?"

"No, not at all."

She closed her laptop and placed it on the couch cushion next to her. "I don't show my writing to many people, you know? I've had some bad experiences with people seeing my work, so I guess it's nerve-wracking."

"I understand. And I'm honored that you asked me to look at it."

The freckles on Skylar's cheeks merged together into a cluster of pink. "Oh, well, I respect your opinion."

"I don't know that I deserve your respect." I scratched my knee; the denim that covered it was growing threadbare. "I do have a question, though."

"Yeah?"

"You said that Mary is actually a serial killer, that she later kills Patrick?"

"Yes."

I glanced back at the pages. "Are you trying to explain her homicides here, with her belief that life after death is better than the life we know? Does she believe she's really just freeing her victims?"

Skylar seemed contemplative as she rubbed her nose with the back of her hand. "Partly. But she's also reacting to a patriarchal society that condemns her for pursuing a man while simultaneously persecuting her for being alone. Mary is driven to murder because her only other options are to die emotionally, or to commit suicide."

I nodded like I understood. "Interesting." I grabbed the pages and stood. "I think I'll read the rest of this in my room."

The temperature-change between the living room with its gas fireplace warmth, and the rest of the condo without it, was a shock, so when I reached my bedroom, my first instinct was to wrap myself in the fleece blanket that covered my bed. But there was Jo Beth, reclined and floating above my blanket, staring at her fingers. I was afraid to upset her; we hadn't made physical contact since she'd died and I worried that if my hand passed through her, I'd experience brain freeze a million times worse than the chill I felt now.

"Don't use Skylar's novel to justify anything, Mitch."

I shivered and hunched my shoulders, crossing my arms. How to get her to leave? "I won't. How could I?"

"You could. I bet you will. But if you know what's good for you, you won't."

Then she disappeared. She always took off right after she'd had the last word.

Later that night, my sleep was restless. I dreamt of Mary, Skylar's heroine, standing over by bed with a dagger poised, ready to stab me. When I begged for mercy, I realized it was Skylar standing there, or was it Jo Beth? Then I was unsure if I was awake or asleep, because lately Jo Beth got a kick out of interrupting my dreams. Yet when I opened my eyes, I was aware of no other presence in the room but my own. I got up, travelled the short distance to Bijou's nursery, and once I saw the steady rise and fall of her tiny little chest, I was reassured enough to try and sleep again. But my eyes refused to stay shut and my mind wouldn't stop racing. After another hour of twisting my sheets as I tossed and turned, I gave in, got up, and opened my laptop.

I checked my account balance. That was a bad idea, as it was even lower than I thought it would be. How was I going to be a responsible parent if I couldn't provide for my daughter? All I had to offer her, or to the world in general, were some bartending skills, the ability to teach skiing, and a partial degree in cognitive studies.

Bijou started crying, right on time for her 3:00 a.m. feeding. I swooped in, lifted her, and got her a bottle. As I rocked her, cradled her, and watched her suckle, a cloud of love and protectiveness settled and surrounded me in a dense fog that was impossible to see through. "I'll always put you first," I whispered, though I knew she didn't understand. Someday she would.

After I burped Bijou and put her back in the crib, I wandered down the hall to Skylar's room. I stood outside her door, hesitating, knowing I shouldn't enter. But that dream had seemed so real and she looked so like her sister, who apparently had wanted to kill me. Now I read in Skylar's novel that she also has homicidal fantasies, that she thought of murder as an 'option.'

I cracked open her door, turning the doorknob ever so slowly, praying the hinges wouldn't squeak or that Skylar wasn't having a wakeful night, like mine.

I found her asleep in the big four-poster bed that I knew used to belong to Jo Beth. For a minuscule moment, I allowed myself to imagine being nestled under those covers, holding the girl who stopped my vertigo in my arms. Then Skylar shifted in her sleep, switching from laying on her right side to her left and releasing a long, wistful sigh. Perhaps she could subliminally perceive my presence and some part of her sleeping mind knew I was standing there, watching.

"What do you want from me?" I whispered.

She didn't answer. Her brown hair was fanned out against the white pillow and her lips were slightly parted. At some point in the night she'd pushed down her covers. Her sleep jersey was loose enough to expose one shoulder. If I walked around to the other side of the bed, I'd be able to see more; her shirt hung at such an angle that I could probably get a really nice view of her body if I'd wanted to.

But what I really wanted was to see inside her mind.

Chapter 48

Skylar

"Mom, I've come to a decision."

I sat at her bakery counter and watched as she arranged a fresh batch of blondie bars onto a tray. Her eyes shot toward me but then went back to the task at hand. "Are you breaking up with Gavin?" she asked.

"What? No!" As my carefully garnered composure evaporated, I scrambled for a response. "I mean; I don't know for sure. But why would you say that?"

"Because you seem ambivalent about him."

"I do?"

Mom put the last blondie bar on a plate and set it in front of me. "If you are planning on ending things, you should do it soon. Leading Gavin on will only hurt him more."

"That's what Mitch said."

"You're talking to Mitch about your relationship with Gavin?" Mom's raised eyebrows shouted her disapproval.

"Mom! What's up? When did you become a police interrogator?" I took a huge bite of the blondie bar, which was buttery and divine, and spoke as I chewed. "Stick to baking. You're good at it and your cross-examination style scares me."

She laughed. With her hair pulled back, and her makeup-less face relaxed in a moment of happiness, she looked young again. She looked like the mother I'd known before sorrow had etched dark shadows and grief-stained crevices where her laugh lines used to be. "Fine. Sorry. So, what's your decision?"

I took a deep, steadying breath. "It actually has to do with Mitch. I've decided that Jo Beth would have wanted Bijou to have the condo, so we should sign it over to the two of them."

So much for a happier version of Mom; her face immediately turned sour. "We can't sign a condo over to an infant, Skylar."

"But we can give it to Mitch, and then he can live here and raise Bijou in Black Diamond. Isn't that what you want?"

"No." She took a step back as her body tensed. "What I want is to raise Bijou myself, so she can have a stable, normal upbringing."

"Mom—"

She held up a hand to silence me. "Mitch is a nice enough guy, but he'll get tired of single parenting soon and he'll want to move on to his next adventure. Call me ruthless, but I'd rather speed that process along so we can all settle in. Please don't give him an excuse to stick around any longer than he was already going to."

"I can't believe what you're saying, Mom. Mitch is a good father and he loved Jo Beth."

Mom picked up a towel and a spray bottle, and she started vigorously wiping down a counter that already seemed clean. "And I can't believe your abrupt change of heart! Weeks ago, you were convinced that Mitch murdered your sister and now you trust him completely!"

"Because you and Dad said I was crazy for accusing him. Now I know you were right. I see how he is with Bijou, and he and I talk about how much we miss Jo Beth. I won't have Mitch or Bijou shut out of an inheritance that rightfully belongs to them."

Mom aggressively scrubbed at what must have been a stubborn spot of gunk. "But have you thought things through? Mitch is young! Eventually he'll meet someone new and get married and have more kids with her. When that happens, do you want his new family living in Jo Beth's condo?"

Her question sank its imaginary fangs into me as sure as if it was a monster living underneath my bed. "Maybe we could make a provision that if Mitch remarries, the condo becomes mine again?"

Mom looked up from her cleaning. Her cynical laugh made her seem a stranger. "You can't. If you're going to give him everything, it has to be unconditionally."

"All or nothing, huh?"

"You wouldn't ski halfway down a mountain, would you?"

I rubbed my knee. "I would if I fell." My blondie bar was now mostly crumbs scattered across a white china plate and I picked at them.

Would Scarlet O'Hara have signed over Tara to Ashley if she thought it was rightfully his, if she believed that doing so would get him to love her? Maybe, but unlike the soft blondie bar I'd just finished, Scarlet was a tough cookie, and though her love for Ashley was strong, her survival instinct was even stronger. Yet I was no Scarlet, hopelessly in love with a man I couldn't have and unappreciative of the man I *could* be with...well, anyway, love had nothing to do with my decision. I knew there was nothing between Mitch and me, except for the shared bond of wanting to do right by Bijou.

I wiped my mouth with the back of my hand, hoping to return to the graceful, composed young woman I'd been earlier, when I'd walked in here ready to tell my mother how things were going to be. "Fine," I said. "I'll give him everything, unconditionally."

A couple of hours later I got home and once inside, the first thing I encountered was a large backpack, the type that students take when they're traveling internationally and staying in sketchy youth hostels. It was dusty and carried a strong odor, a combo of incense and exhaust. It couldn't belong to Mitch. Everything he owned was somehow pristine.

There was nobody in the living room, but I heard voices, laughter from behind a closed door. I mounted the stairs, taking two at a time, my nerves jangling though I wasn't sure why. Just as I got to Mitch's bedroom and rose my hand to knock, his door swung open and he stood in front of me, dressed in a glow I'd never seen him wear before.

"Hey, Sky! You're back! We have a guest!" Grinning, Mitch pulled me towards his bedroom: it was the first invitation I'd ever gotten into his sacred space. "She's like family to me, and since you and I are family now as well…"

"I get it." I said, knowing I sounded snappish.

"Sorry to show up unannounced," she said, rising from her stretched-out position on Mitch's bed. In a previous life that had been my bed.

In a previous life, Jo Beth would be furious to have Magda here.

Chapter 49
Mitch

Skylar's face immediately changed posture, from expectant child to sulky teen. Why did she have to be so unguarded, so vulnerable? In moments like these, I remembered the vast differences between her and Jo Beth and I became determined to elicit Skylar's smile. I just started talking quickly, hoping that if I could prevent holes in the conversation, the hole in her heart would close as well.

"I'm not surprised she was out all afternoon," I said to Magda, who'd arrived unexpectedly a couple of hours ago. "You wouldn't believe how busy Skylar is! She's always either doing her physical therapy or her class work, if she's not writing her novel or watching Bijou for me, that is. I don't think she knows the meaning of down time."

"Congratulations," Magda said to Skylar, and her ill-fitting comment made me squirm.

Skylar's voice was flint-like. "On?"

"On your niece and on your beautiful condo." Magda flashed her game-show-hostess smile. "Now I understand why Mitch is so happy living here. What better place to raise a child?" She switched her heavy-lidded gaze from Skylar to me. "You're staying here forever, aren't you?"

I wiped my sweaty palms against my blue jean-clad thighs, widening my eyes at Magda. Why would she put me on the spot like that, less than thirty seconds after Skylar had come in? "Could be," I muttered. "Hey, who's hungry? Let's get some takeout!"

"Or we could go out to eat," Magda said.

"No. Bijou is still napping and she doesn't do well in restaurants," Skylar replied.

"Plus, if we stay home, then Skylar can drink with us. I thought I'd make caipirinhas."

I'd made caipirinhas, one of Brazil's most famous types of cocktails, once before for Skylar; that was the night that she'd confessed to writing a novel. *Do you want to read it*, her liquor-loosened voice had asked in a lilting tone. I'd said of course, thinking she'd change her mind after she was sober again. But days later, she presented me with the entire manuscript and now I can't get her story out of my mind.

"Okay!" Magda practically sang as she sauntered out of my bedroom. "Let's get Thai food. I can't remember the last time I had decent Thai."

"Great. I'll go get it right now." I turned toward Sky. "Is it okay if I take your car? Bijou will probably wake soon."

Her shrug emitted a wave of negativity. "Whatever."

I pretended to take her at her word, like I didn't get that she honestly hated the situation, and when Magda declared she would stay behind to "get to know Skylar better" I crossed my fingers that they wouldn't come to blows.

I put on my jacket and shoes, grabbed the car keys, and climbed behind the steering wheel. There was Jo Beth in the passenger's seat. "Tell that bitch that she has to go," she said.

"You used to be best friends," I replied as I put the key in the ignition.

"Yeah, and then she plotted to kill me, so that BFF bond? It's over!"

I pulled out of the parking lot and switched on the heat, though I knew it would be a while before the car warmed up enough for it to work. I took a deep breath, which came out like a puff of smoke. "Are you cold?" I asked. "Do you feel things like cold anymore?"

"What do you think?" She asked.

"I really have no idea. Does your endocrine system function? If not, how does the lack of your adrenal medulla affect your sleep and your emotions?"

She shook her head. "Stop trying to sound smart, Mitch. It's too late to impress me and I'm incapable of feeling anything but fury because I'm dead before my time."

"But I want to understand you."

"Understand this," she hissed, right as I swung a left and nearly drove up onto the curb. "If you let Magda hurt Bijou or Skylar, I will hurt you. If *you* hurt Bijou or Skylar I will kill you. Capiche?"

"I'm not going to hurt either of them!"

"You say that, but Skylar is falling in love with you and you're doing nothing to stop it! And now you brought Magda here. WTF?!"

"Exactly! Having Magda here is the quickest way to curtail any of Skylar's feelings for me."

Jo Beth's spectral head fell back against the car seat and though it made no noise, I could see the cushion bend to her skull. "Why should I believe you?"

"Believe me or don't believe me. You're dead. There's not a lot you can do about it, either way."

"That's what you think," she whispered, so softly I wasn't sure that she'd spoken. When I took my eyes off the road and asked her to repeat that, all I saw was a smoke-like fog where she'd just been sitting. In the cold car air, it was like I'd made a huge exhale.

Chapter 50
Skylar

Even after two caipirinhas I was still miserable, gnawing on an egg roll while Mitch and Magda conversed in Spanish. Magda laughed uproariously at some joke that was so over my head it may as well have entered the stratosphere.

I was drowning in loneliness and my only life-preserver was to think about literature. I thought about how when Jane Austen and the Brontës wrote their novels, they had to hide their "female" concerns away, into the dark and vague nooks of their prose, because if they couldn't appeal to a general (i.e. male) audience, then how would they ever gain respect or notoriety? I sat there, positive that I also had to hide, just like Jane, Charlotte, Emily, and Anne. If I were to show my true feminine heart, surely Mitch would deem it too common, too much like juvenile chick lit compared to Magda's more mature and sophisticated literary fiction. After all, she understood the male mind and how to manipulate it.

"I'm going to bed," I announced after an hour or so. I stood from the couch, dusting fortune cookie crumbs off my sweater.

"But it's not even ten," Mitch said.

"I'm tired."

I walked away before either of them could respond. I went upstairs to my room, a sigh of relief escaping my lips as soon as I closed the door behind me. Thank God. I would stay here all night; there was no way I was getting up with Bijou for a 3:00 a.m. feeding. Let Mitch do it and we'd see how he felt after staying up late drinking with Magda.

No sooner had I changed into my nightshirt when I heard a knock. I opened the door a crack and peeked through. Mitch stood there.

"I came to say goodnight," he said.

"Not necessary." I aimed to shut the door, but his hand jolted out and aborted my mission.

"What's wrong with you?" he asked. "You barely said anything all evening."

"Because you and Magda spoke Spanish the whole time!"

He stepped towards me, opening the door, and filling up its frame. "Not the whole time. But I'm sorry. I miss speaking Spanish and Magda is my oldest friend. That's just what we do."

I jutted out my chin, meeting his eye, signaling that I didn't forgive him, "How long is she staying here?"

"That depends on you. It's your condo, after all. How does three days sound?"

My conversation with Mom this afternoon seemed years ago. It was unfathomable that Mitch knew nothing of my plans to give him everything. "I guess I can't really say no."

"Thank you, Skylar." The corners of his mouth gently pulled into a smile as his eyes turned hazy with affection. "Hey, what were you thinking about all evening as you sat there, moping on the couch?"

"I wasn't moping."

His laugh was like whiteout, erasing the smudges and misplaced words from my dark emotions and making them light, easy to understand. "Okay, whatever you say."

I glanced down at my oversized nightshirt, suddenly aware that I wore no bra underneath, and what's more, my bare legs were exposed. "I thought about literature."

His eyes crinkled as his smile relaxed. "Really?"

"Really." I hesitated momentarily, fearful to trust him after this disastrous evening, but he stood there, gazing at me, like he understood me completely, like he accepted my quirky mind and damaged soul. "Mitch, do you ever feel like you're a fictional character, like your story is still being written? Because I do. I feel that all the time, and then it's like anything is possible."

Mitch took a breath so deep that his broad shoulders sagged. I was conscious of his long-sleeved thermal shirt, of how multiple trips through the washer and dryer must have softened it, and how rewarding it would be to touch it, mostly because I'd also feel the warmth of his skin emanating from underneath.

"I guess I always feel like anything is possible. I *know* that it is."

"What do you mean?"

He rubbed his chin, thoughtful. "I experience stuff... like Jo Beth..." his voice quietly trailed off until silence relaxed over us both.

"What about Jo Beth?" I whispered.

Mitch squeezed his eyes shut and I got the sense that when he opened them, he hoped to see someone besides me standing in front of him. "Nothing," he stated. "Just me being crazy."

A panic button pushed inside me as words from Jo Beth's final voice mail came whooshing back. *Mitch is insane...I can't trust him...He CANNOT be a good father to my baby.*

I stepped back and put my hand on the door to shut it. "You should probably get back to Magda," I said. "If you need linens for the couch, they're in the hallway closet."

"Okay," he said, slightly miffed at my abrupt change. "Everything okay?"

"Yeah, fine. Good night." I started to close the door and he began to walk away, but I called after him. "Mitch!" He turned. "Don't worry about getting up with Bijou tonight. I can do it."

"What do you think?" Gavin asked me. We were at a gallery opening, looking at a sculpture of a giant hand with its thick fingers spread apart.

"I don't understand."

He flicked his bangs from his eyes. "What's to understand?"

I cocked my head, examining it. "I mean, is it waving? I don't think so, but it's not doing anything that hands normally do. It's not holding anything, or flipping us off, or pointing, or punching, or caressing, or well... anything. It's just a static hand. What's the point?"

"Maybe existing is the point."

"That isn't enough."

"Not for you, maybe." He looked self-consciously around the small space, like he was worried that the artist was there and I'd just offended him. "Are you ready to go?"

"Sure," I replied. "I'm hungry."

We left and walked down the block to a new fusion restaurant that Gavin insisted we try as part of our "date night." I let him do the ordering, and as we ate appetizers and salad everything was fine, but once the main course arrived, his mood shifted.

"How long is Magda staying?" he asked.

"Mitch said it would just be a few days." I pushed a piece of sushi into my mouth and chewed. If nothing else, that was an excuse to not talk about Magda.

"I'm surprised you're letting her stay."

Mouth still full, I shrugged.

"I know you're hiding something," he said. "You should tell me everything."

I swallowed down the last bit of raw salmon. "What do you mean, *everything*?"

"Everything!" he nearly shouted, which in the noisy restaurant, barely registered as loud. "You were so sure he was guilty. You were even more sure of Magda's guilt. How can you be so calm while sharing a roof with them both?"

Raising my water glass to my lips, I took a sip, letting the cold liquid distract me. "All I can say is Mitch is different than how I thought he'd be. You've sort of gotten to know him; I'm sure you understand."

Gavin said nothing. He did not take a bite of his quinoa tabbouleh nor did he take a drink of his artisan root beer. He just leaned forward and stared at me until I started to squirm.

"What?" I finally demanded.

"You're into him." Gavin stated this as irrefutable fact.

"No."

"You are." Finally, he moved forward and picked up his fork, but he just used it to push at his food. "I mean, he's very good looking."

"Don't be ridiculous."

"I'm not. Objectively, Mitch is a handsome guy."

"Okay." I shrugged. "Yes, he's tall, dark, and handsome, but that doesn't mean he's my type and it doesn't mean I'm attracted to him. And I'm not."

Gavin let his chin drop and now his eyes were focused on his dinner plate. He managed to gather up bits of quinoa, but his fork's journey from plate to mouth was uninspired and he chewed his food like it was rubber.

"Gavin, come on. Don't be like this."

He took a swig of root beer to wash everything down. "You're not coming to Chicago with me, are you?"

"I don't know."

"Yes, you do, Skylar. Just say it. You'd rather stay here, with Mitch."

Why did my choice have to be between two men? Per Jo Beth, men were nothing more than disruptions, sure to set my life off track. Except, she'd liked Gavin and she'd loved Mitch, so was "choosing myself" even a possible resolution to this story? Plot twists danced in my mind, and I realized that to exit this scene gracefully, I must compose a Pulitzer Prize-worthy answer. I decided to stick as close as possible to the truth—to the truth that wouldn't hurt him. "I can't hate Mitch," I said. "Jo Beth loved him and he's Bijou's father. I wasn't counting on feeling close to him, but I do, and I won't apologize for that."

Gavin's eyes grew watery and he blinked a lot, letting his focus be anything but me.

I continued. "But I don't trust him and I can't leave yet, because of Bijou. I have to stay here for her."

"Your mom could take care of Bijou."

"Jo Beth wanted me to."

His sigh was wide, in through his nostrils and out through all his pores. "You let Jo Beth decide everything for you when she was alive. Now that she's dead, why does she still call the shots?"

I lurched back as if he'd slapped me. "I should let you call the shots instead?"

Gavin twisted up his mouth and furrowed his brow. "I want the best for you, Skylar, which is more than Jo Beth could ever say. It's also more than Mitch or even your parents can say. You're my priority and I'm telling you not to trust Mitch."

"Okay, putting everything else you just said aside, I already told you that I *don't* trust Mitch."

"Right." He laughed bitterly. "Do you know that he and Magda are just after Jo Beth's money?"

My head spun at his arrogance, at his assumption that he knows more about my situation than me. "You don't know what you're talking about."

"I know that they'll do anything to get what they want—even if that means hurting you."

"Gavin, do you really think I hadn't considered those possibilities myself? I'm not as naïve as you believe. I just don't happen to agree with you."

He shook his head. "Please, Skylar. Come to Chicago with me. For your own good, you have to get away from Mitch and Magda."

I should grab this opportunity, this opening for the truth. Both my mom and Mitch were right; the sooner I broke things off the better, and the less Gavin would ultimately be hurt. "Look," I said, my voice heavy with regret, "Gavin..."

"Wait!" He dropped his fork, reached for my hands across the table, and squeezed my fingers with a startling intensity. "Don't. Don't tell me no, not yet. I understand that you're probably not coming to Chicago, but you don't need to tell me tonight. Let me believe you're still considering it, that you're still giving us a chance. And if not, at the very least, promise you'll take what I said about Mitch seriously. Promise not to trust him." His eyes bore into mine. "You owe me that much, Skylar."

I closed my eyes for a moment, remembering all the times Gavin had been there for me. How had I repaid him? With betrayal and with lies. He was right; I owed him that much and way, way more. I opened my eyes and nodded simply, easing my hands from his grip. "Okay. I promise."

Chapter 51

Gavin

Gavin turned his key in the ignition and sat back, thinking he'd let the engine warm up for a moment before he began driving. "Am I taking you home?" he asked Skylar.

"I suppose," Skylar answered. "Where else would you take me?"

Hope rose in his stomach, or maybe that was just gas bubbles from the artisan root beer he'd drunk. "We could go to my grandpa's cabin. I'll build a fire, and we could, you know... hang out."

Shyness muzzled him and kept him from saying what he really thought they could do together, alone in a cabin with nothing but firelight and their body heat to keep them warm. But apparently Skylar didn't need him to spell things out; she seemed fine, rejecting him in the abstract. "I don't think so, Gavin," she said. "We'd have to park so far away, and then hike, and by the time we got to the cabin it would be time to turn around."

"Or..." He let his hand graze her thigh. "...we could spend the night there."

She shook her head. "I have a Brontë test coming up. It's important and I need to study."

"You have a test for your online course?"

"Yeah, I had to schedule it, and they monitor when I begin and when I end, and it's like, a third of my grade. If I reschedule, I'll automatically go down a grade."

"And you scheduled it for tomorrow?"

Skylar kept her gaze straight ahead, watching the frost on the window recede as hot air blasted from the car's vents. She blew a strand of hair off her cheek. "The test is on Friday, actually, but I need to get a good night's sleep so I can spend all day tomorrow studying." She wrapped her arms over her chest and rubbed the sleeves of her parka, a gesture to keep warm. "It's cold sitting here. Can we get going?"

Wordlessly, Gavin put the car in reverse and pulled out of his parking spot. They spoke very little on the ride home; in fact, neither of them said a word. But when he pulled up to her curb, Skylar turned to him and Gavin saw that look in her eyes, the one she often had when they first started dating, the one that said he was important to her.

"Are you mad at me?"

"Of course not," he told her. "I understand that you have to study. Your class is important. And if you get a good grade maybe that will mean getting into Northwestern or The University of Chicago."

"Yeah, who knows?" She leaned in and gave him a lingering kiss on the lips. "Look, I'd invite you in, but with Mitch and Magda around, it would just be awkward. But I promise we'll spend more time together soon, okay?"

Gavin agreed and smiled to reassure her that everything between them was good. Then he watched as she climbed out of the car and walked toward her front door. Through the window, he spotted Mitch passing by, peeking out to see that Skylar had returned home. Magda stood behind him. Gavin's reaction was visceral, like he'd just watched a parent slap his child or had seen a sack of puppies dropped into a lake to be drowned. He couldn't help it; his every instinct told him one thing: Mitch was evil. But what was there to do about it? What should he do right now, tonight?

He wasn't going to go to his grandfather's cabin alone, and he really couldn't stomach going to parents' house again, so Gavin drove to the bakery. Even though he wasn't scheduled to work, he figured he may as well have some alone time to experiment with new recipes. That was when he came up with his best ideas. It could be sort of meditative, baking in the middle of the night, just him and his recipe notebook. He used his key to let himself into the bakery's back door, turned on some music, and measured out the ingredients for blackberry cheese-cake muffins. The first batch was too moist and fell apart easily but he got the right balance on the second batch, and Gavin was just cleaning up when Elizabeth arrived.

She took off her coat, placed it on the rack, and grinned when she saw him. "What smells so good?"

"Blackberry cheesecake muffins." He gestured to the platter where they were cooling. "Have one."

Elizabeth picked one up and bit into it, her eyes widening in delight as she chewed. "Delicious!" she exclaimed after swallowing it down. "I hope you remember the recipe, because once people try these, they're going to demand more."

Gavin stood at the sink, rinsing out the bowl where the muffin batter had been, watching as white liquid clumps disappeared down the drain. "How are you, Elizabeth?"

Her head snapped toward him, as if surprised by his question. "Okay, I guess. Why do you ask?"

"Don't take this the wrong way, but you look tired."

She ran a hand through her hair and leaned against the table where they knead dough. "I am. Grief makes you tired, you know? I don't think the pain of losing my Jo Beth will ever go away."

Gavin remembered back to not so long ago, when she'd been so worried about Jo Beth, calling her throughout the day, trying to decide if she should go to Brazil or not. Once Elizabeth had made the decision to buy her ticket for the next day, her mood had lightened and she'd seemed optimistic at the idea that she could do something concrete to help her daughter. He'd promised to look after the bakery and had even put together a care package of treats for her to take to Jo Beth. Fast forward to now, the present moment, and it was clear that Elizabeth's life had gone off the rails. Gavin knew there was nothing he could do to help; fact was, his previous efforts had gone astray and in the end, he'd been sort of destructive.

"I'm sorry," he told her. "I wish I could make things better for you."

She came over and hugged him. The hug was like fresh baked bread: comforting and hopeful at the same time. "You already make things better for me," she said. "I don't know what I'll do once you leave for Chicago."

Their hug fell away and then the moment of affection was replaced by a subtle, pressing guilt.

Chapter 52
Mitch

On my best days, I consider myself a man of science, and through my own, personal research, I've concluded that evil is not a condition or a disease; it's nothing you can diagnose and it's not tangible. You can't see or touch evil, you can only sense it, and everyone knows that senses are subjective and easily fooled.

That said, while Magda was not pure evil, there was something off about her. I was trying to determine what, exactly, it was.

"When are you coming back to Florida with me?" she asked.

We were on a walk, wearing snow boots and stomping through forested land that was part of the city's park service. I had Bijou in the snugly, bundled up close to my chest. My baby was wide awake due to the crisp mountain air.

"I don't know," I replied. "I like it here. I'm thinking I can teach ski school and maybe Skylar's dad can get me a job at the preschool during the off-season."

"But you'll make peanuts!" Magda passed under a low-hanging branch. A clump of snow fell and landed in her dark hair. She shook it out. "Don't you want to finish your degree? You're too smart to work daycare."

"I like watching the little kids learn. Their choices and reactions as they process sensory input are fascinating."

"Oh Mitch, you're so sweet." She'd been walking ahead of me, but she stepped back, and though the path was a little too narrow for us to walk side by side, she took my hand and we continued down the trail together.

"You know I'm not that sweet," I told her. "You understand me better than anyone, actually."

"Of course I do. I know all your secrets, Mitch."

For better or for worse, that was true.

Years ago, after the whole Amanda Butler debacle, I'd kept to myself, scared that if I became involved with another girl it would end in a natural disaster. The police never even questioned me about Amanda; hours after she'd been declared missing, her body washed up onto shore and the autopsy found she'd drowned at approximately 10:00 p.m. the previous night. Nobody had known I was meeting her, and even I wasn't sure what had happened. The police believed me when I'd told them I knew nothing and they let me go. After that I stayed quiet, studied hard, and after school I would skateboard up and down the streets of my neighborhood.

There was a skate park about half a mile from the apartment complex where my dad and I lived. One morning I was practicing my ollies and backslides, feeling at peace as the sunrise turned everything pink. Then a dark-haired girl in a bright red t-shirt showed up. It seemed as if her board was just a natural extension of her feet, the way she glided over pavement, up and down the concrete slopes and inclines. After a while I forgot about my own skating and I just stood watching her. She went down the largest ramp fast as a lightning bolt and then skidded to a halt right in front of me.

"Hi, Mitch," she said.

My jaw dropped. "You know me?"

Her laugh was like jingle bells. "Duh. We sit next to each other in math." She started to skate away, but glancing back she said, "Shame about what happened to Amanda Butler."

"Um, yeah."

Sweat formed at the back of my neck and under my arms. My heart began to pound. Did she know? Did this girl somehow understand my culpability? I skated towards her, but she was so fast that she just became a bright red blur. But the bright red wasn't simply from the fabric that covered her; she had this dusty aura, a crimson cloud that followed her everywhere, settling over her head and behind her back like lethal butterfly wings.

We skated for a while and then went our separate ways, but I thought about her all weekend. On Monday morning in math class I sat down next to her, marveling at how I'd never noticed her before.

"Hi," I said, squinting to see her face, which was blurred by scarlet. I guessed the aura was a permanent thing for her. "I don't remember your name."

"It's Magda," she replied.

"I'm Mitch."

There was her jingle bell laugh again. "I know."

Looking into her eyes, I sensed that she knew a lot, but if any information was new, she'd probably still understand. "Did you know that your aura is like, bright red?"

Magda raised her eyebrows. "Tell me more."

Then Mrs. Palmer came in and class started, so my explanation of the impossible would have to wait. Yet over time, through school lunches where we sat at the last table by the cafeteria's exit, on lazy walks home, or on breaks at the skate park, I told Magda what I saw and how I'd come to believe that sensory perception was as subjective as people's' taste in music or food.

"Just because you experience the world one way and I experience it another, that doesn't make either of us right or wrong, or sane or crazy," I explained.

She always acted like she agreed, so I confessed, told her about Amanda Butler, and as the years passed, I also told her about other disturbing incidents that I couldn't rationalize to anyone else but Magda.

Now here we were, again at an impasse as we walked through the snowy forest.

She squeezed my hand. "Mitch, whatever reservations you have, whatever potential guilt you might be feeling—it will all go away soon enough."

But if something like guilt existed, how could it just magically go away?

"Magda," I said, "Do you remember how, back in Middle School science class, we learned that everything in life is formed by atoms, and that matter is just atoms hugging each other because their electrons compel them to?"

"I guess."

"But I never agreed with that theory, because what about the stuff in life that isn't formed by matter? What about your red cloud, or Amanda's tidal wave, or Jo Beth's ghost?"

Magda stopped walking and released my hand. "You've seen Jo Beth's ghost?"

I hesitated telling her only for a moment. "I see Jo Beth all the time and I don't think she's going away. It's like her atoms are hugging my atoms, because our electrons won't accept that death kills, or that guilt can be dissolved."

Magda raised up on her toes, ballerina-like, so close that her red aura surrounded the three of us. She leaned in, smooshed Bijou against my chest, and kissed me on the mouth. I swooned, not with desire like a heroine from one of Skylar's favorite novels, but because my head felt so light I thought it might float away. My dizziness was back in full force and I had to grab Magda's shoulder to steady myself.

"What was the kiss for?" I asked.

"For being honest."

"If I can't be honest with you, I can't be honest with anyone."

"Exactly."

Chapter 53
Skylar

What was I afraid I'd find? Release papers from a mental institution? A journal full of paranoid ramblings? I knew I'd come across neither as I snooped through Mitch's room, yet I snooped anyway, hoping I'd uncover evidence of his good will and sanity. He didn't own much. Maybe he'd left most of his possessions behind in Santiago. There were three books on his shelf: *The Time Machine* by H.G. Wells, *The Universe in a Single Atom* by Dalai Lama XIV, and *Religion and Science* by Bertrand Russell and Michael Ruse. I was ashamed that I'd read none of them.

His closet held a few flannel shirts on hangers, jeans and sweaters that lay folded along the top shelf, and on the floor was a pair of sneakers, a pair of dress shoes, and some Tevas. His snow boots were missing; he must have been wearing them. I sighed, closed the closet door, and leaned against the wall, scanning this room that used to be mine. A lot of my stuff was still in here, like my high school ski trophies that sat on a high shelf above my old bed, and a bulletin board stuck with note cards on which I'd copied down lines from my favorite novels. One from *Jane Eyre* caught my eye:

"I can live alone, if self-respect, and circumstances require me so to do. I need not sell my soul to buy bliss."

I remembered when I copied that one down; it was shortly after Jo Beth had shown me the *People* magazine with the guy who'd murdered his wife and unborn child. *Promise that you won't fall for the charming, handsome guy,* she'd said and I'd made her that promise repeatedly. So, when I saw this declaration of independence in *Jane Eyre*, I'd believed them to be words I would live by.

Yet Jo Beth had broken her own promise. Now I was finding it more and more difficult to stay true.

My eyes focused on the night stand, which was actually a tiny little dresser with drawers large enough to hold a few sundry items. I went over and pulled open the top one. Inside I found some Carmex, a couple of "Double A" batteries, and a notebook and pen. I leafed through the notebook. It was full of lists.

Places to visit*:*

Bermuda Triangle

Moscow

The Galapagos

Page after page was like this, each with its own heading, like *Things I'm Scared to Try*, or *Celebrities I Want to Meet*. For each heading, there was a list of items, and often there were checks beside them. For example, under *Games to Learn to Play*, both "chess" and "backgammon" had been checked off. Had learning those two been accomplished? I sat on the edge of the bed and paged through the whole notebook. It must have been very old, because the beginning entries were written in faded ink and in handwriting that looked less mature, more like chicken scratch. The further back I got in the notebook, the more evolved the lists became.

Philosophies to Incorporate into My Daily Life*:*

Cognitivism

Existentialism

Moral Skepticism

I didn't know anything about moral skepticism, but if it was what it sounded like, Mitch believed right and wrong were relative. I'd have to look it up later.

One list particularly caught my eye. It was labeled ***The Biggest, Most Stupid Mistakes I Could Ever Make***. There were several reasonable items, like number three: *Digging Where There's Power Lines* and number two: *Letting Harm Come to Bijou*. But when I read number one, *Having Sex With Skylar*, I felt the wind knocked out of me. Okay, sure, I could see how it would be a bad idea for Mitch and me to hook up. But it would be a worse mistake than hitting a power line or than letting someone hurt his baby daughter? I was offended, but underneath the offense lay the revelation that he thinks about me, that he's attracted to me.

At the end of the book was a list that began on the last page and worked its way backwards. It was the longest list by far, and unlike the others, it wasn't labeled. The first item was, "tidal wave in Florida", and number two was, "red cloud." Then it went on for a couple of pages, with things like "phantom limb?", "power outage every time we speak," and "talking cat."

Toward the end came Jo Beth's name. Then it was repeated in item after item:

Jo Beth shows me how to make formula

Jo Beth rides shotgun

Jo Beth threatens me about Skylar

A lava rock formed in my stomach and burned all the way up to my heart. What the hell did any of this mean?

"What are you doing in here, Skylar?"

I dropped the notebook and jolted up, breathless with guilt. "Mitch!" I paused to hyperventilate and he just stared at me. Was that malevolence in his eyes, or betrayal? "I..." I stammered. "Where are Magda and Bijou?"

He leaned against the door frame casually, like he was waiting in line for something. "I dropped Bijou off at your Mom's. Magda went back."

"Went back where?"

"To Florida."

His face was impassive, occupied by two huge brown eyes that refused to blink. I couldn't read his emotions, so I had no idea how to proceed. Before I figured it out, he came towards me, picked up the notebook, and looked at the last page I'd been reading. I stood there feeling the weight of his written words, wondering if maybe I wasn't so culpable for having read them. Perhaps it was something I ought to have done a while ago.

"What's that about?" I asked.

He tossed the notebook onto his bed and stood so close to me that it became hard for us not to breathe in the same rhythm. "I like to make lists," he whispered.

"Yeah, I get that. But I don't understand the ones about Jo Beth. And why would she threaten you about me?"

He squeezed his eyes shut. "The last list in the book is about dreams I've had." Speaking seemed to cause him physical pain. "I dream about Jo Beth a lot, and in one dream, she told me to stay away from you."

His eyes were still closed and he looked so innocent that I just couldn't be scared. Instead, all I wanted was to ease his pain. I cupped his cheek with my hand and his eyes shot open. The air between us was warm and cold at once, like the tugging that could produce a tornado. "Why?"

"Why, what?" he asked.

"Why did Jo Beth tell you to stay away from me?"

He tilted his head down and pressed his forehead to mine. "It was just a dream, Skylar."

Our lips weren't touching, but God, did they want to be. I put my arms around his shoulders. He put his arms around my waist, circling me and holding me close. "Have you had any other dreams about me, Mitch?"

"All the time."

"Me too."

Then, finally, he kissed me with such concentration that my entire body heated with desire. His chest crushed against mine and it was entirely different than what I'd felt with Gavin or even with Frank. This was a hunger that could never be satiated, yet his kiss fulfilled me all the same.

But as quickly as it began, it ended when he abruptly dropped his arms to his sides and stepped back. That made me feel like I'd been plucked from my warm bed and thrown outside into a cold, cold night.

"No," he struggled to say. "This can't happen." He ran his hand through his hair, obviously trying to slow his breathing. One glance down at his crotch and I knew he was as aroused as I was, maybe even more.

"I understand," I said. I started to back out of the room.

"Sky?"

Mitch was sitting on the edge of the bed, right where I had sat only moments ago, when I'd invaded his privacy.

"Yeah?"

He took a sharp inhale. "I'm sorry."

Chapter 54

Mitch

I wasn't planning on kissing Skylar. Talk about lack of self-control.

"What were you thinking?!" Jo Beth demanded. She appeared almost as soon as Skylar had retreated to her room.

"I don't know. At first I think I was just trying to distract her from my list journal…"

"You and that stupid list journal!" Jo Beth's face was bright red, which surprised me, because up until now death had made her sort of pasty. "That's no excuse."

"I know!" I hung my head in misery. "But the closer I get to her, the more normal I feel and it's not just that. When I'm with Skylar, the world makes sense." Jo Beth gave me a skeptical, raised-eyebrow look and I knew she didn't understand. "I guess we've gotten too close, living here and taking care of Bijou together. She's so much like you, sometimes I forget that she *isn't* you."

"That's bullshit, Mitch. Don't give me that line, *oh, she reminded me of you*! Please!"

"What do you want from me?"

Jo Beth sat at the window sill and the light from outside blended into her, making it hard to distinguish her form. "You have to go. You can't stay here."

"You're right. I'll leave with Bijou in the morning."

"Where will you go?"

"To Florida."

"To be with Magda?" Jo Beth laughed ghoulishly. "Hell, no."

"Don't I get any say at all?" I was aware of how whiny I sounded, but I couldn't help it. My life had spun out of control.

"Why should you get a say? I didn't get any say about being poisoned, now did I?"

There was a plunging sensation in the back of my head. Black dots floated in front of my eyes and behind them were sparks like fireflies. I reached for something, anything, to ground me so I wouldn't pass out. "You weren't poisoned, Jo Beth. You died from an embolism caused by amniotic fluid."

"Sure, Mitch. Keep telling yourself that." She floated in front of me and I blinked several times, trying to focus on her eyes as she gazed deeply into mine. "You remember what happened, right?"

I rubbed my face, desperately grasping for reality. "I didn't kill you," I muttered, urgently wishing it was true.

Chapter 55

Skylar

I ran from my old room to my new one. I was headed toward my closet of ski gear, because I needed to be outside, carving tracks down the white crest of a mountain. What good were desire and angst if I couldn't pound them out by slapping my skis against the snow? I mean, screw it. My knee was almost healed. I'd go skiing against my physical therapist's advice and suffer the consequences. But as I went to my closet to change into snow pants, my gaze snagged on my laptop, which sat innocently atop my dresser. Before I even reached for the snow pants I made a detour, grabbed my computer, and plopped down on my bed. Maybe I'd just found a more productive outlet for my torment. The raw emotion spinning through me could be fuel for my novel.

I opened the file and scrolled down to where I'd left off: the pivotal love scene between Mary and Edmund.

Mary wrestled with her self-control. She pushed him away but he wouldn't have it. As his kisses travelled down her neck and burned her skin, a chilling recognition eroded her consciousness. She belonged to him and even murder couldn't change that.

"Leave me now," Mary insisted. She pressed her hands against his chest, creating room enough to speak. "You don't understand what I am."

"I understand enough," he answered.

"No, if you did, you would realize that we can't be together." She struggled from his grasp, stood, and tucked her tangled auburn locks behind her ears. Cheeks flushed with desire, eyes watering from anguish, she faced him. "You stay. I will leave and never come back."

"No." He stood and peered into her eyes. "You must not deceive yourself, Mary. You must not deceive me. If you do, you have killed us both."

She could tell him how close he was to the truth, how he teetered on the edges of her dark reality, but to do so would be to sacrifice his love, and with no possible recourse.

"The privilege of leaving me doesn't belong to you," Edmond continued. "There is no force of God or power on earth that can truly separate us. If you attempt to leave me, you will break my heart and I will wish to die from the pain of unrequited love. Without your kisses, without your breath against my cheek, I will drown in a dark, unforgiving sea and I will long for you, my life raft, with each broken breath that pulls me u nder."

My fingers hovered over the computer keys. Christ, I'd made Edmund practically beg Mary to kill him. But I couldn't let her do it. She had shed the blood of several other suitors but now I realized that ultimately, she couldn't wield that knife again. Because every time I pictured Edmund's throat being slit, it was Mitch's eyes I saw widening in betrayal and disbelief as the knife entered his flesh. Phantom sobs began at the back of my throat, a mixture of bile and tears, and I understood that love and hate are not opposites, that instead they sit next to each other on a circular spectrum with no real beginning and no real end.

I sprang from my bed, went to my closet, and grabbed those snow pants after all. I quickly changed clothes, gathered up all my ski gear, and left the house making as little sound as possible.

Soon I was travelling up the ski lift toward my favorite run, *Holy Moguls*, which Jo Beth and I had raced down together countless times. A wave of misery cleaned me out from the inside, washing away any unseemly dust mites of lust or longing. What would my sister say to me now? I squeezed my eyes shut. Jo Beth was dead; she would never say anything to me again, and here I was, falling for a man who possibly had a hand in her death. It was like *East of Eden*, and I was half horrified, half proud, to realize I resembled Charles, the younger, stronger sibling, and Jo Beth was Adam, who was taken in by the charms of a soulless beauty. Yet in the end, it was Charles who left her money; it was he who could never distinguish the line between hate and love.

I heard the familiar groan of my chair reaching the end of the lift. I opened my eyes to the exquisiteness of the mountain and made myself focus. I shouldn't let my mind take such random leaps; Jo Beth never even read Steinbeck. Once I began skiing, I could clear my head, knocking each terrifying thought from my brain with each mogul I bumped over. I didn't fall, nor did I twist my knee in any unnatural sort of way; still, I could feel the strain I'd unnecessarily put on myself. Hours later I limped home, and with every step, my knee whined and protested. But worse was that the closer I got to home, the more tangible Jo Beth's presence (and the sting of her disapproval) became.

When I entered, I expected the condo to be dark, for Mitch to be safely tucked away in his room, or perhaps in the nursery with Bijou. But the living room lights were turned all the way up and Mitch sat on the couch, waiting for me.

"Where'd you go?"

"Skiing," I answered.

He stood and came toward me. "So soon? I thought you had a couple of weeks before the doctor cleared you."

I shrugged. "I was fine." But I knew I would pay for my little adventure tomorrow. I tried to move past him, but he blocked my path.

"Sky, you're limping."

"I'll go elevate my knee and rest."

Mitch put his hand against my shoulder and I tried to resist his touch. "Bijou is still at your mom's. I'm leaving town tomorrow and she wanted as much time as possible with her granddaughter."

I stumbled back. "Where will you go?"

"To Florida. My dad is there... and Magda." He saw me wince. "She's not that bad, Sky."

"You can't let her near Bijou! Jo Beth would hate that more than anything!" I moved toward him like a beggar. "Please. I'll give you everything, this condo, all the money that Jo Beth left me—everything will be signed over into Bijou's name and you'll have discretion over it all until she's grown. But keep Bijou away from Magda."

Mitch's voice was nearly as pained as his face. "I can't do that."

Anger flamed inside me so bright that I saw red. "Yes, you can!" I yelled. "Let my mom raise Bijou; she wants to! You can go be with Magda and I'll *still* hand over all that I have!" Something compelled me to hobble over to the little showcase at the other end of the room. It had been built to display Jo Beth's Olympic medal. The medal sat behind glass, always shiny, always lit from above, yet when Jo Beth was here she'd never even look at it. I'd asked her about that once, and she'd said, "It reminds me that I lost."

I removed the medal from its display and thrust it toward Mitch. "Here. Take this too. It's yours." In a moment of insanity, I pressed the medal against his chest and his hand flew up to grasp mine.

"Have you lost your mind?" he asked.

I pulled away from his touch, took the medal's ribbon, and put it around his neck. "Probably," I responded. "I've lost everything but it doesn't matter. Everything I have already belongs to you."

His puzzled eyes blinked several times in astonishment. He looked down at the medal that sat against his chest and then he looked at me so deeply, so intently, I was sure this was the first time in my entire life I'd ever been seen at all. In a flash, his arms were around me and we held each other, my craziness a virus that I'd just infected him with. We were both close to tears but frantic laughter came out instead, bubbling between us in inappropriate bursts.

"I don't want anything from you," he said. "I've asked for nothing."

"Well, I can't say the same."

He turned quiet, the laughter dying on his lips. "What? What can I give you?"

There we stood, our arms around each other, and I longed to lean against him, to let him carry my weight so that my knee wouldn't hurt so damn much. But I couldn't show weakness, not now.

Not ever.

I sighed. "Jo Beth made me promise her, to never fall for the charming, beautiful guy. She said that guys like you are trouble, so I swore I would never, ever, give my love away. Now I see that I was wrong to make such a promise. At the time, I assumed that I understood love, but I knew nothing."

His fingers grazed my hairline, my earlobe, my bottom lip. "And now?" he asked gently.

"Now?" My laugh was soft, meant to caress. "Now I understand even less."

My fingers reached back to massage the tendons in the back of his neck. They were tight like thick, coiled wires, which was why, when he started to unzip my fleece with a quivering, uncertain hand, I was shocked at the contrast between hard and soft. After he removed my fleece and my silk thermal shirt and then my bra, I stood naked from the waist up in front of him. I tugged on his sweater and he complied by lifting his arms and letting me pull it up and off over his head. I'd seen his tattoo before, when his shirtsleeves had been pushed up, but now I let my fingers brush over the tiny pi symbol on his bicep, and then I let my fingers brush over his shoulders and chest too.

He sighed, like my touch made him quiver. "You're the beautiful one," he said.

Intuitively, my body curved toward his and he let his hands explore the lines of my back and hips, up and down the contours of my stomach and chest, and then I was gathered into his arms. Our warm, pulsating bodies pressed into each other. Our mouths met in a series of slow, profound kisses that left me feeling weak yet strong.

After several moments, I had to pull away and look him in the eye. "Are you sure this is what you want?" I asked.

"Oh, Skylar..." his voice was desperate. "It's not about what I want, it's what I need and I need you. I need you to make the craziness stop."

Under the glaring living room lights, Mitch's eyes were as dark as the cold night that had descended outside. But inside we were warm, and that enduring heat—born of our kisses and thriving as our bodies merged together—that is what will stay with me whenever I think of our night together.

It's what I'll remember whenever I think of Mitch.

Chapter 56

Mitch

I didn't sleep that night. I lay in bed, naked next to Skylar, her body pressed to mine and her head against my shoulder. I was scared to close my eyes, sure that the moment I let my guard down Jo Beth would start shaking the walls and rattling the windows, throwing objects, and turning from semi-benevolent spirit to full-on poltergeist.

And I wouldn't be able to defend my actions, except that the only time I felt peace was when I held Skylar in my arms.

Maybe Jo Beth understood, maybe she forgave, for she didn't haunt us that night. The next morning, however, brought its own brand of trouble. I heard the door open at around 5:30 a.m., and thinking I knew who it was, I threw on sweatpants and went downstairs. I was surprised to find Gavin in the kitchen. He was preheating the oven. A pan of what looked like cinnamon rolls sat on the kitchen counter. "Isn't it kind of early to be dropping by unannounced?" I asked.

Gavin pivoted toward me. If he was startled, he didn't show it; he just flicked his bangs from his eyes. "Skylar knew I was coming. Her online Brontë exam is scheduled for this morning and I'm bringing her breakfast. She likes waking up to the smell of baking cinnamon."

I laughed before I could stop myself.

"What?" he demanded.

I shook my head. "Nothing." I went toward the refrigerator, feeling Gavin's suspicious eyes on me. They pressed into my bare back as I drank directly from the orange juice carton.

"I'll just go say good morning to Skylar," Gavin murmured and I gagged slightly on the last gulp of OJ.

Skylar was most likely still asleep in my bed.

"I'll get her," I said, shoving the carton of juice back into the refrigerator and swinging the door shut. I bolted out of the kitchen and sort of jumped in front of Gavin, blocking his path upstairs. "I was about to take a shower, anyway. I'll just knock on her door and tell her to come down."

Gavin narrowed his eyes and he sniffed, like an animal trying to determine a scent. "Skylar's *my* girlfriend," he said. "She's coming with me to Chicago and we're in love."

"Okay."

He looked me up and down. "Okay. I don't need you acting like you own her."

Did he know? Could Gavin see into the past so that now, the heat of his hatred was rising like the temperature of the oven he'd just turned on? "Sure," I said. "I just thought I'd knock on her bedroom door, that's all. So..." I looked at the space between Gavin and me, thinking if I could just walk away from him, that this awful, awkward moment would be erased. I coughed away the orange juice acid that still lingered on my tongue. "I think I'll go do that."

I began to back away but I hadn't had time to turn around when Gavin lunged toward me, his fingers landing firmly around my neck. His thumbs burrowed into my throat, cutting off my air supply. I flailed my arms out and jerked my body back and forth, trying to punch him or at least escape his grasp, but I'd been taken by surprise and that weakened me. I felt as if my eyes would pop out of my head when he squeezed, harder and harder as he strangled my life away.

Then, mercifully, he released my throat. It was a mere second of freedom. As I rasped to regain my breath, Gavin stepped into the kitchen but instantly he was back, holding Skylar's heaviest, thickest pottery mug. He used the thing like a set of brass knuckles, swinging and clobbering me in the temple.

After that, everything went black.

Chapter 57
Gavin

Gavin didn't believe in redemption nor did he believe in God. To him it was obvious: we're here for a very short time and when we die, that's it. The candle flickers out, we've made our exit, and it would all be so tragic—except we're dead, so we don't know the difference.

After all, there are certain universal truths when it comes to the human condition. We all occasionally catch colds, get hangnails, feel constipated, and realize how powerless we are against bureaucracy. On the same note, everyone dies. There's nothing spectacular about death; it's just a matter of course and not a big deal. Sure, loss sucks, but that's more about the people who are left behind than about the person who kicked it. And what if somebody's death was a positive thing, like a shot to vaccinate you against some terrible disease?

Honestly, his intentions really were good. Well, at least they hadn't been bad. Not exactly bad, anyway.

Months ago, Skylar had been about to leave for her Olympic training camp and Gavin could feel her pulling away. He'd blamed Jo Beth. If it hadn't been for Jo Beth, Skylar wouldn't have had Olympic aspirations and she wouldn't always have been on the brink of abandoning him. One night when he was particularly upset about it all, Gavin released some steam by going to the bakery and whipping up a batch of lemon bars, which he'd packed full of ground pistachios and coconut milk.

He never thought Jo Beth would actually eat one of them, but he'd had fun imagining it; how she'd get sick and gag, break out in hives, stop breathing, maybe even die.

Then Elizabeth stopped by the bakery and gave him instructions for how to 'handle things' while she was in Brazil. He'd put the lemon bars into a box and handed it to her. "Here," he'd said, "don't go empty handed. They're lemon bars, and you can tell Jo Beth that you made them yourself."

Elizabeth, flushed with happy anticipation at the idea of seeing her daughter, had taken the box from him. "Oh Gavin," she'd said. "You're so sweet."

When Gavin heard that Jo Beth had died he was surprised, but he wasn't sorry. For all he knew, it really was an amniotic fluid embolism, which (he'd read online) can cause a fatal allergic reaction. *Or* maybe it was the lemon bars. He'd never know, and really, did it even matter? Jo Beth had been dragging Skylar down. Skylar had needed to be set free from the constant fear that she wasn't meeting her sister's standards.

"When did you get here?" Speaking of Gavin's dream girl, there she stood, wearing her robe, and rubbing her eyes. She sniffed. "Are you baking cinnamon rolls?"

"And I made coffee!"

He filled a mug with French roast. She barely smiled when he handed it to her, as if she knew he'd just used that very same mug to pummel Mitch. But that was impossible. "Was Mitch up when you got here?" she asked.

Gavin paused like he was thinking. "Not that I know of, unless he left without saying hello."

Skylar sipped her coffee and leaned against the counter. "Maybe he went to get Bijou," she said, sort of to herself.

"Where's Bijou?"

Skylar looked up like she was surprised to find him still in her kitchen. "She's at my mom's." She took another sip of coffee, looking off into the distance, obviously thinking about anything but Gavin.

He moved towards her, took her coffee mug, and set in on the counter. "We have a few minutes before the cinnamon rolls come out of the oven," he said, reaching into her robe, cupping her breast, and kissing her neck. "Let's go upstairs."

She pushed his hand away and stepped back, closing her robe. "Gavin, not now."

His temper flared, but only on the inside. Gavin kept his voice level, calm, like the reasonable guy she knew him to be. "Why not? This is the first time in weeks that we've had the place to ourselves."

Skylar bit her bottom lip, hesitating for a moment. "I'm sorry, Gavin. I know you don't want me to say this, but I can't go to Chicago with you." She paused, perhaps to search his face for permission to continue. He didn't flinch, but kept himself open. "In fact," she continued, "I think we should go back to just being friends."

He nodded and gave her a smile. "Sure. Whatever you want."

Skylar's mouth twisted in surprise. "Really? You're okay with that?"

Of course he wasn't okay. But Gavin figured she needed space, space which he would give her, and when she came back to him things would be even sweeter between them.

The timer on the oven beeped.

"Wow," he said. "We had a lot less time than I thought." He moved toward the oven, grabbed an oven mitt, and took out the tray of cinnamon rolls. "It's a good thing we didn't go upstairs. These would have burned. There's nothing worse than burnt cinnamon rolls."

Chapter 58
Skylar

My cinnamon roll didn't go down easy. What had I just done? Gavin seemed fine, licking the cream cheese frosting off his fingers and sipping his coffee, but I feared he was just putting up a good front. What if I had just destroyed him? With Jo Beth gone, Gavin was my best friend, the one person I could count on for understanding, the only guy who was unequivocally on my side. He must have noticed my slow bites; he must have seen me blink away tears. "What is it?" he asked sympathetically, when, after my treatment of him, he was the one who deserved compassion.

"I don't want to lose you as a friend."

"You won't." He reached out across the table and squeezed my hand. "We'll get through this, Sky."

I hiccupped. If he'd known that I'd cheated on him twice now, he wouldn't be so sweet. "I don't deserve you," I said in a soft voice.

"You let me be the judge of that."

There was a knock on the door.

"Are you expecting someone?" Gavin asked. "It's awfully early. I wonder who it could be."

"I'll go see." I knew Mitch would never knock; he'd just let himself in, but hope banged inside my chest nonetheless. When I opened the door and saw Magda on the other side, my cinnamon roll threatened to come up.

"Hello," she said in her affected, generic accent. "Is Mitch ready to go?"

"Go? Go where?"

She shifted her weight and I glanced down, noticing the suitcase by her feet. "Mitch didn't tell you?"

"Tell me what?"

"Huh." She looked past me. "He said he'd ask you to drive us to the airport."

Gavin came over and put his hands on my shoulders. "Is there a problem?"

"No, not really," Magda responded, though he hadn't been talking to her. "But now I'm sorry I sent that taxi away."

I shrugged off Gavin's hands and spoke to Magda. "I thought you were in Florida."

"No..." she drew out the one syllable as if it were five, implying that I was dim, incapable of comprehension. "I stayed in a hotel last night. Mitch said it would be best. I guess you don't like me much?" She arched an eyebrow and laughed.

I refused to respond.

"Anyway," she continued, "Mitch and I have a plane to catch and we need to get a move on." She turned toward Gavin. "Any chance *you* could give us a ride to the airport?"

A flush crept up Gavin's neck. "I have no idea where Mitch is, but he isn't here. And even if he was, there's no way in hell I'm giving you a ride, not when you helped murder Jo Beth."

"Gavin!" I yelled.

He yelled back. "You know I'm right, Sky. Why are you being so polite?"

"Never mind," Magda said. Her chest caved in and she seemed smaller. "I didn't kill your sister," she said in a scary-quiet voice. "Jo Beth was capable of murder, not me." She paused, straightening her shoulders, and regaining her composure. "Anyway, if you see Mitch, can you please say that I'm looking for him?"

"Did I mince my words?" Gavin's face now matched the red of his neck. "Neither of us will ever do you a favor. Now go away!" And with that, he slammed the door.

I stood there immobile, unable to process all this new information. I couldn't figure out which new nugget held the most shock value: Magda was still in town, Mitch was missing but he'd planned to leave for Florida today, or that Gavin was a badass. It was all too much, and I'm ashamed that I just couldn't process. I held my hands over my face and began to cry. Gavin had been watching me and instantly he folded me into his arms.

"Hey, don't worry," he said. "Mitch and Magda might make it to Florida, but we'll still prove their guilt. We'll make them pay for what they did."

I knew it wasn't right to lean on him, but I let my cheek rest against Gavin's sturdy shoulder anyway. And I sobbed.

Chapter 59
Gavin

Gavin knew why Skylar was crying. He wasn't too stupid to understand that she was in love with Mitch, that she thought he was leaving her, that she felt betrayed after Magda's appearance this morning.

"Hey," he said, in the most soothing tone he could manage. "It's going to be okay."

"I need to call my Mom," she said. "We can't let Mitch take Bijou."

Inwardly, he groaned. It occurred to him, not for the first time, that it might have been better if Jo Beth had eaten one of those lemon bars before giving birth, rather than after. Because now Skylar was obsessed with Bijou, and she was just as chained up as she was when Jo Beth was alive. Maybe even more. But then again, Gavin reasoned, a lot of babies die in their sleep when they're just a few months old. Perhaps he'd made a mistake, but most likely it could be easily corrected.

"I was headed to the bakery anyway," he said. "Your Mom should be there already, so I can talk to her about everything."

"If Mom's at the bakery, then Bijou must be with Dad." Skylar removed herself from his arms. "I'm getting dressed and going over there. I just hope Mitch hasn't gotten to him first."

Skylar raced upstairs and was back down in less than two minutes, wearing jeans and a fleece sweatshirt, her hair pulled back into a sloppy ponytail. She grabbed her purse and car keys, limping more than she had in the last week or so. "Did you do something to aggravate your knee?" he asked.

"What?" She looked at him like he was speaking pig Latin. "Don't worry about my knee," she snapped. "We have to get to Bijou."

"I thought you'd scheduled your online Brontë exam for this morning."

Exasperation skipped over Skylar's face. She shook her head. "Never mind; this is more important. I'll just have to reschedule."

"You can't reschedule; your grade will go down."

"Gavin, do you think I care?" Skylar charged toward him, toward the front door he was standing in front of.

He crossed his arms over his chest in defiance. "I thought you wanted to get accepted into a better school for next year. This course was a chance to prove yourself."

"Yes, but protecting Bijou is more important. Get out of the way, Gavin."

"*I'll* protect Bijou. You worry about your exam."

"Gavin!" She looked ready to use force, to move past him so she could get through that door and to her niece.

He placed his hands on each of her elbows. "Really, Sky. I can talk to both your parents. I can take care of Bijou. Trust me. Please." He looked directly into her eyes. "Please, can't you trust me?"

Chapter 60

Skylar

I told Gavin I'd trust him to handle things.

What else could I do? He was right that if I wanted a chance of getting accepted into a good literature program for next year, I had to do my best right now. But the last thing I wanted was to worry about a Brontë novel, not when my life had become a Brontë novel. My situation felt even more hopeless than Lucy Snowe's. She was the protagonist of *Villette*, the book I was to focus on for my exam. Lucy had nothing; she was without nerve, without good looks, without family, without money. Her life was a breathing suffocation and she'd never be free, not until she could stop internalizing each rejection that came from all the men she knew.

Now I sat at my desk, wracking my brain for something worth writing.

Critics say that Villette *was the writer's final effort to be at peace with her own loneliness and thwarted romance. They say that Charlotte threw her heart into creating literature as a substitute for love and perhaps there is justification to psycho-analyze the author. However,* Villette *is not simply a novel written by a female; it's a work that captures what it means to be a female: all the burdens and expectations that society puts* on women, and all the burdens and expectations that women put on themselves.

I paused my typing and rubbed my forehead, searching for examples. Surely the burdens and expectations for women in 1800s England weren't all that different from 21st century United States. I could feel myself on the brink of making an epic connection between feminist theory and literary history, of perhaps pinning down the sexist societal norms that still exist today. In fiction, a male's character arc is about the search for adventure, or for answers to life's big questions. But a female character is only ever on a quest for love, and often she'll find a bad man who leads her to take poison, to drown herself, or to throw herself in front of a train. My fingers itched to type about the injustice of it all, that if an attractive woman character stays single, she must be evil and doomed to die a horrific death. Conversely, the ugly single women might get a longer lifespan, but she'll still be pigeonholed as the protagonist of a "feminist" novel.

Ugh. My computer screen remained blank. I had to figure out how to put all of this into coherent thoughts, and I had to relate it, specifically, to Charlotte Brontë and *Villette*. I think I could have done it. I know I would have tried, but then my phone buzzed. There was a text.

And it was from Mitch.

Chapter 61
Mitch

My morning had been rough.

It wasn't enough that Gavin nearly strangled me to death before he pummeled me with Skylar's least-favorite coffee mug. He then put me in the hot tub to die.

"Mitch!" Jo Beth hollered at me and I swear she also yanked on a fistful of my hair to lift my face out of the water. It was the first physical contact we'd had since she'd died.

I spluttered out a liquid cough before I gasped for air. "What's going on?" I managed to rasp.

"Gavin left you in the hot tub so it would look like you'd drowned," Jo Beth explained. She made a tsk-tsk noise. "Seriously. Did he think nobody would notice the bruises around your neck or that gash on your temple?"

My head started to droop. Sitting up required way too much energy. But then Jo Beth drew back her hand and slapped my cheek so hard it stung. "Ouch!" I cried. "That was sort of unnecessary."

"You need to climb out of here!"

I looked around to get my bearings. Gavin had tried to make my drowning scenario seem realistic; I'll give him that. There was a towel neatly folded on the nearest patio chair and my sweat pants lay in a heap on the ground, leaving me naked in the hot tub. I caved my body in and turned from Jo Beth. She noticed my actions and laughed. "Now is not the time for modesty, Mitch."

"The last time we were alone before you died, you broke up with me. Remember?"

"I didn't mean to hurt your feelings. Now get out of here! Skylar and Bijou are both in danger!"

The bubbles were on full blast and the heat of the water produced steam against the chilly morning. That blow to my temple still felt like a knife through my brain and my throat burned. But more than anything, I was tired. I could just sink down in the bubbly warmth and drift away.

It would be so soothing.

Another wet, stinging slap. "GET UP!"

"All right, all right." I hoisted myself out of the hot tub and went for the towel, my movements slowed and pained. I began to shiver but that quickly turned to shaking, and all I could think about was how much I wanted to get back into the safety of that warm water. But I resisted temptation, dried myself off, and put on my sweat pants, which were damp from sitting in a puddle.

I went for the door, my wet hand sticking to the freezing metal of the doorknob. "It's locked," I said.

"Doesn't matter," Jo Beth said. "You can't go inside now, anyway. Gavin is still in there."

It felt as if there was a wrecking ball swinging inside my head. Teeth chattering, I said, "So what do I do?"

Jo Beth gave me an exasperated shrug. "You figure it out!"

"Thanks, but that helps me not at all!" I pried my hand from the doorknob, but now my bare feet were sticking to the frozen pavement. "Do you have any constructive suggestions?"

Jo Beth was still in the hot tub and steam swirled into her ghostly form. "I'm doing the best I can, okay? But Bijou is your responsibility now, Mitch. It's up to you to protect her. Make sure you protect her from Gavin."

Then the hot tub started bubbling over like a witch's caldron, and the steam became so thick, so intense, that it swallowed Jo Beth whole. The world began to spin at a breakneck speed, but I stood still, my feet frozen to the ground. I had to place my faith in science, in the belief that the universe perfectly supported my life form. I could only forecast future trends and life-changing events if the world was designed for me, as opposed to my being a victim of a happy accident. But speaking of happy accidents, I reached down into the pockets of my sweatpants.

And I found my cell phone.

Chapter 62
Gavin

When he was eleven years old, Gavin and his grandpa spent their weekends going to the farmer's market, or driving to Denver to visit exotic food shops so they could find a specific ingredient like shitake bacon or oatmeal flour. Then they'd haul their finds into the kitchen and cook up something delicious. Gavin's grandfather would stir whatever was on the stove, occasionally presenting the wooden spoon to Gavin for a taste-test. "Cooking is an art, Gavin." He'd raise an eyebrow every time he said this. "So be subtle. And be detailed."

Gavin cherished spending time with his grandfather, and cooking was Gavin's favorite thing to do. His dad didn't understand why Gavin preferred cooking to playing sports, and his mom worried that he had no friends his own age. But being with his grandpa felt more natural than anything else. They'd communicate through creation and their edible science projects were all they needed to bond them together.

Then Gavin's grandpa got cancer. At first, his prognosis was okay because it hadn't spread to the lymph nodes. "I'm going to be just fine," he'd said. "I'll always be there for you, Gavin."

"Do you promise?" Gavin had asked.

"Yup. I promise."

At the time, Gavin was a kid and no adult had ever truly let him down. He believed what his grandfather told him, and luckily the cancer went into remission. For a while it seemed like everything would work out. But it didn't. The cancer came back and then it killed Gavin's grandpa in less than three months. Gavin's mother came home from the hospital one night, climbed the stairs up to Gavin's room, and delivered the bad news. "Grandpa passed away tonight, Hon." She'd sat next to him on his bed, her arm around his shoulders. "I know this is hard, but we can be happy that he's in a better place now."

Gavin was too numb to cry. "Grandpa lied. He promised that he'd always be there for me and now he's gone."

"Oh, Gavin." His mom's voice was choked with emotion. "Grandpa didn't lie. He'll still always be there for you; only now, he'll be watching down on you from heaven. That's even better, right? You have your own personal angel."

Gavin thought about this a lot. Was his grandpa more useful to him dead than alive? It took a major leap of faith to believe that, since there was no real evidence that his grandpa was watching over him and doing the whole guardian-angel thing. Perhaps all that was left of his grandfather was a pile of decomposing flesh and bones, a lifeless body buried in the cemetery along with all the other dead people. And there were so many dead people; if you really thought about it, all the people who had already died *way* outnumbered the ones still living. And what if being dead meant no after-life, no altered consciousness, and no prospect of heaven and/or hell? It was entirely possible that being dead meant being nothing, and if that was the case, was there even a point to life?

But then Gavin remembered his grandpa's words of wisdom: *Be subtle. Be detailed.* Perhaps the same principles that applied to art and cooking also applied to life itself. Bigger doesn't equal better and the after-taste is as important as what's going down. That's when Gavin decided that all bets were off. Death was inevitable, and since he wouldn't know what dying was all about until his own time came, any false sense of morality, spirituality, or anxiety about the whole thing seemed silly. He might as well make the most of things while he was here, try not to get too attached to his life, and, for lack of a better metaphor, skip the salad and have seconds on dessert.

Now he stood in the bakery, bending over baby Bijou, making silly faces and kooky noises. "I can't expect you to take her," Elizabeth said. "Not on your day off."

"I'm surprised Joseph didn't take her to his nursery school," Gavin replied.

"She's too young, and they have strict rules about that sort of thing there. I don't think Bijou's even had all her shots yet." Elizabeth sighed as she punched some bread dough, flour rising and settling on her cheeks. "I don't trust Mitch to make sure she gets them, either. He seems to have his head in the clouds."

"Well, you can't let him take her away. It's as simple as that."

Elizabeth rubbed at her eye and a pasty white streak appeared where her hand had been, probably a mixture of flour and tears. "I don't have a choice, Gavin. If Mitch wants to take Bijou to Florida, I can't stop him."

"But he lied! He told Skylar that Magda had left town, and then she showed up this morning, looking for him. She said they were leaving together and you can't let that happen. We all know that Magda is dangerous, that Jo Beth didn't want her baby anywhere near her."

Elizabeth gave the bread dough a few more vigorous punches. Meanwhile, Bijou was getting fussy, strapped into her baby chair and squirming to get out. Elizabeth looked up and as soon as her eyes settled on her granddaughter, she melted. "What are you suggesting, Gavin?"

"Let me take her. My grandfather's old cabin is pretty remote and I can hide her up there. Mitch won't be able to find her."

"But don't you think he'll figure it out eventually?" Elizabeth asked.

With any luck, Gavin thought, Mitch would be found dead, drowned in the hot tub, and the issue would be moot. For the record, Gavin had had no intention of killing Mitch. Something inside him just snapped at the way he'd been prancing around Skylar's kitchen, shirtless and obviously satisfied from a great night of sex. Gavin knew Mitch had sex with Skylar. He could smell it on him.

But after he'd knocked Mitch out, Gavin had realized his mistake. He'd been neither subtle nor detailed, and it was too late to change what he'd done. Gavin knew that killing Mitch with his bare hands or with a kitchen utensil would be both difficult and messy, and besides, Skylar would come downstairs soon, so he had to think fast. He couldn't let Mitch wake up, because then he'd tell her what had happened, and if she wasn't already in Mitch's corner she certainly would be then. He scrambled for a solution and a hot tub drowning was the best he could do.

Now that he was getting Mitch out of the way, it seemed practical to take care of Bijou as well. Two more deaths would send the family reeling, but when the dust settled, Skylar would be his again and he could skip straight to his endless, just desserts. Nothing would tie her to Black Diamond anymore but she'd be heartbroken enough that the thought of setting out on her own would be too difficult. Plus, he'd blame Bijou's "crib death" on himself; he'd sob and pull his hair out, and Skylar would know how much he needed her support. She'd definitely come to Chicago with him then.

He unsnapped the baby chair belt from around Bijou's waist and lifted her from her chair. "Magda said that their plane tickets are for today. Hopefully when Mitch can't find Bijou, he'll give up easily and just get on that plane." Gavin bent down, grabbed the handle of Bijou's diaper bag, and swung it over his shoulder. "It's worth a shot, anyway."

Elizabeth came over, ran her hand over Bijou's downy head, and kissed the top of her nose. "Okay," she murmured. "Take my car. It has a baby seat."

Chapter 63

Skylar

Magda swung open the door to her hotel room, silently letting me in. She gestured to Mitch, who wore a white terry-cloth robe with a *Marriott* insignia on the breast pocket. His hair was wet and slicked back like he'd just come out of the shower, and he held a bag of ice to his temple.

"Are you okay?" I asked.

"Yeah." His head was still, like it hurt to nod. "Did you bring me some clothes?"

I handed him the gym bag I'd brought and he pulled out a pair of jeans, a sweatshirt, underwear, shoes, and socks… all the stuff he needed.

"Thanks, Skylar." He got up woozily and headed for the bathroom to get dressed.

When the door to the bathroom clicked shut, Magda said, "Mitch should be getting checked out at the hospital. He almost died, you know."

My heart stammered. I wasn't prepared to see him looking so vulnerable and I also wasn't prepared to find Magda in his hotel room, broadcasting the notion that they'd been intimate. All Mitch's text had said was, *It's an emergency and I'm worried about Bijou. Please bring me shoes and clothes and I'll explain everything.* He gave me the hotel room number, but that was it. Now I was torn between jealousy, concern, and an urgent panic that had solely to do with my niece.

"I'm just here for Bijou," I said. "Where is she?"

"Your mom wouldn't say."

"What do you mean, 'my mom wouldn't say'?"

Magda shot me a look of pure contempt. "I mean that Mitch called her and she wouldn't tell him where Bijou is."

The bathroom door opened and Mitch emerged, dressed in the clothes I'd brought him. He walked like he could be knocked over with a push from my pinkie finger. "What's going on, Mitch? I just failed my Brontë exam, so you'd better tell me everything."

He sat on the edge of the bed and I got the sense that he couldn't let himself get comfortable for fear of passing out. "I will tell you everything, but you have to promise to believe me."

I took a short, shallow breath, and my ribs hurt from the anger I wanted to release. "Why should I believe you about anything?" I pointed to Magda. "You told me she'd gone and yet she's still here."

"I'm sorry I lied," Mitch answered. "But it's been nearly impossible trying to figure out how best to handle things, when I have *her* telling me what I can and cannot do."

By "her" he must have meant Magda. I crossed my arms over my chest and let my eyes travel the length of the room, to where Magda stood, looking innocuous in her gray sweatpants and black turtleneck. I had to admit, she certainly didn't seem like she was dressing to seduce, not today anyway.

"You can't use your controlling girlfriend as an excuse for lying to me, for using me—"

"No." Mitch spoke with a strong, quiet tone, closing his eyes as if meditating. "Magda is not my girlfriend and she's not who we should be worried about." He reopened his eyes and the sudden intensity of his gaze weakened my knees. "Skylar, I'm sorry, but Gavin isn't who you think he is. He tried to kill me today and now he wants to hurt Bijou."

I laughed.

The idea was so ridiculous, what else could I do? "Gavin's a murderer?" I swallowed back my laughter, for Mitch was emanating a seriously solemn vibe. "Thanks for the warning. I'm glad you're okay. Good luck in Florida, but if you think you're taking my niece with you, get ready for a major legal battle—"

"Skylar!" He jolted up from his sitting position and came toward me. "My journal, and the list in the back?" He widened his dark eyes in question and I nodded to indicate that I remembered. "They were all things that have *happened* to me. Since she's died, Jo Beth has taught me to make formula, and she rode shotgun, and she keeps telling me to stay away from you. But even though I went against her, she still saved my life this morning, after Gavin knocked me out and left me to drown in the hot tub. And before she disappeared into a cloud of steam, she told me that I have to protect you and Bijou from Gavin."

I sucked in a deep breath. "How can you possibly expect me to believe this?"

Mitch placed one hand on each of my shoulders, gently, reminding me of the tenderness we shared last night. My body flushed with the memory.

"I don't know," he said. "But if we let Gavin get close to Bijou and something bad happens, how will we ever forgive ourselves?"

Chapter 64
Mitch

Skylar called her mother, who told her that Gavin had taken Bijou to his grandfather's cabin. "I'll go get her right now," said Skylar. "And I'll call you once she's safely with me."

"I'm coming too." Anticipating an argument, I added, "She's my daughter, Sky. You can't stop me."

Skylar pursed her lips, ready to shoot me down, but before she could, Magda chimed in. "I also want to come."

Even though my head was still pounding I spun toward her. "No," I told Magda. "That's a bad idea."

"Mitch..." Her voice was even, overly patient, like she was speaking to a small child. "You can't keep shutting me out. Remember our plan."

"What plan?" Skylar asked.

"Mitch promised that we'd move back to Florida with Bijou," Magda answered.

I turned back toward Skylar, feeling stuck between them. "That's not entirely true," I said.

"When did you make her this promise?" Skylar asked, her face all pinched. "Was it before or after my sister died?"

"After. But I don't know exactly when," I told her honestly. "Everything has been so confused. I can't always remember what I'm agreeing to."

"Give me a break," Magda said. "Estás conmigo o no?"

Was I with her or not? Weeks ago, I'd told Skylar that if she didn't love Gavin, she should break things off. But I hadn't followed my own advice. With my shoulders sagging, I faced Magda. "Lo siento. Pero se acabó." I watched as her face fell, knowing I needed to repeat myself in English, so Skylar could bear witness. "We're over, Magda."

I didn't have time for Magda's tears, or to make the apologies I most likely owed her. Instead, I kissed her on the cheek, wished her a safe flight back to Florida, and then as quickly as possible, Skylar and I were in her car. She broke the speed limit driving to the cabin, which was isolated, with no driveway and no parking.

"Wait here," Skylar said. "It's better if I just go. I'll hike up to the cabin and get Bijou, but if I'm not back in forty-five minutes, call the police."

"Hell, no," I said. "I'm coming with you."

"Mitch, I think that's a bad idea."

"I think it's a bad idea that the guy who tried to murder me this morning is alone with my daughter this afternoon. I'm coming with you and you can't stop me."

Skylar puffed out air through her nose but said nothing. She started walking and I followed. We travelled through the snowy terrain and to keep my panic at bay I thought about how long ago the earth may have resembled a giant snowball, covered in an ice that was called "the big freeze." Now I could pick up a handful of snow, mold it into a sphere, and throw it against a tree. It would shatter, just like my world would shatter if Gavin hurt Bijou.

Finally, we reached the cabin and Skylar put her index finger to her mouth, as if to quiet me, though I'd been silent. She pointed, gesturing that I should stand off to the side, so Gavin wouldn't immediately see me when he opened the door. I did what she wanted, and then she knocked on his door.

"Gavin? It's me, Gavin. Are you there?"

After a moment, the door opened and I heard Gavin's voice. "Hey," he said. "This is a surprise. How'd your Brontë test go?"

"I think it went okay," she answered. "At least it's over. Can I come in?"

From where I stood I'd been able to see Skylar, shifting her weight in Gavin's doorway. But then he opened the door wider, she entered, and the door slammed behind her. I stood there, the icy wind cooling me on the outside and my anger heating me from within. How long should I wait before I just burst into that cabin?

"Poor Mitch," Jo Beth said, and I started at her sudden appearance. "Nothing ever completely makes sense to you, does it?"

I whispered my reply. "Tell me what to do, Jo Beth. Give me some answers."

She laughed softly. "Oh, Babe, I wish I had answers. Tell you what... I know now that you're not responsible for my death. Does that make you feel better?"

My relief at hearing this was so great that I reached for her, to hug and spin her around. Of course, my arms just grabbed at air and we both laughed at my stupidity. "How'd you figure it out?" I asked.

She shrugged. "Some things are better left unexplained." Her face turned serious. "But Mitch, just because you didn't kill me doesn't mean you don't still owe me. I died a seriously flawed person, but I was trying to be better. Now I need you to be the best version of yourself—for Bijou and for Skylar."

"I'm not sure how to do that, Jo Beth."

"Of course you aren't. I mean, are you ever sure about anything?"

I considered this like it was the question for the ages. "I thought I was sure about you and me, that we should be together. Even when I found you in bed, clutching that knife, I still thought we could be happy. And then when you died, I was sure my life was over too."

"But it's not."

"It almost was. Without you, I would have died this morning. Tell me how I'm supposed to get by without you."

She gave me that sad smile of hers and somehow, I knew that it would be the last time I'd ever see it. "It's simple, Babe. Don't be afraid of who you are."

Then she was gone, like she'd melted into the snow.

I thought it was a fitting resting place.

Chapter 65

Skylar

"How long has she been asleep?" I asked.

"I don't know. Maybe twenty minutes?" Gavin leaned in and gave me a kiss. "I think she's out for a while. Do you want to go for a hike?"

"A hike?" I struggled for a good answer. "You mean, we'd leave Bijou here, alone?"

"What's going to happen to her?" Gavin asked. "Besides, we won't be gone long."

My mind sprinted, weighing the pros and cons. If I agreed to go, Mitch would see us leave. He'd probably, hopefully, notice that we weren't carrying Bijou, and then he could race into the cabin, grab Bijou, and I could meet him at the car.

But what if Gavin had something planned? What if he fixed the stove so that it would burst shortly after we left and Mitch couldn't rescue her in time? Or, what if Mitch was lying about Gavin trying to kill him this morning? What if Mitch was the dangerous one?

I decided to stall for time. "What were you doing before I got here?" I asked. "Cooking?"

"Just jotting down some notes for recipes," Gavin replied, and I noticed his notebook resting on the counter.

Check the notebook, Sky. Jo Beth's voice was sudden and strong, like a siren inside my head. I didn't analyze the phenomenon, I just opened my mouth and went with the first thing I could think to say. "Gavin, would you mind checking the roof?"

He cocked his head in confusion. "What?"

"I thought I heard some snow cracking against the roof. With all the melting that's going on, I'm worried it might cave in. Can you go look?"

He gave me a funny look but went to put his shoes on. "Sure, Sky. Anything for you."

As soon as he was out the door, I grabbed his notebook and began furiously leafing through. I didn't know what I was looking for or why, but I quickly found the page I hadn't known I needed to see:

Lemon Bars:

THE CRUST:

1 cup all-purpose flour

¼ cup confectioners' sugar

¼ teaspoon kosher salt

½ cup cold, unsalted butter, cut into small pieces

2 cups pureed pistachios

THE FILLING:

2 eggs

1 cup sugar

2 tablespoons all-purpose flour

1 teaspoon grated lemon zest

4 tablespoons fresh lemon juice

1 cup coconut milk

Gavin's secret lemon bar recipe used pistachios and coconut milk! And he had known about Jo Beth's allergies. But why? Why would he make them, just so Mom could take the lemon bars to Santiago and let

Jo Beth scarf them down on the morning of her death? That seemed like a risky plan, hardly foolproof, and heavily reliant on circumstance. Still, it seemed pretty clear that he'd intended to hurt my sister. I threw the notebook across the room like it was a bomb I could detonate, wishing I could take Gavin's life in the explosion. It meant nothing. It meant everything.

Bijou stirred, a soft baby sigh escaping from her sleeping form. I ran to her pack-n-play and lifted her. "Sorry, Sweetie," I said. "But we have to go."

I found her woolen baby snuggly but I didn't want to take the time to zip her noodlely arms and legs into it. I just wrapped it around her, patted my jean pocket to make sure I had my car keys, swiped Gavin's notebook, and quietly slipped out through the front door.

Gavin and Mitch were arguing and they didn't notice me leave, at least not at first.

"You tried to kill me, you sonofabitch!"

"Prove it."

"Stay away from my daughter. Stay away from Skylar, or *I* will kill *you*."

Their yells turned to grunts as their conflict morphed from verbal to physical. I ran past them, hoping they'd be too consumed with each other to notice my presence, but no such luck. I was about twenty feet away when I heard Gavin yell.

"Skylar!"

I ran faster, hugging Bijou to my chest. Athlete that I am, I got pretty far, pretty fast, but Gavin's legs were longer than mine. He didn't have a bad knee and he wasn't carrying a baby. Too soon he caught up, tugged on my arm, and spun me around.

"You almost made me drop Bijou!" I yelled.

Gavin's face was beet red. "Where are you going?"

"Home! I'm taking Bijou home with me, where she belongs. Don't call me and don't come over. You and I are through."

His breathing quickened and his panicked eyes darted all over the place, until they settled on his notebook, which was jutting out of my jacket pocket. He tightened his grip on my arm.

"Why do you have my notebook?"

His obvious panic convinced me that I held incriminating evidence. My anger boiled over. "Because it's proof that you wanted to kill my sister! Why? Why would you want Jo Beth dead?"

His whole face seemed to grow a size, as confusion and shock settled into his features and his mouth hung open for a couple of seconds before he spoke. "I did it for you, Sky. You needed to escape the control she had over you. It was an act of love."

"Oh yeah?" I murmured, softly, like I understood. He relaxed his grip on my arm ever so slightly. "That's the most fucked up thing I've ever heard. Go to hell!" I simultaneously kneed him in the balls and yanked my arm free. After that, I made a run for it.

I got about two inches away.

Gavin reached for my bad knee and yanked it in exactly the right direction, so it would give me the maximum amount of debilitating pain. I yelled in agony and fell to the ground, my arms tightening around Bijou, protecting her at all costs.

Gavin stood over me. In less than a second he'd picked up a rock and now he swung it back, aiming for my temple.

"You're a whore!" He yelled. "I gave you everything. I would have done anything for you!"

I'd have killed him if could. Just like Mary, the fictional character I'd created, if I'd had a knife right then, I would have stabbed Gavin in the heart and I would never have looked back.

"Skylar!"

This time, the yell didn't come from Gavin. It came from Mitch, who would never get to me in time. But suddenly Gavin faltered and then he winced, for there was a loud cracking sound: the sound of stressed out snow.

None of the signs were there. The temperature had been steady all day and the snow wasn't fresh. There was maybe three inches of thick, melting slush on the ground. Yet somehow, a torrent was released, and it tumbled towards us in an icy, angry ball. It was an avalanche and it was headed straight for Gavin, Bijou, and me.

"Move, Skylar, move!" Mitch yelled.

I scooted away from Gavin. And then I witnessed the most incomprehensible thing ever. I could almost see Jo Beth in the middle of the frosty, piercing force that rolled furiously like a tumbleweed. Even crazier, it was as if the avalanche knew its intended victim and had a purpose and aim as the snow claimed Gavin, swallowing him whole.

He barely had time to scream before he was swept away.

Afterwards, the earth stood still, exhausted from such tremendous activity. But Mitch kept moving until he caught up to Bijou and me.

"Sorry," he said, breathless. "I couldn't run very fast. I'm still struggling from this morning."

"What the hell just happened?" I asked.

Mitch just gazed innocently down at me, as I sat with his daughter in the snow. "It was a force of nature, Sky."

Chapter 66
Mitch

Skylar and I were both in shock but we managed to drive home, arriving safely at the condo with Bijou in tow. With everything that there was to talk about, we stayed remarkably silent. But hours later, after Bijou was down for the night, Skylar found me outside, sitting in the hot tub where I'd almost drowned.

"I'm surprised you want to be out here," she said, "considering recent events."

"Yeah. I don't know." The water bubbled around me, creating steam and loosening my tense muscles. I stretched and let my head lean back, so I could stare at the sky. "It's like, 'What the hell? I have nothing left to be afraid of.' You know?"

Skylar removed her long t-shirt to reveal a bikini underneath. She climbed in and sat across from me so that we weren't even close to touching. "I guess you had a lot to be afraid of, before?"

I wanted to reach for her but instinct told me not to. "I have a feeling that's over."

"You think Jo Beth is gone now?"

"I do. But it wasn't her that I needed to be afraid of. It was myself."

She thought for a moment, the crease between her eyebrows prominent, but then her face relaxed into something that wasn't quite a smile. "And Gavin," she said. "I guess we both needed to be afraid of him."

"Yeah."

We stayed silent; the gurgling bubbles the only sound between us. "Do you think he's dead?" Skylar's whisper was barely perceptible over the hot tub's noise, but I heard her just enough.

"Yeah..." I sighed, grabbing the tub's edges as if to steady me, though my vertigo was gone. "Today, with the avalanche, that wasn't the first time something like that had happened to me. I sort of have a history..."

Another deep breath, and I launched in, telling Skylar everything: Amanda Butler and the tidal wave, Magda and her blood red cloud, Jo Beth's earthquakes, Jo Beth's ghost. I finished with today's events, telling the avalanche story as if Skylar hadn't seen it with her very own eyes.

"But for some reason," I said, "I have a feeling that today was a culmination, and now all the weird stuff is going to go away." I looked past Skylar's unblinking eyes, up towards the sky. "Or maybe I'm just crazy. If you think so, and if you don't want me around Bijou, then I'll leave. Your mom can raise her if that's what you believe is best."

"You'd be okay with letting Bijou go?"

"No. Letting her go would be awful, but hurting her would be even worse."

Skylar sounded choked up. "I know you'd never hurt Bijou. You're not capable of it." I let my eyes find Skylar's face once again. Her lips were parted, already forming thoughts she'd yet to speak. "I think you should raise your daughter. But what about Florida? What about Magda?"

"I don't need Magda anymore," I said.

"Why not?"

"She's always been the one who knew how crazy I am and she at least pretended to understand. But now, with you…" I let my words hang, momentarily resting, because they were too big to be rushed. "…with you, I'm cured." I couldn't help it; my hands reached for her and my body bent forward, desperate to touch Skylar. She got up, quickly travelled the short distance of the hot tub, and settled into my arms.

"I don't want you to change, Mitch," she murmured between kisses.

I promised that I wouldn't.

I never heard from Gavin again; nobody did. Skylar and I believed that the avalanche had swallowed him whole, that it made him disappear. But we couldn't tell his parents that. We just said he'd been alive and well when we'd gone to get Bijou, and after that, we had no idea what had happened. His parents conducted a search for a while, but eventually they began to believe that he'd simply run off, and he didn't want to be found. Meanwhile, Elizabeth was happy that I'd agreed to stay in Black Diamond so that she and Joseph could help raise Bijou. Skylar's knee never healed enough for her to be competitive in skiing, though she kept skiing for fun. More importantly, she finished her novel and was accepted into Oxford University, to study both literature and creative writing. I dreaded having to say goodbye.

After all, I was terrible at goodbyes, what with my penchant for natural disasters.

But eventually we stood at the curb, her father's car idling while he waited for Skylar to climb in so he could drive her to the airport. At that moment, I found I could focus on the beginning and not on the end. "Go knock 'em dead," I said, hugging her and speaking into her hair.

"Not literally, right?" She laughed as she pulled away, so I laughed back. But then her face turned serious. "Take good care of Bijou," she said. "And remember, no matter how far apart we are, and no matter what else happens, a part of me will be with you."

"I'll always love you, Skylar."

"Me too, Mitch."

She sniffed back tears and I wiped mine away. I knew this was goodbye.

And I knew that was okay.

Chapter 67

Skylar

TEN YEARS LATER...

"Come on, Aunt Skylar! Ski faster!"

Bijou raced down the mountain, mastering a slope that Jo Beth and I had skied together many years ago. I tried to keep up. Bijou was barely a tween but she was faster than me. And while she was too young to be skilled, her potential far exceeded my own. That was all right; I'd made my own set of choices, putting aside my Olympic dreams for travel, for writing, and for a career in academia. Occasionally I managed to fit in a romantic relationship, but nothing yet had stuck. Now I was visiting Black Diamond, staying with Mitch and Bijou in Jo Beth's old condo, and trying to resist the temptation of falling back with Mitch (which I'd already done a handful of times over the years.)

Bijou skidded to a stop and waited, letting me catch up. "Are you and my dad going to get married?" Her question was so sudden, so out of the blue, that my mouth hung open for a second before I could answer.

"No!" I exclaimed. "Why would you even ask that?"

"Because you two act like you love each other."

My breath came out in a puff. "Come on," I said. "Let's ski."

We continued at a slower pace so that it was possible to talk. "I wasn't much older than you are now when your mother made me promise that I'd never fall for a charming, handsome guy. Your dad qualifies both as charming and as handsome, don't you think?"

She made a face. "I guess. But why did my mom want you to make such a stupid promise?"

"I guess she wanted me to be complete, all on my own."

Bijou sighed before she dug her poles into the ground and pushed off. "I don't even know what that means," she said over her shoulder, as she gained speed.

"I didn't either," I shouted after her. "But I think I do now."

Then again, maybe I'd never really understood my sister and what she was truly capable of. Had Jo Beth caused the avalanche that took Gavin? She'd certainly been prone to creating drama, but over the years I had come to realize Mitch was her equal in extreme, sudden events. Neither could be controlled and neither could be explained. I stood for a moment, watching my niece speed down the mountain. She was so like her mother. Bijou was a force of nature, capable of causing an avalanche, capable of succeeding at whatever she set her mind to.

I looked toward the sky and then around at the snow. "She's beautiful, Jo Beth," I whispered. "And she's strong. She gets her strength from you."

I skied on, content to have fallen behind. That way if Bijou fell, I'd be there to pick her right back up. "You're my favorite, Bijou." My voice was swallowed by the wind, but it didn't matter. Even if she couldn't hear me, maybe her mother could.

"I love you best of all."

THE END

Did you enjoy reading *Just Like the Bronte Sisters*? If so, click here to see Laurel Osterkamp's other books on Amazon. And get ready for more emotionally compelling women's fiction and contemporary romance! Also, you can subscribe to Laurellit.com for free bonus reads, updates, and special offers.

Other Books by Laurel Osterkamp

The Side Project
Beautiful Little Furies
Favorite Daughters
Murder at Styles Resort
The Standout
The Next Breath
The Holdout
Starring in the Movie of My Life
Following My Toes

Dear Reader,

Thank you for reading *Just Like the Brontë Sisters!* I realize there are hundreds of thousands of books available for you to choose from, and since I'm a relatively unknown author, I'm especially honored that you chose to read one of mine. My biggest challenge as an author is reaching new readers, but that is where you can help. If you enjoyed my book, please consider posting a review on Amazon. Positive customer reviews are the biggest/best way to attract new readers. It doesn't have to be long or fancy, but if you and write a review I will be extremely grateful.

Thanks!

Laurel Osterkamp

9 781933 826882